SINS OF DECEPTION

VALERIE WILCOX

BERKLEY PRIME CRIME, NEW YORK

SINS OF DECEPTION

A Berkley Prime Crime Book / published by arrangement with the author

PRINTING HISTORY
Berkley Prime Crime edition / June 2000

The Penguin Putnam Inc. World Wide Web site address is http://www.penguinputnam.com

ISBN: 0-425-17507–3

Berkley Prime Crime Books are published by The Berkley Publishing Group, a division of Penguin Putnam Inc., 375 Hudson Street, New York, New York 10014. The name BERKLEY PRIME CRIME and the BERKLEY PRIME CRIME design are trademarks belonging to Penguin Putnam Inc.

PRINTED IN THE UNITED STATES OF AMERICA

10 9 8 7 6 5 4 3 2 1

In memory of Richard A. Usselman

ACKNOWLEDGMENTS

I am grateful to the following people for giving so freely of their time, technical assistance, and encouragement: Rita Gardner, Pam Baillargeon, Tomette Copp, Julia Stroud, Ph.D., of Shrink Write, Officer P. B. Nicholls and his fellow officers of the Seattle Police Department, Lieutenant S. M. Bourgette of the Bellevue Police Department, Detectives Henri Hardenberg and Denny Gulla of the King County Sheriff's Office, Joe S. Sando of the Indian Pueblo Cultural Center in Albuquerque, NM, Anna Cottle and Mary Alice Kier of Cine/Lit Representation, and, as always, David H. Wilcox. Thanks, guys.

. . . Come away, o human child!
To the waters and the wild
With a faery, hand in hand,
For the world's more full of weeping than you can
understand . . .

—From *The Stolen Child*,
W. B. YEATS, 1886

SINS OF
DECEPTION

ONE

ON THE WATER everything is true. It is only when you've been on the water, sailed its moods, breathed its secrets, and experienced its power that the saline scent of truth will manifest itself. And once you've felt its pure, exacting touch, you cannot return to shore unchanged. The manner of its arrival—as a fine mist gently nudging at the edge of your consciousness or as a violent tidal wave crashing at your soul—matters not. What matters is the remembering. It is the remembering that allows you to discard all the false and pretentious trappings of your life. It is the remembering that gives you the power to rise above the desperate everyday struggle and seize the life you crave. A life that is real. A life that is authentic. A life that is yours.

You want to succeed in life, Kellie darlin'? Then get out on the water. Find the wind and hoist your sails. Listen to the screeching gulls, the luffing sails, the rushing water; taste the salt spray on your tongue; feel your

*hair whipping against your face; and breathe in the
clean, pure sea air that carries the one true life you seek.
And remember.*

PAUL CRENSHAW WAS one of the good guys. And if
you suggested otherwise, I'd be the first to call you a
fool. I suppose you'd be right in claiming that I had a
favorable bias toward the man because of our long
friendship. But if you talked to anyone who knew him,
you'd get the same reaction. Paul was a loyal friend,
loving husband and father, and a successful engineer
who went out of his way to help those in need. I admit
that you never really know a person, but in Paul Crenshaw's case, the private persona matched the public persona to a tee. So when he was handcuffed and hauled
off to jail at gunpoint, I was more than a little shocked.
Not to mention pissed. Even before his untimely arrest,
my first trip as skipper of a chartered sailboat hadn't
been what I would call fun and games. But I'd sort of
expected a few bumps. After all, it was a new venture
for me. What I didn't expect was to have my business—
and ultimately, my life—nearly destroyed.

At first, everything was just peachy. My clients and I
had left Seattle on a balmy September morning a little
over a week before. The four of us were aboard a bor-
rowed forty-foot sloop called *Picture Perfect* which at
the time seemed aptly named, given the weather and
company. Our destination was the San Juan Islands, a
cluster of emerald jewels tucked away in the northwest
corner of Washington State.

The trip was a reunion of sorts. Paul and Sharon Crenshaw had been my next-door neighbors for almost fifteen
years, but after my husband's death, I sold our family
home and moved aboard my sailboat at Larstad's Ma-

rina. We'd stayed in touch for a while, but as often happens, we'd drifted apart in the last couple of years. I felt more than a little guilty about the break since I was their fourteen-year-old daughter Tiffany's godmother. I'd been thinking about reestablishing contact with the Crenshaws for some time—especially since my own daughter had essentially left the nest. Cassie attended college in New York, and her visits home were all too infrequent. So, when Paul and his wife signed up for my first charter trip, I was delighted. The only disappointment was that Tiffany couldn't join us. But as Paul explained, "She just started a new school year."

The trip was also a celebration. Paul's engineering firm had just been awarded a major contract with Larstad's Marina. The marina's status as Seattle's premier boating facility had been in jeopardy ever since Coho Marina had opened for business six months previously. Larstad's had already lost several long-time clients to the ritzy new facility, and more were threatening to leave as soon as a slip became available. In an effort to prevent further bail-outs, old man Larstad had decided to enlarge and update his namesake marina.

The expansion project, while welcomed in many quarters, wasn't without opposition. Many feared that their moorage rates would be raised, while others were concerned that the additional slips would have an adverse impact on the environment and place an unmanageable burden on the various amenities at the marina. I hadn't taken a position on the issue except to recommend Paul's firm, Pierpont Engineering and Construction, for the job. Although I doubted that my recommendation carried much weight with old man Larstad, Paul was very grateful for my help. I think the charter trip was his way of thanking me.

Martin Petrowski, Paul's best friend and construction

supervisor at his firm, had also signed up for the charter. I didn't know Martin that well, but I was immediately drawn to his quirky sense of humor and easygoing manner. Although somewhat preoccupied, Paul was in a good mood when we first got underway. So, too, were Sharon and Martin. The downturn in everyone's spirits began the minute Jason Petrowski, Martin's seventeen-year-old son, stepped aboard the boat.

Because of some conflict with his schedule, he joined us after we left Seattle. We picked him up at the public boat dock in La Conner, a picturesque little town in the middle of tulip country. As we cruised through the Swinomish Channel toward our first night's anchorage, I tried to figure out what the problem was. I'd never met him before this trip, but Jason seemed like a nice kid. A little moody perhaps, but not surly or foul-mouthed like some of the teens I'd had in my classes when I taught high school.

At six foot five, he towered over his father, but they shared the same breathtaking good looks. Deeply tanned despite their fair skin, they both had sandy-blond hair, green eyes, and a body that screamed, "Look at me, I'm a jock!" But Jason played down his athletic prowess, clearly embarrassed by his father's endless recitation of his own glory days on the gridiron.

Martin didn't pay much attention to his son, but Paul and Sharon acted as if the kid were some kind of pariah. They avoided him as much as is physically possible on a forty-foot sailboat. For the life of me, I couldn't understand why he made everyone so uncomfortable. I found him polite, eager to help with chores, and a pretty good sailor. If Jason had done something to offend the Crenshaws, why invite him along? As the week wore on, the kid's presence cast such a pall over the group that even the pristine beauty of the San Juan Islands and excellent sailing conditions failed to excite anyone. Including me.

"I wish I'd never come," Jason muttered as we sat side by side at the helm. We were alone in the cockpit, having just raised the sails after exiting the Port Sidney Marina in British Columbia, Canada. We'd spent the previous day on Vancouver Island and were now enroute to U.S. waters. In the distance, a green and white ferry navigated Haro Strait, the broad, watery expanse that links the San Juan Islands with their neighbor to the north.

As had become their practice, the rest of the group had found other things to do, and crewing wasn't it. For the past couple of days, Paul had been hiding out in the cabin with his briefcase and a stack of paperwork while Sharon and Martin staked out separate territory for themselves on the forward deck. At the moment, Sharon had her nose buried in a romance novel, and Martin had stretched out on the bow to catch some rays. Although seemingly contented when engaged in their own activities, there was no mistaking the tension that marked whatever personal interactions took place. Basically no one was a happy camper.

"Why *did* you come?" I asked Jason.

He glanced at Martin and shrugged. "Don't ask me. It was my dad's idea."

I tried to think of something positive to say, but at that point I was pretty much wishing I was somewhere else myself. I usually manage the sailing school at Larstad's Marina, but I'd been trying to get a charter service going for a long time. It wasn't until my best friend, Rose Randall, was chosen as the marina's new general manager that old man Larstad finally conceded that the idea had merit—especially since he didn't have to put out any cash for a new boat. A friend I'd helped through a difficult time a while back volunteered her sloop free of charge for the inaugural charter. I'd been thrilled by the prospect of spending an entire week sailing in the San Juans with my friends and hoped that the trip would be the beginning of a profitable side business for Sound Sailing School. Now all I hoped to do was get back to Seattle without tossing someone overboard.

Then, suddenly, everything changed when the killers arrived.

Jason spotted the first one. "Oh, man! Look at that!" He pointed to an area some hundred yards off the starboard bow. My eyes traced a line from his finger to a spot where a huge black-and-white orca exploded out of the water. Like an ungainly ballerina, the breaching whale returned to the sea with a resounding splash.

The noise so startled Martin that he jumped to his feet. "What the hell was that?"

Another whale, smaller than the first, performed a similar maneuver. When its tail slapped the water, Sharon threw down her book. "Oh, my God! Did you see that? What *was* it?"

I slowed the boat by turning into the wind. "Orcas," I said. "A mother and her calf."

"Killer whales!" Jason shouted.

When a third and a fourth whale popped out of the water, Sharon screamed. "Kellie, get us out of here!"

I turned the wheel and adjusted the sails so that we traveled parallel and slightly to the rear of the whales at the same speed as the calf, the slowest member of the pod.

"What are you doing?" Martin shouted.

"Trying not to separate the mother and her calf."

Jason grabbed the binoculars. "This is way cool."

"Is everything all right?" Paul asked as he scrambled out of the cabin. "I thought I heard someone scream."

He carried a sheaf of papers in one hand, but I doubted he'd been working while he was down below. His khaki shorts and tank top were wrinkled, and his thick, curly brown hair was matted on one side as if he'd been napping.

Jason grinned and handed him the binoculars. "We're surrounded by killers, man."

"Actually," I said, "they're Orcinus orca, the largest member of the dolphin family."

As Sharon and Martin joined us in the cockpit, Sharon propped her Versace sunglasses on her head and looked at me quizzically. "Dolphins?"

Paul adjusted the focus on the binoculars and peered through the lenses. Although a little round-shouldered and not as strikingly good-looking as his friend Martin, Paul Crenshaw was still capable of making women run into walls. He was thirty-five and tall with a wiry body that, despite a few extra pounds around the belly, looked fit and youthful. He turned to his wife and said, "Whales are a relative of the dolphin, honey. Dolphins, porpoises, whales—they all belong to the same order of marine mammals." He handed her the binoculars. "Here, take a look. They're beautiful."

She hesitated. "Aren't whales dangerous?"

"Not if we don't do anything to aggravate them," I said. "We're positioned far enough away from the pod that it shouldn't be a problem."

"Whales are so awesome," Jason said. "We studied them in school. Mr. Cohen told us about these two orcas in Antarctica that actually tipped an ice floe up, dumping a sleeping seal right into the jaws of a third whale."

Martin laughed. "Talk about your team players."

"You got that right," Paul said. "Strength and a co-operative hunting strategy. The dual punch allows them to feed on nearly anything that crosses their paths."

Frowning, Sharon handed the binoculars back to Paul. "I don't like the sound of that." Sharon's Nervous Nellie routine was no act. Ever since I'd known her she'd been afraid of one thing or another. She refused to fly and even avoided elevators if she could help it. Although two years older than her husband, she seemed almost childlike at times, an impression that her high-pitched, singsong voice only reinforced. She was thin and plain but, thanks to good makeup and expensive clothing, managed to look quite beautiful. Beautiful enough to keep people from claiming she'd snagged the likes of Paul Crenshaw because of her father's money.

Paul put his arm around his wife's shoulder, "Don't worry, sweetheart. From what I've read, there has never been an authenticated report of killer whales eating humans."

"Besides," I said, "if they should begin to exhibit defensive or aggressive behavior, we're out of here."

The possibility of a confrontation with the killers sparked a lively discussion. And for the first time since he'd come aboard, the group was actually interacting with Jason. He proved to have a wealth of information about whales and their habits—everything from the female's estimated life span of fifty to sixty years to the sixty-two separate sonarlike clicking sounds they produce underwater. "They're amazing creatures," he said. "But thirty years ago, sportsmen in Canada complained so loudly about local orcas eating salmon and threatening the safety of boaters that a machine gun was installed overlooking the Strait of Georgia to kill or drive away the whales."

Sharon shook her head. "How barbaric."

"Yeah. Well, fortunately, the gun was never fired."

Any animal that can swim one hundred miles in a day is quite capable of making sudden appearances or disappearances. And so, as quickly as they'd come, the killers were gone. But the welcome change in the group's mood lingered long after the whales' departure. By the time we'd reached our destination for the night, I was beginning to think that my charter business might succeed after all. Unfortunately that was just wishful thinking, because as we would soon find out, the whales weren't the only killers around.

TWO

A WATERY HIGHWAY system of broad straits and fjordlike channels links the approximately two hundred islands known collectively as the San Juans. But I use the term "island" loosely. For starters, just when is a rock big enough to be called an island? How many rocks make a reef? Is a reef an island? What about tidal changes that cause rocks and reefs to appear and disappear and split apart or join together? How you answer those questions can inflate the number of islands to as high as seven hundred. Although the actual figures may be disputed, there is no doubt that of the four larger islands—Lopez, Shaw, Orcas, and San Juan—San Juan Island is the largest, both in terms of territory and population. It's also the site of the county seat and the only incorporated town in the archipelago.

The island's early settlers were no fools. They recognized prime real estate when they saw it—gentle, rolling farmland for raising crops and cattle, thick forests for building cabins and fences, and fine harbors for providing sheltered access to the shores. Today's settlers, while no less astute, are primarily retirees, artists, authors, and dropouts from the rat race. Folks who believe in the crazy notion that air without smog, beaches without litter, highways without traffic jams, and starry nights without obliterating city lights is a good thing.

Good anchoring spots are plentiful around San Juan Island, but my clients wanted to spend the night at Roche Harbor Marina where they could take advantage of the tennis courts, pool, and other trappings of a modern resort. Our first stop, though, was the on-site customs office. Since we'd been to Canada and were reentering the United States, we were obligated to check in with customs before going ashore.

When the marina had expanded its facilities a while back, they moved the customs office to the main pier just inside the harbor proper. The white clapboard building was brand new, but surprisingly low-key for a government facility. Except for the signs and flags designating the small, unassuming structure as an official U.S. Customs Office, it could have passed for a one-room schoolhouse. Roche Harbor is a popular destination, and when summer is in full swing, you often have to wait in line to check in at the customs pier. But it was several days after Labor Day when we arrived, and boating traffic was light. I let Jason take the wheel while I readied the mooring lines and fenders for docking.

For a novice, Jason took to sailing like a natural. He skillfully guided the sloop into the harbor and pulled alongside the pier as if he'd been doing it all his life. As usual, he made light of the accomplishment with a laid-back, "no big deal" pose. When I gave him a thumbs-up sign, though, he broke into a grin that stretched from ear to ear. As I stepped off the boat to secure the mooring lines, I caught a glimpse of Martin congratulating his son with an affectionate slap on the back. It was the first warm gesture that had passed between them since the trip began.

It was my responsibility as skipper to clear our vessel through customs before anyone disembarked. While the others waited aboard *Picture Perfect,* I went inside the office. As far as offices go, it wasn't much—just a counter that functioned primarily as a dividing line between the public and the inspector's gray, government-issue desk. The desk was uncluttered and held a computer terminal, keyboard, and a bunch of spiral-bound notebooks. Some kind of official-looking paperwork was neatly tacked to the bulletin board on the wall behind the desk. Although there were three windows in the small structure, they appeared to be painted shut, which probably explained why the room was so hot and stuffy. It also reeked of Obsession perfume and tuna fish. Two customs inspectors were on duty, which struck me as sort of unusual since it was so late in the boating season.

"May I help you?" This from the source of the perfume—a petite, twenty-something blonde in a starched, dark blue uniform. Despite her youthful appearance, she looked official in her perfectly creased slacks and short-sleeved shirt with the U.S. Customs insignia embroidered on the pocket. But there was something about the way she smiled that seemed forced, as if she had to prove that she wasn't just playing dress-up. She stood behind the counter while her associate wolfed down a sandwich (most probably tuna) at the room's lone desk.

"I'm the skipper of *Picture Perfect,* a charter boat out of Seattle with four clients aboard. We've been to Vancouver Island and are returning to the U.S."

The guy behind the desk looked up suddenly. He was

a big man around forty or so with a tiny bald head, turnip ears, and a generous beer belly. He wiped a blob of mayonnaise from his mouth with the back of his hand. "You say you're on *Picture Perfect?*"

I nodded. "That's right."

He shot the blonde a look I couldn't decipher and, after pausing long enough to stuff another bite into his mouth, waddled over to the counter. I waited while they turned their backs slightly and conferred. After a moment the big guy returned to his desk and sat down. He glanced back at his young partner, then tossed his half-eaten sandwich aside and started pecking furiously at the keyboard. She, meanwhile, grabbed a clipboard and walked around the counter to where I stood. "Show me your vessel," she said sternly.

A customs inspection isn't all that unusual, but her attitude surprised me. Most of the time when inspectors ask to come aboard your boat, they do so politely and with a little less edge to their voice. I wasn't sure what I'd said, but I'd evidently raised some kind of red flag with these two.

I looked at her nametag and smiled. "My name's Kellie Montgomery, Ms. Wainwright. And I'd be happy to show you *Picture Perfect.*"

With Inspector Wainwright following on my heels, we left the office and boarded the sloop. Jason and Martin were still in the cockpit, downing a couple of cold drinks. "Don't mind us." Martin grinned as we climbed aboard. "We're just having a little father-son bonding moment." He rummaged through the ice in the cooler and grabbed a second can of Bud Lite for himself and a Coke for Jason.

Inspector Wainwright eyed the cooler and frowned. "How much alcohol do you have on board?"

Martin gave the blonde the once-over and then

belched loudly. "Not nearly enough, sweetie. Not nearly enough."

Wainwright dismissed him with a withering look and turned to me. "Where's the rest of your group?"

"I assume Paul and Sharon are in the cabin. They said they wanted to change into their tennis clothes."

"Get them up here. I need to check everyone's ID."

That was a new one on me. Inspectors routinely search vessels for contraband, illegal drugs, or whatever else happens to land on their hot sheets, but rarely do passengers have to show any kind of identification. "Our ID?" I asked.

She extended her hand palm side up to Jason. "You first," she said. As Jason forked over his driver's license, I opened the hatchway and called to Paul and Sharon.

"Is this really necessary?" Martin asked, frowning.

Inspector Wainwright jotted something on a form attached to the clipboard and then handed Jason's ID back to him. "Now yours," she said to Martin.

He paused as if considering her request. But instead of reaching for his wallet, he raised his beer can in a salute before tilting his head back and swigging noisily.

When Paul and Sharon joined us in the cockpit, Paul asked, "What's this all about?"

"Customs inspection," Wainwright answered. "I'll need to see your ID, sir. Yours, too, ma'am." Her tone was something akin to a burly motorcycle cop who'd just caught us careening through a school zone at a hundred miles an hour.

Sharon's brown eyes darted from Wainwright to her husband and back again. "Oh, my." Her hands fluttered at her side like a bird with a broken wing. When she spoke again, her little-girl voice was strained and breathy. "Uh, my license is in my purse, and I . . . Oh, what about my passport? Should I get that for you, too?"

Wainwright nodded curtly, and Sharon scurried back inside the cabin. Paul reached for his wallet just as the other inspector came barreling out the office door. "Freeze!" he shouted.

Of course, we didn't do any such thing. We all whipped around and stared openmouthed as Wainwright's beefy partner planted himself in a shooting stance. The cannon-sized gun he aimed at us struck me as a rather extreme attention-getting device, but it worked. He got our undivided attention. I didn't know what kind of a shot the guy was, but I wasn't about to argue. As far as I'm concerned, whoever holds the gun makes the rules.

"All of you," he boomed. "Put your hands on top of your head!"

"Including Inspector Wainwright?" Martin quipped, seemingly amused by the absurdity of the situation.

Wainwright whirled to face him. "Asshole! You heard the man. Get your hands on top of your head. Now!"

Martin rolled his eyes but held his tongue and complied with her order.

By this time, Sharon had located her purse and popped out of the hatchway. She opened her mouth to speak, but the bizarre scene shocked her into silence. For half a second. Then she let loose with everything she had.

"On a scale of one to ten," Martin said, "I'd have to give that scream a ten."

I KNEW THAT Paul Crenshaw was no criminal. When Inspector Wainwright handcuffed him, I was certain that she had made some kind of terrible mistake. "What are you doing?" I asked incredulously. "Paul hasn't done anything."

"That's where you're wrong," she said brusquely. She signaled to her partner, who then marched him back to their small office at gunpoint. "The rest of you are free to go now, but if I had my way, you'd all be detained as accessories."

Martin snorted, "Accessories to what? A kangaroo court? Paul hasn't done a damn thing, and you know it."

"There's a warrant out for his arrest," Wainwright said with a triumphant smile. "We were notified to be on the lookout for your vessel. Ralph verified it on the computer while I checked your IDs. The authorities will be here soon to pick up Crenshaw."

I'd wrapped my arm around Sharon's shoulder, and she clung to me now as if I were a life ring. The way she was trembling convinced me that I was all that kept her from slumping to the floor. I asked the questions that I was sure she'd ask if she could. "What are you talking about? What authorities? What warrant?"

"Murder. Paul Crenshaw is wanted for murder by the Port of Seattle police."

THREE

"THIS IS BULLSHIT!" Martin Petrowski slammed his fist on the office counter and glared indignantly at the customs inspector. The amused indifference that he'd shown initially aboard *Picture Perfect* had given way to raw anger. Martin had been the first to scramble off the boat when Inspector Ralph Freiden led Paul away, and we'd all quickly followed suit. We'd congregated in the hot and stuffy customs office to demand some sort of explanation for the inconceivable predicament in which we found ourselves. An explanation that was not forthcoming. Martin's outburst simply reflected what we were all thinking and feeling.

Inspector Freiden cast his heavy-lidded eyes onto Martin. "I think not, sir," he said. "Your friend here is in deep doo-doo, and you'll find yourself in the same barnyard slop if you don't keep your opinions to yourself."

Martin leaned across the counter as if to grab the inspector by his shirt. "You fat fuck. I oughta—"

"Marty, that's enough." Paul sat in a metal chair next to the inspector's desk, his hands still cuffed. "There's no need to get so excited over this. Obviously there's been some kind of mistake. As soon as the sheriff arrives, we'll get it all straightened out."

"Paul's right," I said. "You know how computers are. Press the wrong key, and they hiccup and spit out garbage. It could've just as easily issued an arrest warrant for the pope."

"Which would've made more sense than arresting Paul," Martin said with a sneer directed at Freiden.

The inspector put one hand on his holstered weapon and eyed Martin cautiously. "You'd best step away from the counter, sir."

Martin didn't budge.

Freiden's partner, Ms. Wainwright, had been following the exchange from the doorway. She approached the counter now with a tense but determined stride. Itching, no doubt, to take Martin down. Despite her small stature, I had the feeling that she probably could—and relish the opportunity. But she didn't get a chance. Paul diffused the situation by telling Martin to back off.

"Whatever you say, Paul," he shrugged. Moving to the spot vacated by Wainwright, he slouched against the door and said, "But this damn nonsense better get cleared up when the sheriff arrives, or we're talking a major lawsuit here." He took a pack of Marlboros from his shirt pocket and shook a cigarette loose. He'd been carrying the pack around with him during our entire trip, but this was the first time I'd seen him open it.

"You can't smoke in here, sir," bristled Inspector Wainwright.

Martin snorted. "Don't tell me that's against the law, too."

"As a matter of fact, this is a government building, and—"

"Give me a friggin' break." He paused long enough to light up and then bolted from the office. Jason hesitated a moment and then trudged after his father.

Sharon gripped my hand. "Oh, dear," she cried.

Paul gave his wife a reassuring smile. "Marty'll be okay."

"But, Paul," Sharon said, "maybe I should call Daddy. We might need a lawyer."

Paul shook his head. "I don't need a lawyer, honey. I haven't done anything wrong. This thing isn't going to come down to a lawsuit, either. Everything's going to be just fine." He nodded toward the door. "Kellie, why don't you take Sharon and the others up to the restaurant for something to eat? They said it would be a while before the county sheriff makes it over from Friday Harbor."

"I want to stay here with you," Sharon protested.

Paul smiled again and said, "No, you go on. I'll be all right."

Sharon wouldn't drop it. "What if the sheriff comes while we're gone?"

For whatever reason, I could see that Paul wanted some time to himself. I figured that Sharon could benefit from a time-out as well. "It's okay, Sharon," I said. "The restaurant has a balcony overlooking the parking area. We can keep an eye out for the sheriff while we eat."

"I'm not hungry," she said in a last-ditch effort to stand by her husband.

Martin walked back into the room and said, "Good God, Sharon, that's not the point." Taking her by the arm, he steered her toward the door. "Nobody's hungry, but we're going to do what Paul says."

There's something about the ritual of eating, even the

pretense of eating, that is oddly comforting. Hungry or
not, we ordered comfort food and plenty of it. As I suggested, we sat outside on the restaurant balcony. We had
a nice view of the marina and the hotel's flower garden.
The restaurant was located in an elegant old building
that was once the home of John McMillin, a young Indiana lawyer who, in the 1850s, built the largest lime-
producing company west of the Mississippi.

While we ate, I tried to distract everyone by making
small talk about the resort. I launched into a history lesson of sorts, relating how John McMillin had ruled the
company and its town for fifty years and became one of
the richest and most influential men in the state.

Jason was the only one who seemed remotely interested. "How'd the place wind up as a resort?" he asked.

"After his death, McMillin's son operated the family
business until the lime deposits began to play out. In
1956, the company town was sold, and the lime kilns
that had produced the valuable ingredient for making
cement were shut down shortly thereafter. Subsequent
owners restored the deteriorated warehouse, hotel, and
other buildings and turned the McMillins' former property into the first-class resort you see today."

Jason and I carried the conversational ball until it became obvious that we weren't distracting anyone from
thinking about Paul and what might lie ahead. Our halfhearted exercise had lapsed into an uneasy silence when
our waitress, a pert redhead with a dimpled grin, returned to check on us. Glancing at our plates, she asked,
"Is everything all right? You've hardly touched a thing."
Possessing what my grandfather used to call "a good set
of bow thrusters," she sidled up to Martin and added
with a flirty wink, "Is there something else you'd like
instead?"

Jason sneaked a quick look at her ample bosom and

blushed furiously when his father said, "Getting a little hot out here. Maybe you'd better bring us another round of drinks."

The waitress laughed and sashayed off to the bar.

"I should've called Daddy," Sharon said, pushing her plate to the edge of the table.

Martin groaned and lit his third cigarette of the day. Exhaling, he said, "Why don't you forget Daddy-o for once, Sharon. Paul's a big boy now. He can take care of himself."

She didn't seem to register the comment or the harshness in his voice. "I wish I had my cell phone with me. I could probably still reach him at the office."

"Jesus," Martin said under his breath. He turned toward the bar. "I think I'll go see what's keeping that gal."

Then Jason excused himself, saying he'd meet us back at the customs office. Left to ourselves, Sharon and I fell to talking about Paul. Or, I should say, Sharon talked about Paul. I listened. "It's our anniversary next week, you know." She sighed. "Seventeen years."

I murmured some congratulatory words, realizing somewhat sheepishly that I'd forgotten all about their anniversary—something I never would have done if we'd still been neighbors. When Wendell was alive, we always celebrated the occasion with Paul and Sharon. That I'd forgotten the date tugged at my heart because it meant that I'd also forgotten my own anniversary, since Wendell and I were married on the same date as the Crenshaws. In our case, it would've been twenty years.

I was thankful Sharon was too caught up in her own problems to remember the date's significance to me. I didn't think I could handle any expression of sympathy, no matter how well intended. For as much as I liked to think I've succeeded in dealing with Wendell's death, the pain never goes away. I've stuffed it down deep inside somewhere, but it always manages to sneak up on me at the oddest moments. I drank the last of my iced tea and changed the subject. "How's my goddaughter doing these days?"

Sharon shook her head. "Let's not go there, okay?"

Fourteen-year-old Tiffany was the light of her life. I was puzzled by her reluctance to talk about her daughter, but didn't pursue it, knowing how difficult raising a teenager could be. My own daughter and I had had plenty of problems over the years. If Sharon and Tiffany were at odds with one another, I wasn't in the mood to "go there," either. As I struggled to think of a safe topic, a brown and white sedan pulled into the parking area alongside the flower garden. The emblem on the door read: *San Juan County Sheriff.* I scooped up the check for our meal and stood. "Sharon, we better get going. The man of the hour has just arrived."

SHERIFF DEL SLOAN was about fifty with a marathon runner's build and a narrow, unlined face that suggested more than a passing acquaintance with the wonders of plastic surgery. His dark, neatly trimmed beard contrasted sharply with his pale complexion and the wispy blond hair that sprouted from his head like annoying weeds. Judging from the black roots, he was overdue for another Grecian Formula treatment. When he opened his mouth to speak, his straight white teeth were an orthodontist's delight. Since he was still wearing a retainer, it was a safe bet that he was still paying the bill, too.

I figured the sheriff for a man on the make based on the telltale white band on his ring finger and the not-so-subtle upgrades in his appearance. But he was all business when he addressed us. "This is the drill: I'll be escorting Mr. Crenshaw to Friday Harbor where he'll be held until the homicide detectives from Seattle can pick him up."

"But, Sheriff," Martin protested, "there must be some mistake. Paul hasn't committed any crime." I didn't know if it was because of the drinks he'd had earlier, but Martin seemed much calmer now. Unlike the way he'd acted with the customs inspectors, he treated the sheriff with respect and so far had refrained from making any wisecracks or disparaging remarks.

Sheriff Sloan clutched a piece of paper in his hand and said, "Not according to this arrest warrant."

Paul shifted in his chair and asked, "What does the warrant say, Sheriff? We don't know any of the details."

The sheriff eyed him carefully. "I guess you're entitled." He scanned the document briefly and said, "The Port of Seattle police allege that you killed a twenty-two-year-old woman by the name of Jewell Jessup. She was found aboard your yacht at Larstad's Marina."

Shocked silence all around. Then Sharon gasped, "No! That's impossible."

When the rest of us found our voices, it was to echo Sharon's sentiments. But Paul actually seemed relieved. "Sheriff," he said, straightening his shoulders, "I'm positive now that there's been a computer glitch or something. You see, I don't know any woman named Jewell Jessup. Nor do I own a yacht—at Larstad's Marina or anywhere else. My friends here can tell you that."

"That's right," I said nodding, vigorously. For a moment I felt relieved, too. The facts were so obviously wrong that I was sure they'd gotten Paul mixed up with someone else.

"And you are?" asked the sheriff.

"Kellie Montgomery. I'm the skipper of the charter

boat *Picture Perfect* and I work at Larstad's Marina. I've known Paul Crenshaw for many years. You can believe him when he says he doesn't own a yacht or know this woman."

I thought I sounded sincere and convincing, but Sheriff Sloan wasn't buying it. Nor did he seem interested in anything Martin or Sharon had to say concerning Paul's innocence. He cut them off with an upraised hand. "That's quite enough. Save your comments for the homicide detectives. Right now I've got a prisoner to transport to the county jail."

FOUR

THE SAN JUAN County Jail was located in Friday Harbor, some six miles southwest of Roche Harbor. Since Sheriff Sloan refused to allow any of us to accompany Paul in the patrol car, we were forced to find our own way to town. Public transportation from the marina was limited this time of year, but Martin and Sharon managed to catch a ride on a shuttle bus shortly after the sheriff and Paul left. The customs inspectors had made a big fuss about not leaving *Picture Perfect* tied up at their dock, so Jason and I stayed behind to move the sailboat to one of the visitor slips at the marina.

"Are you sure you don't want to go with them?" I asked Jason as his father and Sharon boarded the bus. "I can take care of the boat by myself."

"I know that," he said. "But I'm the last person Paul would want tagging along with him right now. He hates me."

Surprised, my first impulse was to defend Paul. While

it was true that he hadn't exactly been overly friendly to Jason during our trip, I didn't think he hated the kid. But I knew telling Jason that he was wrong about Paul wouldn't get me anywhere. Credit that insight to the battle scars I'd accumulated while raising Cassie. Instead, I asked, "Want to talk about it?"

"Nope."

Insight number two: Don't push it. "Okay," I said, and we headed back to the customs dock in silence.

As we climbed aboard the sloop, Jason said, "Thanks, Kellie."

I'd kept my mouth shut. Not always easy for me to pull off, but so appreciated when I do. "You bet." I nodded. "Now, let's get this rig squared away."

The squaring away took the better part of two hours. After the harbormaster assigned us a guest slip, we pumped out the sewage, filled the water tanks, and hosed off the salt water that clung to the surface of the sloop like sticky tape.

I hauled out the sail covers from the storage locker and handed them to Jason. "Think you can finish up here? I'd like to see if I can hitch a ride into town."

"Sure thing," he said. He draped the mainsail cover over the boom and began to unfold it. He caught me watching him and stopped. "What? Isn't this how you said to do it?"

I smiled my approval. "*Exactly* how I said, Jason."

He tossed me a skeptical look. I got the impression he wasn't used to being complimented. "Yeah?"

"Yeah."

He waited, correctly assuming I had something else on my mind.

"This charter trip sure has turned out differently from what I expected," I said.

"You mean Paul getting arrested and all?"

"Well, yes. I'd never have expected that in a million years. But right now I was thinking about you."

He propped his arms atop the boom and tilted his head at me with a puzzled expression. "Me?"

"Yes, you. I never expected such a competent first mate."

He gave me an "aw shucks, ma'am" look.

"I mean it, Jason. I'd go sailing with you any day."

He smiled broadly. "Watch out, I may take you up on that."

"Promises, promises," I said, hoisting myself onto the dock. "I'd better scoot now or I'll miss the last shuttle to town. There's no telling how long this thing with Paul is going to take, so you're on your own until we get back."

He gave me a sharp salute. "Don't worry, Captain. Your first mate will keep an eye on the ship while you're gone."

I laughed and waved goodbye. It was the last laugh I'd have for a long time.

I WAS THE only passenger on the Ford minivan that served as the island's main transportation system. The portly, white-haired driver took my money and told me to watch my step. I think he was afraid I'd smash the little brown fluffball that slept in the middle of the aisle. "I'm Gus, and that there is Traveler," he said. "Never leave home without her." The dog raised its head and cocked one ear slightly. "Isn't that right, girl? Never leave home without my itsy-bitsy Travel-poo."

I headed for the rear of the bus and sat down. "Travel-poo" stunk like the real thing, so I opened a window. The late afternoon air was chilly, but it felt good. I zipped up my windbreaker and let the breeze do what-

ever it wanted to my hair. I didn't mind, since the short
red frizz I call a hairdo always looks a little windblown.

Gus eyed me through the rearview mirror. "Gonna be
a short autumn," he said. "Temperature's supposed to
drop down to thirty-five degrees tonight. Dang unusual
for September."

I ignored the weather report and concentrated on the
sights outside my window. Vibrant red and yellow
leaves slowly fluttered to the ground like giant painted
snowflakes. The last rays of the setting sun cast everything in a golden glow. Autumn is my favorite time of
year, and I wanted to savor every colorful minute of it.
The savoring lasted just twenty minutes before Gus
ground the bus to a halt and announced our arrival in
Friday Harbor.

Friday Harbor is known as the nautical Times Square
of the Northwest. They say that if you stand on the wa-
terfront dock long enough, every cruising boat in Washington will eventually pass by. According to the
guidebooks, Friday Harbor plays host to around twenty
thousand overnight boats each year, and an equal number stop briefly to refuel, shop, or clear customs. When
you consider that the island town is also accessible by
car via the state ferry system, you're talking a lot of
visitors lining the pockets of the local merchants.

The town itself is an enchanting mix of old and new
structures—some shopping-center modern, some his-
toric but beautifully renovated, and still others nostal-
gically decrepit. It's your basic tourist trap with a
plethora of tacky souvenir shops and eating joints interspersed with fine galleries offering quality work by local
artists and craftsfolk. I like to hang out at the Harbor
Bookstore when I'm in town, but this visit wasn't for
pleasure. I hotfooted the four blocks to the sheriff's office like a power walker on steroids.

I tried to convince myself that everything had been cleared up by now and Paul and the others were sitting in a bar somewhere, laughing over the whole stupid ordeal. But with each passing block I conceded that that notion was about as unlikely as Seattleites giving up their daily espresso fix.

Sure enough, cold hard reality hit me square in the face as soon as I entered the squat stucco building that served as the county's law enforcement headquarters. The lobby was about the same size as the customs office in Roche Harbor and just as utilitarian in decor. I didn't register much else because of the uproar in progress.

Two men in gray suits with the unmistakable look of "the law" struggled to subdue an uncooperative prisoner. It took me a moment to realize that the prisoner they were using for a punching bag was Paul Crenshaw. His white tennis clothes were disheveled and ink-smudged, his brown hair a loose tangle over wild, angry eyes. Although handcuffed, he managed to retaliate against his captors by using his head as a battering ram. He also got off a few good kicks before Sheriff Sloan rushed into the room, pump racking a shotgun. He leveled the weapon at Paul and yelled, "On the floor, slimeball!"

Sharon screamed as the two suits grabbed Paul's arms and threw him face first onto the floor. The bigger of the two lawmen ground a snakeskin boot into the middle of Paul's back while the other pressed a service revolver against his left temple.

Paul didn't move except to shout, "I didn't do it! I didn't do it! You have no right to treat me like this!"

Sharon screamed again and lunged toward the threesome like a mother bear intent on protecting her cub. But Martin restrained her by wrapping both arms around her. "Calm down, Sharon!" he yelled over her piercing screams.

The sheriff waved the shotgun at Sharon and Martin. "Get the hell out of here before she gets hurt."

Martin prodded Sharon toward the door, and together we dragged her outside. She didn't stop the hysterics until Martin slapped her in the face. "God dammit, Sharon, you're just making things worse."

She whimpered a little and then fell silent. Although I knew it wasn't the case, she looked as though she'd been roughed up by the lawmen, too. Her usually salon-perfect hairdo was a disheveled tangle, and her face was as white as the tennis clothes she wore. I asked her if she was all right, but she didn't answer. Her vacant and unseeing eyes reminded me of the famous photo of Jackie Kennedy aboard Air Force One when Johnson was sworn in as president.

I turned to Martin. "What happened in there?"

He glanced at Sharon and then lit a cigarette. "Looks like the murder warrant's valid. We tried to talk some sense into those two homicide goons, but they wouldn't listen to anything we had to say. They're taking Paul to the King County Jail in Seattle which, as you saw, didn't sit too well with him."

Didn't sit well? Talk about an understatement. Getting hauled off to jail isn't exactly the highlight of anyone's day, especially when you're innocent, but I was surprised by Paul's reaction and told Martin so. "Paul should be calling a lawyer, not putting up a fight. It will only make things worse."

Martin took a long drag on his cigarette before responding. "He did call a lawyer—or, I should say, Sharon called her father. Herman will see to it that Paul gets the best defense money can buy."

"But resisting arrest . . . that seems so out of character for Paul."

"I guess you never know *what* someone will do when they're under pressure."

"Did they give any more details about the charges?"
I asked.

"Just to say that the evidence against Paul is rock
solid."

"They have actual physical evidence?"

Martin shrugged. "Apparently." He looked over at
Sharon who was hugging herself and shivering in her
skimpy tennis skirt. He took off his jacket and draped it
over her shoulders. "There isn't much we can do for
Paul right now. But Sharon's another matter."

"Right," I said. She had the look of someone teetering
on the edge of a breakdown. "What do you suggest?"

"I'm going to see if we can get a flight out of here
on Kenmore Air. They fly to Seattle on a regular schedule. Meantime, could you go back to the boat and tell
Jason to pack up our gear? I'll send a taxi for him."

BY EIGHT O'CLOCK that night, my first charter sailing
trip was officially over. While the homicide detectives
transported Paul to Seattle in an unmarked sedan via the
state ferry system, Martin, Jason, and Sharon, despite
Sharon's fear of flying, caught a seaplane bound for the
city by way of Lake Union. That left me to sail *Picture
Perfect* back to Larstad's Marina by myself. I didn't
mind sailing solo. Although I regretted the troubling way
the charter trip had ended, I was grateful for the opportunity to unwind by myself. The weather was coopera-
tive—just enough wind to make it interesting but not
enough to make me work up a sweat. Despite the annoying roar of a jet ski jumping the wake behind a powerboat now and then, it was a quiet, peaceful journey.

I had just approached Whidbey Island when I considered cranking up the engine. The wind had essentially
died, and the sloop was struggling to maintain even two

knots. While I was reluctant to abandon the quiet that the gentle sails offered, I did want to get home sooner than later. As I was preparing to start the engine, a swift-moving dark shadow passed along the starboard side. Startled, I watched as it passed underneath the bow and swam along the port side to about fifty yards in back of the stern. Within seconds, two more shadows followed the same course. Suddenly there were six shadows, three on each side of the boat. They moved through the water like torpedoes, passing each other underneath the bow and racing back to the stern for another go-round.

I grinned broadly when I realized what was happening. Despite the sloop's slow pace, its tiny wake had attracted some fun-loving Dall porpoises. My playful companions had black and white markings that made them look like round little versions of the killer whales we'd seen on our way to Roche Harbor. I'll take porpoises jumping my wake versus a jet ski any day, but they only stayed for fifteen minutes. Remembering how excited Jason had been when he spotted the orcas, I wished that he'd witnessed the porpoises, too. Especially when one of them turned on its side and eyeballed me eyeballing it.

When I finally arrived in Seattle I'd had plenty of time to think about what had happened to Paul. It all seemed like a bad dream. Or someone's warped idea of a joke. Anything but the nitty-gritty truth. I'd almost succeeded in pushing the whole unpleasant episode out of my mind by the time I rounded the breakwater at Larstad's. But as soon as I stepped ashore, I ran smack-dab into reality—in the form of a TV news crew.

"Look, it's that boat Crenshaw was on when he was arrested!" someone shouted. That's all it took. Before I'd finished tying the spring lines, a microphone was shoved in my face, and a reporter bombarded me with questions.

FIVE

I'M NOT PARTICULARLY media savvy, but I know enough to spout the standard party line when under attack. "No comment," I said firmly as I walked away. The reporter and her cameraman gave chase. And a fine chase it was. The faster I walked, the faster the questions flew. The reporter doing all the flinging was Danielle Korb, a freelance journalist I'd had dealings with before. I didn't know that she'd landed a job with the local CBS news affiliate, but it wasn't too surprising. The twenty-three-year-old woman was smart, dazzlingly photogenic, and personable. That she was also a conniving, persistent little snip was just an added bonus.

Danielle and her cameraman followed me all the way to the administration building. I intended to find Bruno, the marina's big, badass security guard, and sic him on them. But the only person in the lobby was Todd L. Wilmington, a.k.a. the Weasel. Wilmington is old man Larstad's nephew, a fact he believes gives him some kind of preferred status around here. We all agree. The preference being that we'd just as soon he'd go away. The man has no real purpose in life except to make mine difficult—a talent he has honed to a fine art. He's a tall, gangly, thirty-five-year-old still struggling to make it past puberty and losing mightily.

He gave me a smarmy smile. "Well, well, well, if it isn't the wandering sailor."

"Where's Bruno?" I asked.

He looked at Danielle and winked. "On a smoke break. Why? You have some kind of security problem?"

The wink and Danielle Korb's giggly response said it all. She still had the Weasel thinking they were some kind of item. He'd fallen for her the day they'd met, and Danielle, bright girl that she is, never hesitated since then to take advantage of the situation. Never mind that Larstad's Marina is supposed to be a secure facility with electronic gates to keep riffraff and nosy reporters off the premises. If Danielle wanted inside the marina, all she had to do was flutter her eyelashes, and the Weasel would slobber all over himself trying to make it happen.

The Weasel took a step closer and waved his bony hand in front of my face. "Hello. Earth to Kellie. I repeat, do you have a problem?"

They say the tongue weighs practically nothing, but very few people can hold it. Including me. "Guess not." I shrugged. "But you might want to do something about your problem."

"*My* problem? I don't have any problem."

The Weasel is a legend in his own mind. "Oh, that's right. I forgot. You're a problem *solver*."

"Huh?"

"A problem solver. You know, someone who fixes things." I motioned to Danielle and her cameraman.

"Like explaining to your uncle why Larstad's Marina is on the evening news."

The Weasel shrugged. "Don't be silly. I'm confident that Dani won't put the marina in a bad light."

Danielle smiled smugly. "Of course not," she said.

I raised my hands in surrender. "Okay," I said to the Weasel, "but maybe you can explain something to me, then. Wasn't a murdered woman found aboard a yacht here?"

The Weasel hesitated, not sure where this was heading. "On Paul Crenshaw's yacht," he said finally.

"And what is Paul Crenshaw's connection to the marina? Besides allegedly having a yacht moored here?" I asked.

"Oh, Kellie, you know the answer to that," Wilmington said impatiently. "His engineering firm was awarded the contract for the marina's expansion. So what?"

"Think about it, Todd. Larstad's Marina and Paul Crenshaw are practically joined at the hip right now. A TV crew running free on the docks filming whatever and whomever they please isn't exactly in our best interest."

Wilmington folded his arms across his sunken, almost nonexistent chest and said, "I'll be the judge of that."

"Okay, you're the man. Now, if you don't mind, I have business with the harbormaster." I headed for the elevator, but Danielle blocked my exit.

"Just one question, Kellie. Are you and Paul lovers?"

"No! What kind of a question is that?"

"The first one you've answered," she said with a sly grin. "Look, I'm just trying to get some background on Crenshaw."

"Then try the library. They have an excellent reference section."

Danielle ignored the barb and continued. "From what I've been told, you've known the family for a long time.

I'd hoped you could fill me in on what they're really like."

"Then you hoped wrong. As I said before, I have no comment."

"Who are you protecting? Paul or his wife?"

I reached around Danielle and punched the elevator button. Made believe it was her perky little nose.

"Okay, okay. Maybe you're not Crenshaw's lover. But the police say he *was* having an affair—with the murdered woman, Jewell Jessup. Do you know her, too?"

The elevator doors opened, but Danielle had positioned herself so that she blocked my entrance.

Assuming my best tough-girl look, I growled, "Get out of my way, Danielle."

I don't think she was the least bit intimidated, but she did move aside. "Talk to you later, Kellie," she said sweetly. "We'll do lunch or something. My treat."

In your dreams, lady, I thought.

I exited the elevator on the third floor where Bert Foster, my former brother-in-law and harbormaster, had his office. And a cushy office it was, too. It'd been old man Larstad's until he took semiretirement on the golf links, leaving all his furnishings to Bert. The large, ornate room was festooned in oak and brass, Oriental carpeting, oil paintings, and leather furniture as soft as melted butter.

Bert was a lovable, easygoing sort who just happened to luck into a good deal. He'd been harbormaster for over ten years now and had used his connections to help me get a job running the sailing school. Without my job and an employee discount on the out-of-sight moorage rates, I'd never have been able to afford one night in a guest slip, let alone live aboard my sailboat, *Second Wind.* Larstad's has all the amenities the affluent yachting types prefer, including an on-site yacht brokerage, an upholstery and sail repair shop, a yachting apparel boutique, and two fine restaurants—the Topside Bar and Grill for casual dining and the elegant Pacific Broiler for more formal occasions.

"Hey, Kellie," called Bert as soon as he saw me walk in the door. "Glad you're back." He was sitting at his oak desk, but quickly pulled himself upright and gave me an affectionate hug. Bert's a big man. Fat might be a more accurate adjective, but I prefer to think of him as a roly-poly, six-foot-tall teddy bear.

"Glad to be back. But I have to tell you I didn't much like the reception committee that greeted me down at the dock."

He scratched his balding head. "What committee?"

"Channel Seven News."

"What? Don't tell me Danielle Korb is back again."

"Sorry."

Bert muttered a curse under his breath. "I ran her out of here the day that Jessup woman's body was discovered." A worried look crossed his pudgy face. "I beefed up the security around here on direct orders from old man Larstad. Assured him that I had things under control. If he finds out about this, I've got some explaining to do."

"Don't beat yourself up, Bert. The Weasel's behind the security breach. He let Danielle Korb and her cameraman onto the premises."

"And I just escorted them off," said a voice behind us. Rose Randall stood in the doorway with an amused look on her face. "This general manager role definitely has its moments. I pulled out all the stops, powerwise, and sent them packing." She chuckled. "But the best part was watching the Weasel stumble over himself, trying to apologize to Danielle for my quote, insensitive attitude, unquote."

Bert laughed. "That's what I love about my little Rose." At five-foot eleven, Rose was hardly little, but she was as pretty as her namesake flower. Slender, blond, with curves in all the right places, she could've had any man she wanted. That the man she chose was a forty-something, balding, overweight Bert Foster confused a lot of people. But the relationship seemed to work. I loved Rose, too. Her attitude and everything else. At twenty-five, she was a certified public accountant, the marina's new general manager, and one of the best friends I've ever had.

She kissed Bert on his chubby cheek and then sat down on the leather couch next to me. As usual, she was dressed for success. Today she wore a double-breasted gray pantsuit accented with a designer scarf at the neckline. I hate to mention what I had on, but it was my usual dressed-for-mediocrity outfit—jeans and a sweatshirt.

"Wow, Rose! You've changed your hairstyle." I'd always admired her long straight hair. Now it was almost as curly as mine.

"I got a perm yesterday," she said, patting the tight curls. "Do you like it? Tell me the truth."

Since she seemed to be asking for some reassurance that she'd done the right thing, I told her what she wanted to hear. Then I quickly steered the conversation to what I wanted to hear—the status of the case against Paul Crenshaw.

"He's been released on one million dollars bail," Bert said. "Provided by his father-in-law."

"It'll never go to trial," I said with a forced bravado. "He doesn't even own a boat."

Bert and Rose exchanged a look.

"What?" I asked.

"They've got a mountain of evidence against him, Kellie," Rose said. "It doesn't look good, I'm afraid."

"What kind of evidence?"

Bert said, "We read in the newspaper that his finger-prints were found at the murder scene, and there are credit card receipts linking him to Jewell Jessup. Are you ready for this? Seems she was an employee of Premier Escorts."

"An escort service? That sounds a lot like—"

"You guessed it. The high-priced service is really a front for a prostitution ring."

I shook my head. "No way! There is just no way Paul would be mixed up with a prostitute."

"We agree," Rose said, "but it sure looks like that's the case."

"This so-called yacht he owns . . . what do you know about it?" I asked Bert.

"Just that his signature is on the registration papers. From what I understand, the sales transaction was handled over the telephone and through the mail. I'm not sure what time the yacht arrived at the marina, but it was the day before you left on the charter trip. The same day the police figure the gal was killed."

"How do you know the yacht was at the marina on that particular day?"

"The nightly slip count record. We walk the docks each night and annotate which yacht is in port. Didn't look like anyone was on board, though."

"But someone had to have paid for the moorage. Who handled the paperwork for that?"

"Office staff, but the moorage was paid up for a whole year in advance. Again, all by phone and the mail."

"So we don't know for sure that it is really Paul who owns the yacht."

"Well, the police are convinced that his signature is on the registration papers and the bill of sale."

"Did the dealer or the owner bring the yacht in?" I asked.

Bert shrugged. "Afraid I can't help you with that, either. Since the moorage had been paid and she was already registered, there wasn't any need to check in with the office when they arrived. Could've been a dealer delivery or some other person helping out the owner. Or the owner himself."

Exasperated, I asked, "Do you at least know the name of the yacht?"

"*Sunshine.* A fifty-seven-foot Bayliner. But she's gone now. Towed out of here by the Port of Seattle Police after the body was discovered."

I shook my head again. "I just can't believe this."

Rose glanced quickly at Bert. "Neither can anyone else. And I have to tell you, Kellie, old man Larstad isn't taking the matter very well."

"Worried about the negative publicity, huh?"

Rose nodded. "He has his lawyers reviewing the contract we negotiated with Paul's firm. I think he's looking for a loophole to cancel the deal."

"But Paul hasn't been found guilty yet. Talk about a rush to judgment."

"You're right, but there's a very vocal contingent opposed to the expansion project. Larstad is afraid that they'll use Paul's arrest as a way to bring a halt to everything."

"I wish there was something I could do."

"We all wish that," Rose said. "But right now the case is in the hands of the lawyers."

How encouraging.

SIX

AS ORDERED, DANIELLE Korb and her entourage had left the premises—but not by much. They'd joined a group of placard-carrying protesters across the street from the marina's parking lot. Their signs were hand-scrawled, colorful denunciations of the marina's expansion project: "Bigger Isn't Best!" "More Ducks, Not Docks!" "Just Say NO!" With TV cameras running, Korb worked the crowd for a good sound bite. The protesters, eager to oblige, jostled one another for a chance at her microphone, the evening news, and their fifteen seconds of fame. Some of the marina's employees and boat owners had gathered in the parking lot to watch the show, but I didn't stick around. I'd seen enough of Danielle Korb for one day—or any other. I had a feeling, though, that we'd all be seeing much more of the woman. She chased controversy the way lobbyists chase politicians.

Despite everything, I was glad to be home. I would've

preferred to unpack my gear and unwind from the trip
before dealing with business matters, but I was anxious
to check on things at the sailing school. Not that I was
worried; I'd left Sound Sailing in the able hands of Tom
Dolan. Some people around here thought my lead mechanic was an unlikely substitute—at fifty-five, Tom
was an ex-Navy Seal who had more muscles than man-
ners. I agreed that his people skills weren't tops, but
other than my grandfather, he was the best all-around
sailor I'd ever known. Sort of a lean, mean sailing machine. So, my need to check on things had nothing to
do with Tom Dolan the sailor and everything to do with
Tom Dolan the kitty-sitter.

Besides the sailing school, he'd been taking care of
Pan-Pan, a little gray cat with big yellow eyes who'd
meowed her way into my heart several months back.
She'd been abandoned at the marina and had somehow
wound up in the drink. I saved the panicky feline from
drowning, and she's been with me ever since. I couldn't
wait to see her again.

The sailing school was in a little building at the far
end of the marina. "Little" is the operative word. I'd
spruced up the place with some paint, racing posters,
and signal flags, but you couldn't disguise the fact that
it used to be a storage shed. I'd crammed a long table
and a few chairs in one half of the room and a desk that
doubled as my office and reception area in the other half.
The two sections were separated by a couple of blue
room dividers. It wasn't much, but it was my home away
from home. Apparently Dolan felt right at home, too. I
found him sitting in my comfy leather chair with his
long legs propped up on my desk—sound asleep. His
snoring was louder than a mainsail luffing in a stiff
wind, but Pan-Pan didn't seem to mind. She'd curled up
in his lap and was sleeping, too.

"Tom," I said.

He didn't stir. Pan-Pan opened one eye, blinked, and, seeing nothing of interest, resumed her catnap.

I raised my voice. "Tom. Pan-Pan. I'm home."

Getting no response from either of them, I reached for Pan-Pan. But Tom's eyes popped open and slapped my hands away. Startled by the sudden movement, the cat dug her claws into his pants leg.

"Jeez, woman," Tom said, gently stroking Pan-Pan's neck in an effort to calm her. "Don't you know better than to sneak up on a body?"

"I wouldn't call walking into my own office sneaking."

"Hmmf."

"Well, anyway . . . it looks like you and Pan-Pan have been getting along all right."

"Damn fur ball has been nothing but a pain in the butt," he complained. The pain in the butt had retracted her claws and repositioned herself in the crook of Dolan's arm where she now rested comfortably.

"Is that right?"

He nodded as he scratched Pan-Pan's chin. "She's a finicky eater, too damn independent for her own good, and nothing but a nuisance on a sailboat."

"Guess I'd better take her home right away, then."

With Pan-Pan still cradled in his arms, he swung his legs off the desk and sat upright. "Yeah, I guess so," he said, regarding the cat with undisguised affection. He lovingly stroked her backside a few times. "But maybe you should return some phone calls first."

"To whom?"

He shrugged. "Your brothers, your sisters, I don't know who all. But they've been calling here nonstop. Ever since that Crenshaw business hit the fan."

I have three brothers, two sisters, and an assortment

of shirttail relatives who have nothing better to do than worry about my comings and goings. For the most part, they're a good bunch of people, but I don't always live up to their expectations. Like staying out of situations that wind up on the six o'clock news.

"Anyone call besides my family?" I asked.

Without tearing his eyes away from Pan-Pan, he said, "Just your main squeeze. He's been calling here every hour on the hour wanting to know if you'd made it back yet." A slight smile played at the corner of his mouth. "Must be damn horny."

"Give me a break," I said, reaching for the phone. Tom was referring to Allen Kingston, a Seattle homicide detective I'd bumped heads with a few times when he was investigating cases that involved the marina. Despite his tendency to think I stick my nose into things that I shouldn't (meaning police business), we've become good friends. Well, maybe more than just good friends. I guess "main squeeze" is as good a term as any to describe our relationship. I didn't know about horny but I could always hope.

He answered on the first ring. "Homicide. Kingston."

"Hi."

"Kellie! Where are you?"

"At the marina. I just got in."

"Are you all right?"

Maybe I was tired or something, but the question hit me wrong. Like I couldn't take care of myself. Couldn't go out of town for a couple of weeks without getting into trouble. "Of course I'm all right. Why wouldn't I be?"

"Don't get cute with me, Montgomery. The Crenshaw case is big news around here, and you're right in the thick of it."

I sighed, instantly sorry for my thin-skinned attitude.

"Tell me about it. I got accosted by the media as soon as I stepped off the boat."

"There you go." He waited a beat and added, "I've missed you, Red."

"Really?"

"Big time."

"I've missed you, too."

Tom Dolan rolled his eyes and muttered something under his breath.

I turned my back to him and lowered my voice. "It's a little difficult to talk right now," I said. "When can I see you?"

"Today would be good, but I was called in to take Harper's shift. He's out with the flu. The best I can do is tomorrow night. How about dinner at the Topside?"

"It's a date."

Since Pan-Pan didn't seem in any hurry to leave the comfort of Tom's big arms, I called my family next. After I finished calming everyone's jangled nerves, Tom extricated himself from Pan-Pan long enough to give me a status report on Sound Sailing. As I expected, everything had gone smoothly during his tour of duty. Despite another round of complaints, Tom volunteered to keep an eye on the "fur ball" while I spent the afternoon cleaning *Picture Perfect*.

Usually, cleaning up after a sailing trip wouldn't have been a solo activity. My policy is to enlist my clients' help with the job. They don't always appreciate the opportunity, but I tell them to blame my grandfather. He taught me many things, not the least of which was that the sail isn't over just because you've made it back to shore. As Grampy always said, "You sail it, you clean it." I guess he never figured on having a sailing partner who wound up getting arrested for murder before the sail ended.

Since the sloop wasn't mine, I was particularly concerned that I leave her shipshape and Bristol fashion. That's sailor talk for neat and tidy. Besides hosing down the decks and cleaning out a week's worth of mess in the cabin, I made a thorough check of the sails. This involved inspecting the seams, batten pockets, and corners for wear and tear. Sails usually blow out in these places and, sure enough, I had to drag out a needle and thread to make a couple of repairs before I was finished for the day.

They say keeping yourself busy is a good way to keep your mind off your troubles. I guess that doesn't work when it's other people's troubles because I couldn't keep my mind off Paul and Sharon Crenshaw. I was still thinking about the absurdity of their situation when I came across a little gold ring under one of the seat cushions in the cabin. It looked like a man's pinkie ring, but I couldn't remember any of the men wearing it on our trip. There was an inscription inside that made me believe it was Paul's. *"Yours 'til the sun no longer shines—S."* I figured it must have been a gift from Sharon.

Later, I also found Paul's briefcase. Jason must have missed it when he gathered up all their gear. I reasoned that returning their belongings would give me a good excuse to check on how they were doing. Not that I needed an excuse to visit old friends—especially friends in trouble—but I've been trying to clean up my act lately. In other words, to quit giving people around here something to talk about. Strange as it may sound, there are a few misguided souls in my acquaintance (besides Allen Kingston) who are convinced I'm too curious for my own good. It's a bum rap. After all, what's an inquiring mind for, anyway?

The Crenshaws live in an area of Seattle known as

Greenwood, a kind of old-fashioned neighborhood with a trendy edge, a place where coffee shops mix with espresso bars, where young families live among senior citizens, and low-income housing and custom-built homes worth almost a million dollars sit just blocks apart.

When my husband was alive, we lived in Greenwood, too, right next door to Paul and Sharon. I hadn't been back to the old neighborhood in over four years, not since I sold our house and moved aboard *Second Wind*. But I remembered Greenwood as a community that comes together for block parties and tree plantings, holiday caroling and Seafair parades. A neighborhood where it is still possible to buy a little bungalow on a quiet street without breaking the bank, or start a small business with little more than a dream and watch it thrive in the shadow of chains and superstores. Some people call Greenwood "Seattle's hidden treasure."

My old street was an interesting mix of brick ramblers and Tudors to 1950s-style split-levels and small-frame bungalows. I pulled the Miata to the curb and sat a moment staring at our old house, the only house Wendell and I had ever owned. "The house where all my memories are" is the way Cassie still refers to it. The place hadn't been kept up very well, and the neglect tugged at my heart. Wendell wasn't much of a handyman, but he would've been appalled at the way the current owners had failed to maintain the place. I couldn't see the backyard, but I feared it didn't look much better. Wendell fancied himself a gardener and got a kick out of "harvesting season" when he'd supply the whole neighborhood with his famous beefsteak tomatoes and zucchini. I noted that there weren't any window boxes on the house anymore. When we lived there, the boxes brimmed with colors of the season—purple and pink petunias, cherry-red geraniums, royal blue lobelia, and bright yellow pansies. Enough, I told myself. I didn't come here to wax nostalgic over a life I no longer had.

Paul and Sharon had a brick rambler that also looked different from how I remembered it. Not run-down like my former home, but larger, or something. The drapes were closed, and there weren't any lights on even though it was well past sundown. I hadn't bothered to give them a call before I left the marina and I wondered now if that had been a mistake. It never occurred to me that they might not be at home or that they might not welcome my visit. Based on the media presence at the marina, I was sure they'd had their share of reporter types dogging their every move. Without advance warning, it was entirely possible that they'd think it was some pesky reporter at their doorstep. But Sharon opened the door as soon as I rang the bell.

"Kellie! Come in, come in. I'm so glad you're back."

Her enthusiastic greeting was at odds with her drawn, haggard expression—an image that her perfectly applied makeup failed to conceal. She was wearing a white designer sweat suit, Reeboks, and a pink and white braided headband.

"Are you going jogging?" Sharon had been a fitness buff long before it became fashionable. Her enthusiasm for aerobics was so contagious that she even talked me into signing up for a class at the local health club a few years back.

She slipped off the headband and fluffed her auburn hair. "Well, not outside. I'm afraid of dogs." She waved toward the back of the house and added, "We converted a spare bedroom into a gym of sorts when we remodeled. I use a treadmill for my workouts now. Much less hassle than driving all the way to the Sports Center."

"I don't want to interrupt your routine," I said, holding up Paul's briefcase. "But I thought Paul would need this. He left it on the boat."

She thanked me for my thoughtfulness and set the case on a glass coffee table. After switching on a crystal table lamp, she invited me to sit down. I'd been in this living room many times, but it wasn't anything like I remembered. Casual had given way to formal, and I wasn't sure I liked the result. The pale yellow walls that I'd helped Sharon paint had been covered with striped wallpaper, and the comfy, overstuffed rocker where I'd first cradled Tiffany had been replaced by a thin, Louis-the-something chair. Despite the warm colors—the fabrics in the fancy couches were maroons, hunter green, and golds, and the carpeting was a rich, deep navy blue—there was a cold, sterile feel to everything. I'd always felt a kinship with Sharon's sloppy housekeeping, but everything was uncharacteristically in its place in this elegantly furnished room.

"You're not interrupting anything, Kellie," she said with a sigh. "I've had this suit on for an hour now but I haven't been able to summon the energy to turn the darn treadmill on." She sighed again and slumped into a wing chair across from the couch. "Paul's even worse, I'm afraid. He hasn't gotten out of bed all day. Not that I blame him. The media coverage has been relentless." She pointed to the tightly drawn drapes at the window. "We've been trying to keep a low profile. Paul hasn't even been to the office since his arraignment."

"Is there anything I can do to help?"

She shook her head. "I don't know what to tell you to do. Don't know what I can do, either. Paul's always been the strong one in this family, but he's not dealing with this whole thing very well at all. Not that I blame him. I mean, it's just terrible what they're accusing him of. He didn't even know that . . . that hooker. So he couldn't possibly have killed her." She shook her head again. "It's all just so preposterous."

"What does Paul say about the evidence against him? I hear they found his fingerprints on the yacht where the woman was found."

"That's what has him so bummed out. His fingerprints were on a bottle of champagne. Paul can't explain it. He doesn't own any yacht! And he hasn't even been on a boat this year—except for when we went sailing with you, of course."

"I take it he also doesn't have any explanation for his signature being on the yacht's registration papers and the bill of sale."

"It's a forgery," Paul said as he shuffled into the room. He wore a wrinkled blue and green plaid bathrobe and a pair of black slippers. His unkempt hair was greasy and his jaws unshaven under bloodshot eyes. If I hadn't known better, I'd have guessed he was suffering from a bad case of the flu . . . or a hangover.

He flopped down on the other end of the couch. "Somebody forged my signature on those credit card receipts, too." He sighed despairingly. "But I can't convince the police of that. They've painted me as some kind of monster. Said I strangled Jewell Jessup because of a lover's spat that turned violent." He rubbed his temples and frowned. "What a nightmare!"

"Well, at least they let you out on bail," I said, trying to sound encouraging.

Paul snorted and said, "Only because Herman put up the cash."

"Daddy was happy to do it, Paul. He loves you like a son."

Paul heaved another deep sigh, leaned his head against the back of the couch, and closed his eyes.

Sharon filled the conversational void by launching

into a long discourse about her father's efforts to help Paul. "Our family lawyer doesn't know diddly about criminal law, so Daddy hired the firm of Truman, Scott, and Meacher to represent Paul. They're supposed to have the best defense team in all of Seattle."

"That's good," I said, watching Paul. He was so still that I initially thought he'd fallen asleep. Then I noticed that he was clenching and unclenching his fists. Desperate to change the subject, I made some innocuous remark about the house.

Sharon took the ball and ran with it, telling me all about the remodeling they'd done. The house didn't just *seem* larger, it was—by almost one thousand square feet. "One of the advantages of being married to an engineer," she said, smiling bravely.

It was then that I remembered the ring in my pocket. "I almost forgot. I found your ring, Paul."

He suddenly jerked his head up and stared at me. "Ring?"

"What ring?" Sharon asked.

I pulled the gold pinkie ring from my pocket and handed it to Paul. "I love the inscription on the inside of the band," I said to Sharon.

"Inscription?" she asked.

"You know, 'Yours 'til the sun no longer shines.' "

Paul glanced at the ring briefly and shrugged. "It's not mine." He handed it back to me and rose from the couch. "Maybe it belongs to Marty or his son," he said, abruptly leaving the room.

"Oh, dear," Sharon murmured after he was out of earshot. "He's changed so much since all this mess started. Depressed, the doctor says." She wrung her hands. "I just don't know what to do," she whined, her eyes brimming with tears.

I played with the ring, absently slipping it on and off my thumb as I tried to think of something comforting to say. All I could come up with was another offer to help in whatever way I could.

Sharon removed her headband and used it to wipe her tears. "Thanks, Kellie, you're a love." She was quiet a moment. "You know, there may be something you could do."

"You name it."

"Well, Paul is convinced that he's being framed."

"By the police?"

She shook her head. "No, no. Somebody else. He doesn't know or won't say who he thinks is behind this. But it just occurred to me that you might be able to help us find out—"

I raised my hands to stop her. "Wait a minute, Sharon. When I offered to help, I didn't mean that I would play detective."

"I know that, silly. I wasn't suggesting that you do anything of the kind."

"Then what were you suggesting?"

"Didn't you tell me that you're dating a homicide detective?"

"Yes," I said, not liking where this was heading. I was trying very hard not to screw up my relationship with Allen Kingston. Getting involved in police business, even peripherally, was a sure ticket to splitsville.

"Well," Sharon said, "can't you ask him a few questions about the case?"

"What kind of questions?"

"I don't know. Anything that comes to mind. Our attorney says that the prosecution has to turn over all the evidence they have against Paul."

"There you go, then," I said, relieved. "You don't need more than that."

Sharon shook her head vigorously. "That's where you're wrong, Kellie. I think the police are holding things back. I think there's more to this case than even the prosecution is aware of. And I believe a little inside information from your friend could make a big difference to Paul's defense."

I thought she was grasping at straws and told her so. But nothing I said would convince her otherwise. She kept pleading with me in that plaintive, little-girl voice of hers until I finally gave in. "Okay, Sharon," I said. "I'll talk to Allen. But I can't guarantee it will help matters."

A prophetic statement, to say the least.

SEVEN

THE TOPSIDE IS a casual beer and pizza joint that had been a warehouse at one time. Despite extensive remodeling and a trendy décor by some California designer, it still retained enough of a working-class atmosphere to make it my favorite hangout. Best of all, the food was good, the service fast, and you didn't have to float a loan to pay for your meal.

Allen set his coffee mug on the table and turned his dark, penetrating eyes on me. The infamous Kingston hard stare. "Hell, no, Montgomery," he said. "You know I can't give you any information about the case."

"Can't or won't?"

Again the hard stare. When not angrily staring me down, Kingston's eyes were appealing. Actually everything about him was appealing. He isn't a pretty boy—his nose has been broken three times, he has a scar on his chin, and his ears stick out too much—but his slightly battered, comfortable face suggests vulnerability as well as strength. I suppose you could call him sexy, but I think of Allen Kingston as manly, the kind of man who would protect you no matter what, a man who could fix a leaky faucet or build you a table. Kingston, though, would probably describe himself as just an ordinary guy in his mid-forties who does what needs to be done. Which, unfortunately, didn't include sharing anything about Paul Crenshaw with me.

"Can't," he said forcefully. "It's not my case." He grabbed his coffee mug and slurped noisily. Wiping his mouth, he added, "Hell, Seattle P.D. isn't even involved. The Port of Seattle got the call on this one."

"I realize that," I said. "But surely you know someone at the Port who could tell you what's going on."

Kingston glanced at four young men seated at a table next to ours and said, "See those guys?"

They wore sailing garb and had apparently come to the Topside directly from the docks. From the sound of things, they'd won some kind of race. Loud and boisterous, they celebrated by swilling beer and lambasting their opponent's ineptitude.

"What about them?" I asked.

"They have about as much chance of getting something out of the Port P.D. as I do."

"Oh, come on, Kingston," I said. "Don't be so disingenuous."

He arched an eyebrow and gave me a lopsided smile. "Disin-what?"

"Never mind," I said. I knew a stone wall when I hit it.

Kingston shrugged. "Okay." Downing the last of his coffee, he signaled our waitress for a refill. Like most of the staff at the Topside, Janey was a student at the University of Washington, or "U Dub," as we locals call the school. I listened halfheartedly as Kingston bantered with her about college life. After she'd left, he said, "Nice kid."

"Yeah, she is." I sighed.

Kingston eyed me over the rim of his coffee cup a moment. Then, reaching across the table, he took my hands in his. "Kellie, I know you think I'm being difficult, but the truth is, I just don't know anything about the Crenshaw case." His voice was as warm as his hands.

I was struck by his sincerity. He could be as irritating as hell, but he was also a good guy. Unaffected and loyal. Not hip but comfortable, like a pair of old shoes. As usual, he'd completely disarmed me. "That's okay, Allen. I promised Sharon I'd talk to you. I didn't promise her that I'd get any answers."

"That's good, because I don't have any. But . . ."

"But what?"

"I have heard some things."

"What things?" I asked eagerly.

He released my hands. "Ease up, Montgomery. It's mostly just talk."

"What *kind* of talk?" See what I mean? Irritating as hell.

"Rumor, scuttlebutt, that sort of thing."

I flashed him an exasperated look. "Well?"

"Well, the gist of it is that Crenshaw isn't the Goody Two-shoes you seem to think he is."

"What do you mean by that?"

"For one thing, he has a record."

Stunned, I stared openmouthed as he continued.

"Some kind of juvenile thing. But a record nevertheless."

"What did he do?"

"Not sure. The record is sealed."

I shrugged. "Lots of people get into trouble as kids.

That doesn't mean they become hardened criminals as adults."

"I didn't say he was a hardened criminal. I'm just telling you what I've heard. I don't know much about the murder they're alleging he committed, but it's common knowledge around headquarters that he's run up a string of traffic tickets and a mountain of credit card debt. And despite frequent bailouts from his rich father-in-law, he's on the verge of bankruptcy."

I took that in without comment as Kingston sipped his coffee. After a moment, he said, "So. You've talked to me and kept your promise to Sharon. Now I'd like you to promise me something."

I knew what was coming, but I asked the question anyway. "And what would that be?"

He turned his piercing eyes on me. "That you won't get involved in this thing. That you'll stay out of the case, Kellie."

"It's a promise."

I WAS TIRED when I got home from the Topside. As soon as I fed Pan-Pan, I went straight to bed. Usually my warm, comfy bunk and the water gently lapping against *Second Wind's* hull is so soothing that I'm lulled to sleep like a babe in a cradle. On this night, however, I found myself tossing and turning until the wee hours. The wind moaned in the rigging, and every so often a deep-throated foghorn blasted in the distance. But it wasn't the night sounds that kept me awake. The problem was the promise I'd made to Kingston—and the certain knowledge that I'd be unable to honor it. The so-called rumors he'd shared about Paul had stirred my curiosity. As the night wore on, I cured my sleeplessness by telling myself that it wouldn't hurt anything to do a little investigating—a little. Not much; just enough to answer a few questions I had. It was the least I could do for Sharon. What Kingston didn't know wouldn't hurt him—or us.

The next morning, I cornered Bert Foster in his office and asked him again about how "Paul's yacht" had come to be moored at Larstad's Marina. Unfortunately he had nothing new to add. "Like I said yesterday, Kellie, everything was handled by phone and through the mail. And I never saw the boat come in."

"Could I take a look at the registration forms he supposedly signed and mailed in?"

Bert shook his head. "Sorry, the police confiscated all my records."

"Who found the body?"

Bert eyed me suspiciously. "You aren't going to get yourself mixed up in this, are you?"

"No, no, of course not," I assured him with an innocent smile.

He had my number. "Right, Kellie. I'll believe that when Todd Wilmington stops acting like a know-it-all."

"Okay, okay," I said with my hands upraised. "I am poking around a bit, but I'm not going to do anything to jeopardize the police investigation."

"What about Allen Kingston?"

"What about him?" I asked.

Bert sighed at my defensive tone. "Forget it. I know you're going to do whatever you want, come hell or high water—or Allen Kingston. As far as who found the body, talk to Charlie."

I grinned and said, "Thanks, Bert."

Charlie "the Tuna" Saunders was a live-aboard like me. He had a thirty-three-foot sailboat with a cutter rig. That is, she had two jibs, or, more correctly, a jib and a staysail forward of her single mast. He called her *Tuna*

Delight, a nod to the thirty years he spent hauling fishing lines off the coast of Alaska. I found him below deck working on the boat's engine.

"Got a problem with your fuel line, Charlie?"

He wiped his grease-stained face with a similarly stained rag from the back pocket of his farmer john jeans. "Air leak," he said.

"Oops." I knew what that meant. Diesels don't like air in the fuel supply, and when it occurs, you've got trouble.

"Damn thing went on strike," he added with a grimace. "But I think I've got it fixed now."

"Time for a coffee break?"

Charlie gave me a toothless grin. "Beer break would suit me better."

I held up two bottles of Red Hook. "Thought you might say that."

After we'd settled ourselves inside the cabin, I got right to the point. "Charlie, I heard that you were the one who found that woman's body, the woman they say Paul Crenshaw killed."

He nodded. "You heard right."

"Feel like talking about it?"

"Shit, I've done nothing *but* talk about it. The cops asked me a million and one questions. Not that I minded, considering that's their job and all." He paused to take a long swig. "But what's your interest?"

"Paul and Sharon Crenshaw are old friends. It's hard for me to believe that Paul is a murderer. I thought if I could find out what happened, I might be able to help him in some way."

Charlie allowed as how that sounded reasonable and launched into a play-by-play description of his role in the affair. "The yacht was moored right alongside mine, you know. A brand-new Bayliner. For a stinkpot, she was a real beauty."

"Did you see her when she came in?"

He shook his head. "Nope. She must've been brought in sometime when I wasn't here. No one else I've talked to saw her come in, either. 'Course, that's not so unusual when you think about it."

"How's that?"

"You know how it is at Larstad's. This marina is plumb full of big luxury yachts coming and going all the time. Nobody pays much attention to 'em unless it's something mighty spectacular."

I acknowledged that he was right and tried another angle. "Bert isn't sure who delivered the yacht to the marina. Did you see anyone around who could've been from a Bayliner dealership?"

He shook his head again. "Didn't see nobody until the day I climbed aboard and found the woman—dead."

"How did you happen to go aboard?"

"As usual, I was tinkering around on this here old tub. I'd noticed the port spreader was loose and went up the mast to tighten the bolts." He belched and added, "Seems like there's always some dad-burn thing or another that needs fixin'."

I chuckled and said, "I hear you. Grampy used to say that 'sailor' is an old Gaelic word meaning 'person who is always fixing things.'"

Charlie snorted. "He got that right. Anyways, while I was hugging the mast, I heard a bunch of crows and gulls screeching up a storm. There must've been a dozen or so of them birds dive-bombing the Bayliner. Then I noticed that the door to the main cabin was ajar. Some of the birds were actually making their way inside."

"What did you do?"

"What any good neighbor would've done. I scrambled

down the mast and hoisted myself onto the Bayliner. Figured I'd shoo the birds off and shut the door."

"What made you go inside?"

He pinched his nose. "The stink. I thought some wild animal had been caught in there and died. An animal had died all right, but it was human."

"Where'd you find her?"

"Right inside the main salon. She was just a skinny little thing, lying facedown on the floor."

"The warrant said she'd been strangled."

"Yeah, that's true. Strangled with a fancy silk scarf. But, judging by the bruises all over her arms and legs, she'd been battered around some, too."

"Did you notice anything else?"

"She was a redhead."

"I mean about the scene."

He thought a moment. "There was a half-empty champagne bottle and a couple of glasses on the dining table."

I pressed him for additional details, but he said he couldn't remember anything else. "I didn't take a picture," he said. "Just got out of there as fast as I could and called 9–1–1 from my cell phone."

We drank our beer and chatted for a few more minutes. After I left Charlie's, I decided to check with some of the other regulars around the marina. I knew most of the twenty-five souls who lived aboard their boats at Larstad's, but that didn't mean we were friends. For the most part, the marina's live-aboard contingent was an independent lot, preferring privacy above all else. That's not to say that they were unfriendly; just wary. And it was their wariness around strangers that I was counting on. They generally kept a sharp eye out for the goings-on at the marina. If anyone new, not to mention suspicious, had been to Larstad's lately, a live-aboard had probably taken note. But like Bert and Charlie, nobody I talked to remembered seeing the Bayliner when she arrived at the marina. Nor could they remember seeing anyone in or around the boat or her mooring slip until the day Jewell Jessup's body was discovered.

Knowing that the yacht didn't just float in on its own accord, I was determined to find someone who had seen her. I walked the docks for a couple of hours, talking to almost everyone I met, but learned absolutely nothing. I was just about ready to give up when I suddenly realized that I hadn't checked where everybody hangs out at one time or another. Unlike the live-aboards at other marinas, Larstad's boat dwellers had no monthly newsletter, regular meetings, or organized social functions whatsoever. But they did have a laundry room. Much like the corner grocery store of days gone by, the laundry room was the unofficial gathering place for the live-aboards.

Both washing machines and dryers were chugging away when I entered. The tiny room was a blast of hot air tinged with bleach and soap. Helen Holtzer was the lone occupant, busily folding towels at the corner counter. She looked up when I came through the door and gave me a brief nod. Helen was a plain, rail-thin woman with hair that had turned gray when she was just twenty-one. She was forty-one now, but her laughing blue eyes and dimples made her seem much younger.

"Hi, Helen. Got a minute to talk?"

"Sure," she said, grabbing a towel from her laundry basket and tossing it to me. "Just as long as you help fold. John wants to take *Harmony* out for a spin around Blake Island. I told him this was my laundry day, but he says the wind knows nothing from laundry. If I don't get back soon, he said he'd leave without me." She laughed and added, "The old coot would, too."

"I won't keep you," I said, folding the towel and reaching for another. "I just wanted to ask you a few questions about one of the yachts here at the marina. The one that Jewell Jessup was murdered on."

She shook her head. "Such a sad thing. They say she was a hooker, but that doesn't excuse murder."

I agreed and then asked, "Did you happen to see the Bayliner when she was delivered to the marina?"

"No."

"What about after she arrived? Did you ever see anyone on board?"

Helen paused to pick up a washrag that had fallen to the floor. "Well," she said, brushing off some lint, "just the young woman."

I couldn't believe it. "You saw Jewell Jessup? Before or after she was killed?"

"Before. As it turns out, it was the same night she was killed. I'd been to the grocery store and was totin' a couple of bags when I ran into her. She was sitting atop the dock box in front of the Bayliner's slip. Talked to her, too."

"What about?"

"I asked her who she was. I mean, she was dressed in a skimpy little piece of fabric that anyone could see wasn't going to keep her warm. And she wasn't. She was shivering something awful. She told me that her name was Jewell and that she was waiting for her boyfriend, Paul."

"Paul?"

"Yep. I know what you're thinking, but she didn't offer a last name, and I didn't ask."

"Did she say anything else?"

"Nope. I figured it wasn't any of my business if she wanted to freeze to death and I walked on down the dock to our boat." She shook her head sadly. "Little did I know that she really would die that night."

I asked a few more questions, but Helen didn't have

anything more to add. Could the Paul that Jewell Jessup claimed she was waiting for have been Paul Crenshaw? I found myself wondering just how much I really knew about him. We'd all been so close when we were neighbors. It had taken Sharon and I a little while to warm up to each other, but Wendell and Paul hit it off right away, sharing a mutual interest in computers and sports cars. I remembered the time Paul came tearing into our house, all excited about a used MG he'd seen for sale. He knew how long Wendell had been searching for something we could afford. "It's a bargain, Wendell!" he said. "Just needs a little fixing up, and she'll be a real beauty."

Some bargain. Some fixing up. Those two guys spent a small fortune on parts, not to mention paint, tires, and who knows what else, transforming that old bucket of bolts into something presentable. They were together every weekend for months and months, tinkering on the car. And in the end, their labors paid off. I still have the photo of a beaming Wendell and Paul on the day their "real beauty" took first place in Seattle's classic car parade.

Paul had a few more wrinkles now, but I wondered if that was all that had changed since those days in the old neighborhood. Could he possibly be leading a double life? It wasn't all that unusual. It seemed like there were always stories in the newspaper or on TV about people who'd done just that. Sometimes even marrying and having second families that no one knew anything about. Or had Paul fallen victim to some elaborate frame, as he was now claiming? If so, for what purpose?

EIGHT

THE USUALLY UNFLAPPABLE Rose Randall nearly fell out of her executive chair. "You're going to do what?" she blurted.

"I don't know why you're so shocked. We've both done some pretty kooky things before."

Rose has always been the one person I could count on to support me whenever I got involved in an investigation. In fact, she sometimes even got involved herself. About a year ago I persuaded her to help me scope out a suspicious adoption search and reunion service by pretending to be an adoptee looking for her birth parents. But her promotion from the marina's accountant to general manager seemed to have encompassed much more than title change. Like her new office—spacious but with a conservative beige color scheme and bland, unremarkable furnishings—she'd become quite proper and cautious. Much too proper and cautious for a twenty-

five-year-old. And certainly not as much fun as she used
to be.

"But, Kellie, going to visit an escort service under the
pretext of landing a job there? That's way beyond
kooky."

"It's better than telling them I want to hire some
young stud to squire me around town."

"What's wrong with telling them the truth? That
you're looking into the death of one of their employees."

"I think the term is 'independent contractor.' "

"Whatever. I think you're just asking for trouble."

"What do you mean?"

"Think about it," she said with an exasperated sigh.
"Jewell Jessup was working as a so-called escort when
she was killed. It's not exactly a low-risk occupation."
She opened the phone book and flipped through the
pages. "There must be a hundred escort services listed
here." Running her finger down the page, she rattled off
some of the names: "Blonde Affair, Cherry Connection,
Tryst, Playboy Centerfolds, All-Leather Fantasies, An
Exotic Companion, Soft Touch . . . My God, Kellie, they
even have a service called Bored Housewives."

"And your point is?"

"Do any of these outfits sound legitimate to you?"

"I've called some of those places. What you usually
get is a recording asking you to leave your name and
number so that they can get back to you." I didn't see
the need to mention how provocative some of the re-
cordings were, the sultry voice purring, 'Hey guys, looking for something hot to do with two?' Instead I told
her, "Premier Escorts, Jewell Jessup's former outfit, has
an office on Broadway. Most of the others don't even
bother with such niceties."

"And that makes Premier legitimate? Because it has
an office?" she asked with arched eyebrows.

"No, of course not. It's been pretty well established that Premier Escorts is a front for prostitution."

"That's what troubles me. I don't understand why the police haven't shut it down."

"From what I've heard, all these services get around the legal issue by claiming that they are just providing a referral service. Escorts only. And escorts are perfectly legal. What the independent contractors and the clients do after they meet is strictly up to them."

Rose closed the phone book and gave me a no-nonsense look. "What exactly are you hoping to learn by masquerading as a job applicant at Premier?"

"Something about Jewell Jessup and her supposed relationship with Paul Crenshaw." I summarized my conversation with Helen Holtzer. "I want to find out if the boyfriend that Jewell was meeting that night had been with her before. Whoever does the referrals at Premier should be able to tell me whether he ever came in to the office. Maybe how the referral payments were handled. You never know what you'll learn until you ask a few questions."

"Sounds like a long shot to me. What makes you think they'll share that kind of information with you?"

"I don't. But I won't get any information unless I try."

She sighed again. "I still think it could be dangerous."

"Well, I'm not actually going to work as an escort. But I want them to think I'd like to. And that's why I've come to you."

She reared back in her chair, folded her arms, and gave me the eagle eye. "Here it comes. I knew you'd rope me into this scheme somehow."

"Look, you don't even have to leave your office. All I want you to do is fix me up a little."

"Fix you up?"

I nodded. "You know, make me look presentable.

This is supposed to be an upscale escort service. Meaning it's for men of means who will pay well for a woman of class. Like a Vassar graduate; someone with brains and not just a bimbo. Someone who is sophisticated and well dressed." I touched my hair. "Obviously I need a little help if I'm going to play such a part. I was hoping you could do something with this tangled mess. Maybe loan me that blue silk blouse of yours that goes so well with my suit."

It took some doing, but I finally convinced Rose to help me. "I'll probably regret this," she must've said a dozen times. Despite her best efforts, I don't think I looked like a sophisticated anything when I walked into Premier Escort Services' office an hour and a half later. But I did look good. Maybe even high class in my Ann Taylor suit, pearls, and Rose's silk blouse. She'd worked true magic with my hair, which meant the frizz was under control for a change.

If I'd had any misgivings about my intended ruse, I'd shoved them aside. So, too, my promise to Allen Kingston. It's fair to say that I'd gotten carried away with my "little investigation," but there was no backing out now. I'd already entered the escort facility in question, a small but well-maintained storefront on Broadway. The discreet gold lettering on the windows read: *Premier Services*. No mention of escorts. It could have passed for a real estate office.

The office staff consisted of a receptionist who invited me to sit in the chair next to her desk. She was a young woman—younger than I'd expected—who looked as wholesome as apple pie. Just your basic girl-next-door type with strawberry-blond hair worn in a short, sporty style. She even had freckles and dimples. But she also had a figure that, while not Dolly Parton caliber, certainly did wonders for the simple basic black dress that she wore. She introduced herself as Sandy.

I suddenly felt very old and foolish but I plowed ahead anyway. "My name's Kellie, and I came about a job. Are you hiring?"

Sandy might've been young and beautiful, but she was sharp—and suspicious. "You've worked as an escort before?" she asked, her face and body language clearly indicating that she didn't think such a thing was remotely possible.

"Oh, yes," I lied. "I've been in the business a long time."

"Where was that?"

"Here and there. Mostly L.A." It was the first city that popped into my head, but it was probably the worst mistake I could've made.

"Really?" she said with a sly smile. "I used to work there, too. What was the name of your outfit?"

I tried to remember a name from the list in the Seattle phone book. Surely Los Angeles had something similar. "It was several years ago," I said. "You probably haven't heard of it. Cozy Companions."

"Ever get busted?"

How was I supposed to answer that? *You're definitely in over your head, kid,* I told myself. *You should just bag it now before you really mess things up. Take Rose's advice, explain to Sandy what the real purpose of your visit is, and take your chances.* But I wasn't ready to give up that easily. "I was only busted once," I said straight-faced.

"Cozy Companions bail you out?"

Isn't that what pimps did for their girls? I figured it must work the same way with the escort business. "Yep. And I was back in business that same night."

She frowned and was quiet a moment. I could tell that she was studying me and I tried to remain calm. This interview wasn't going at all the way I'd anticipated. I looked nervous and felt even more so. For the first time I noticed that Sandy and I weren't alone. At the far corner of the room I noticed a conversational grouping of two leather wing chairs and a small couch. A woman in her mid-thirties, looking every bit the Vassar type I'd tried to emulate, sat on the couch idly flipping through a magazine. She had an angular face and sullen, deep-set brown eyes that caught me staring. She gave me a friendly nod, but I got the impression that she felt sorry for me.

Sandy, meanwhile, had stood up. "Thanks for coming in, but we don't have any openings at this time."

Talk about the bum's rush. She showed me to the door so fast that I didn't even get an opportunity to switch gears and 'fess up. As I stood on the sidewalk trying to decide whether I should go back inside and explain what I really wanted, the woman from the couch sauntered out the door. She walked past without looking at me and said, "If you want to talk, Starbucks on Pine Street. Ten minutes."

I'D BEEN WRONG about her age. Her name was Abby, and she was only twenty-two. She was originally from a small town in Indiana and had come to Seattle to attend the university on a scholarship. But unlike the college kids who worked at the marina, Abby had drifted into the escort business to supplement her scholarship funds. She'd only been an escort for eight months, but she said it felt like eight years. "I want out," she said simply. "I just can't take it anymore."

I didn't know why she'd pegged me to confide in but I didn't question her motives. We ordered our drinks and continued talking. After a few minutes it suddenly dawned on me that she thought I was an undercover cop. I decided to run with it for a while. "How did you make me back at the office?" I asked.

She smiled through capped teeth. "Same way Sandy did. That part about getting busted. You should've been more careful. No outfit would hire you back after a bust. Not with the contract hanging out there."

"Contract?"

She looked at me as if I was trying to make her life more difficult. "You know, the contract the service makes us sign saying we don't do sex acts. If they bail us out on a soliciting charge and put us back to work, you vice cops would be all over them. Unless this Cozy Companions or whatever you called it was run by a complete idiot, you'd have been fired. Otherwise L.A. Vice would've shut them down for sure."

What she said made sense. "Right," I nodded knowingly. "Aiding and abetting prostitution." I smiled and added, "My first undercover assignment, and I blew it big time."

"But can you help me?" It was a request tinged with extreme weariness and sadness.

I weighed what I should say. Being straight with her might just make her clam up. But if she trusted me, there was always the possibility that she could tell me something that would help Paul's case. Maybe she even knew Jewell Jessup. Since I'd already struck out once today, I wasn't anxious to repeat the experience. On the other hand, I wasn't keen on impersonating a cop but I thought it would be a lot easier to pull off than my previous role. I decided to keep the pretense going for a while longer. "Why do you want my help?" I asked.

Despite makeup, her young-old face looked so sallow and her body so thin that I wondered if she was on drugs. She seemed to be struggling to find the right words. "I . . . well . . . it's just . . . Don't get me wrong. I like the money, okay? In eight months, I've made more than my mother earned from her crummy job teaching kindergarten in two years. And she has a master's degree!" She held out her hand. "Take a look at this." The ring she sported made the Hope diamond look puny. "But . . ."

"But what?"

"It's hard, you know. Especially when you lose . . ." She paused to sip her coffee. With trembling hands, she set the cup on the table and continued, "A friend of mine got murdered recently."

Bingo. "Jewell Jessup?"

She grimaced a yes.

"And you're scared that what happened to her might happen to you?"

With a half-shrug, she said, "That's part of it. It's a risky business, all right. Not as risky as working the street, but it's still unpredictable as hell. Walking into a stranger's hotel room can be a real adrenaline rush. Mostly, though, it's just sleazy." She was quiet a moment, and then the tears began to flow, streaking her face with black mascara.

"For the last eight months I've been doing whatever vile act any stupid jerk who flashed enough cash wanted. And for what? A Rolex? A shopping spree at Tiffany's and Saks? We never had much money in my family, but my mother—the same woman who could barely afford to shop K-Mart—never abused me, never neglected me, never did anything but love me. She's the only person who has ever loved me, but not now. Not after the things I've done."

Abby dabbed her tear-and-mascara-streaked face with a napkin and then used it to blow her nose. "The truth is I hate myself. I'm just a piece of trash in an Armani dress."

What could I say to that? I feel your pain?

After an awkward silence, she smiled bravely. "So. There you have it. You asked me how you could help . . . Well, like I said, I want out. But I want to do more than just get out. I want my self-respect and dignity back. I want to feel good about myself again. Basically, I want to put Premier out of business. I guess what I'm saying is that I want to go C.I."

"C.I.?"

"Confidential informant," she said. "You're a cop, don't you know what . . . wait a minute here." Her brown eyes bore into mine. "Just who the hell are you, anyway?"

I thought she was going to bolt when I came clean. Instead, she walked to the counter and ordered another latté. When she came back to our table she said, "I thought the police arrested Jewell's killer."

"I think they have the wrong man. That's why I came to Premier. I'd hoped that I could learn something about Jewell and her clients."

"What do you want to know?"

"If anyone ever saw her with Paul Crenshaw. How he paid for her services. That type of thing."

"Okay, I can help you. But it's gonna cost."

When I opened my handbag, she shook her head. "I don't need your money."

"What then?"

"You said earlier that you knew some homicide dick."

That's not exactly how I'd described Kingston, but I nodded anyway. Why'd I ever try to bolster my credibility by mentioning him at all?

"I'll tell you what you want to know if you'll do something for me."

Here we go again, I thought. Shades of Sharon Crenshaw.

"Talk to your friend for me. Find out from him who I can talk to in the vice unit. Get me a phone number of someone righteous. Someone I can trust."

My love life was doomed.

NINE

MY CONVERSATION WITH Abby lasted another hour. She was open and frank with her answers, and I learned a lot about the escort business but not much that I thought would help Paul Crenshaw's case. Abby had never seen Paul. "They don't like us to know each other," she explained. "The girls, I mean. Some of us get a lot more callbacks than the others. They don't want us comparing notes, learning who's earning more tips and such. Spares the cat fighting, I guess."

"But you said Jewell was your friend."

"Yeah, I met her at the university. She was a student, too. We had English Lit together."

"Did she ever talk about a boyfriend named Paul?"

Abby laughed bitterly. "We don't refer to our johns as 'boyfriends.' I think Paul had to be a regular, though."

"How do you figure?"

"Look, Premier is one of the higher-end joints. That means our clientele is pretty much confined to repeat customers. You wouldn't believe the men I've met. Doctors, lawyers, high-tech millionaires. New clients are screened very carefully and usually don't get anywhere unless another client refers them to the service. Makes it harder for the vice cops to infiltrate and bust us."

"How are you paid?"

"Very well. It's not uncommon for me to get a thousand-dollar tip."

"I understand. But how does the referral service get their cut?"

"It depends on the service. Some outfits have a special bank account that can be accessed by the girls. They take the money from the john and then deposit it right away. Others have a mail drop or a safe deposit box. Premier had us drop off our daily earnings with Albert."

"Albert?"

"Big fat Albert, the collector. We paged him after we were done, and he met us at a prearranged location to collect the referral fee. Say you got a hundred and eighty dollars, the service would take eighty and you'd keep the rest."

"Are there any records of these transactions?"

"Yeah, that happens. We take credit cards, you know. And some of the girls keep their own records. The little black book you hear about in the movies."

"Did Jewell have a book?"

"I don't know."

"So let me see if I've got this straight. The prospective client calls the phone number listed in the phone book—"

"Or the number listed in one of our ads. Premier advertises in *The Stranger* and the *Seattle Weekly.*"

"Okay, he sees the number and calls. A recording or somebody like Sandy answers the phone, takes his name and phone number and—"

"Asks about any preferences he might have. You

know, two at a time, blondes, redheads, or a specific girl."

"Then the referral service calls the girl."

"Well, not by phone." She unclipped the pager from her waistband. "We all wear these. When we get a page we call in to the service. Then we're told the client's name and where to meet him. Usually a hotel but sometimes in an apartment the client's got set up. That's about it. We do the deed and then drop off the money with Albert."

All very interesting. The problem was, it didn't prove a thing. The man Jewell Jessup met the night she was murdered could've been Paul Crenshaw or an imposter using his name. If she kept a black book, I figured the police had it by now. But unless she'd taken a photo of him and pasted it in the book—which was highly unlikely—how would anyone know the man's true identity? Seizing Premier's credit card receipts wouldn't prove anything, either. Paul claimed that the receipts the police had already confiscated were forged. He'd probably say the same about Premier's. Before leaving, though, I gave Abby one of my business cards in case she thought of anything else.

Just to make sure that I'd covered all the bases, I stopped by Olympic Yacht Center on Lake Union before heading back to the marina. Since Olympic is the only Bayliner dealer in the area, it stood to reason that whoever purchased "Paul's yacht" bought it there. Sure enough, a talkative sales associate told me that *Sunshine* had been purchased by a Mr. Paul Crenshaw and delivered to a prepaid slip at Larstad's Marina. As Bert Foster had said, the sale was handled over the phone and through the mail. "That's a rather expensive item to buy over the phone," I said skeptically. "Isn't that kind of unusual?"

"No, ma'am," the salesman said. "Actually phone sales account for seventy percent of our business." I was amazed, particularly when he said that the price tag on a fifty-seven footer was around eight hundred thousand dollars. The rich, I thought; they do live differently.

I felt frustrated and let down after my day's outing. All in all, I'd made a piss-poor showing as an investigator. As disappointed as I was, it was my talk with Abby that had truly depressed me. What a sordid business she'd gotten mixed up with. I didn't know how I was going to approach Kingston about her, but I vowed to do it soon. I made another vow as well: I was finished with sleuthing. I would keep my promise to Allen Kingston and not get involved. And I kept that promise—for almost twenty-four hours.

My good intentions came undone with one phone call from Sharon Crenshaw. She called the next morning just as I was scrounging up something to feed Pan-Pan. Tom Dolan was right about one thing: my little cabinmate was a finicky eater. I made the mistake of spoiling her early on, and now she turned up her nose at regular cat food, insisting with loud, plaintive meows that only chopped liver will satisfy her discriminating palate. She was still meowing when I stopped to answer the phone.

I recognized Sharon's voice, but there was a lot of static on the line, and she kept fading in and out. "Kellie! I'm so glad . . . you! . . . to come . . . away!"

"Sharon, I can't hear you."

"What?"

"I said I can't hear you!"

"Oh, it's this d . . . cell phone." She explained that she was in her car and on her way home. At least that's what I thought she said. The battery on her phone was apparently dying, and there were too many gaps in the transmission to be sure. I suggested that she call me when she got home.

"Better yet," she said. "Can you come . . . ?"

"What?"

"Can you . . . my house? . . . show you something that . . . oh, Paul, Paul."

Filling in the blanks, I assumed that she wanted me to come over to her house. But what did she say about Paul? "Sharon, is Paul home?"

"Paul? He's . . . on a walk . . . can you come over?"

"I have a class right now, Sharon."

"Please! . . . found something important . . . explains everything . . ."

Our botched communication was getting tiresome. "Listen," I said, "I'll call you just as soon as I'm finished with my class."

The line went dead. "Sharon? You there?" I slammed down the receiver. Cell phones! I hate the dang things. Especially in cars. Talking on the phone while driving is an accident just waiting to happen. I know they're a godsend in an emergency, but such a hassle when they don't work properly. Despite the poor transmission, I thought Sharon sounded excited about something. Or maybe she was upset. It was hard to tell what her state of mind was, but if I had to guess, I'd say she was upset. My friend has always been worry-prone, but it seems like everything has upset her since Paul was arrested.

For a fleeting moment I thought about canceling my class and heading over to her house. Then Pan-Pan clawed at my legs and reminded me of my responsibilities. I'd call Sharon later. I fed Pan-Pan her meal of choice and then headed off to class.

I didn't get far. The Weasel spotted me walking down the dock and, undeterred by my *don't-bother-me* look, blocked my path. He was accompanied by a tanned, well-heeled man in his late thirties to early forties who flashed a killer smile when Wilmington introduced him. His name was William Starkey. Despite a graying crew cut, he was about as sexy as they get in Seattle. He had the classic chiseled jaw and tall, athletic physique favored by Hollywood; probably did a thousand stomach crunches a day.

That Starkey was hanging out with the Weasel made me question his judgment, but he was probably new to the marina and didn't know any better. I figured that he must be worth a bundle, though, if Todd Wilmington was squiring him around. Whenever he wasn't busy annoying me, the Weasel could usually be found fawning over the marina's wealthiest clients.

"What can I do for you, Todd?" I asked, pointedly looking at my wristwatch. "I have a class in about ten minutes."

"You missed the meeting."

"Okay, I'll bite. What meeting?"

The Weasel nudged Starkey with his elbow. "This is exactly what I was telling you about."

Starkey looked amused, but the Weasel didn't notice. He was too busy giving me what for. "Surely you can't be serious," he said incredulously. "You mean to tell me that you've forgotten about the anniversary celebration?"

He meant the marina's fifteenth anniversary. Old man Larstad had decided that some sort of celebration was in order, and Wilmington had jumped on the idea. He'd given himself the job of coordinating the affair. No one else wanted the job, but the Weasel performed it with a zeal that was downright frightening.

"I don't mean to tell you anything, Todd. That would be impossible."

Starkey laughed out loud. When he tilted his head

back, I noticed a thin, white scar along his jawline. Somehow the scar made him look even sexier.

The Weasel stiffened and said, "Just make sure you don't forget our next planning session. It's Friday afternoon at three o'clock."

I assured him that I'd be there with bells on. With a "nice meeting you" wave to Starkey, I trotted off to class.

My students were four women who were almost ready to graduate from the basics class. They'd been a little unsure of themselves when they first started, but had become confident, enthusiastic sailors. As was our practice, we met in the Sound Sailing classroom before heading out to the dock. Today's topic was anchoring.

"As you can see," I said, pointing to the array of anchors I'd assembled on the table, "there are many different kinds of anchors." I gave them a rundown on the characteristics of each, beginning with the Danforth, one of the most common sailing anchors, and finishing up with the Bruce, a solid-piece anchor introduced on North Sea oil rigs. "The various anchors you see here perform differently," I told them, "depending on whether you're dealing with sand, mud, grass, or rock." Gesturing toward the anchors, I asked, "Now, what do all of these anchors have in common?"

Carrie, the youngest member of the class and something of a cut-up, was quick to respond. "They sink?"

Once the laughter died down, I led them through the main points:

- They have holding power. Thanks to one or more prongs or points called flukes, which dig into the bottom like a shovel, the anchor is secured in place.
- They have a long arm, or shank, providing mechanical advantage to help the flukes dig in.

- They have some sort of feature to help keep the flukes dug in when the boat pulls from a different direction.
- Despite their holding power, they can be "unstuck" with relative ease.

I ended the session by discussing anchor rode—the line and chain that attach the anchor to the boat. "As you might expect, just any old rope won't do for your anchor line," I told the women. "What do you think you need?"

Again, Carrie was the first to respond. "A rope that is pretty strong."

"That's right," I said. "Strong enough to hold your boat in whatever conditions you might encounter."

Marlene asked, "How about nylon? Would that be strong enough?"

"As a matter of fact, nylon rope is recommended for anchor lines," I answered. "It's stretchy enough to absorb the surging load without yanking the anchor out, and it's resistant to chafing."

After a short discussion about how to determine the proper length of rode to put out when anchoring, we headed for the sloop we'd use to practice what we'd learned in class. We spent the next hour at a small cove near the marina, dropping hook. As each woman took a turn overseeing the anchoring process, I explained how to alleviate some of the difficulties they encountered. For the most part, they did very well. We finished with a few safety tips and then returned to the marina.

As soon as we'd moored and cleaned up the boat, I called Sharon as I had promised. When I didn't get any answer I was a little annoyed—and then worried. Didn't she say she was heading straight home? I was convinced now that my earlier hunch was correct: Sharon *was* upset. But too upset to come to the phone? It was probably just my imagination working overtime, but I decided to check on her anyway. I hopped in the Miata and arrived at the Crenshaws' house fifteen minutes later. I purposefully avoided looking at my old house this time. After parking curbside, I bounded up the steps to their home. I was all set to ring the doorbell when I noticed that the front door was slightly ajar. Now I was definitely worried. Sharon was a locked-door freak who'd never dream of leaving the front door open—even on the hottest summer day.

Stepping inside, I shouted, "Hello! It's me, Kellie."

Silence.

"Hello! Anybody home?"

Apparently not. I hesitated, then called out again. "Sharon? Paul?"

No answer.

The creepy stillness made me shudder. I glanced around the living room, but nothing looked out of place. I pushed aside my fears and decided that Sharon and Paul were probably in the backyard. Sharon said that they often ate their lunch on their newly installed deck. It was a little cool and breezy for outside dining, but I figured it wouldn't hurt to take a look. I strode through the living room and into the kitchen where French doors led to the wraparound deck. But I never made it to the deck.

Sharon was in the kitchen, lying facedown on the floor by the double oven. She had on the same jogging outfit she'd worn the night before. I thought she'd fainted until I knelt beside her and gently turned her head to the side. A bright red silk scarf had been wrapped so tightly about her neck that her swollen and contorted face was almost unrecognizable. My heart raced a mile a minute as the reality of the situation crashed down on me.

I checked her pulse. It was an instinctive response that came from the training I'd received when I was a volunteer paramedic. I'd seen plenty of corpses during my two-year stint with the paramedics, but that didn't make Sharon's death any easier to take. No training or experience ever prepares you for murder, especially the murder of someone you know and care about. I said a quick prayer and then forced myself to examine her more closely.

I figured she couldn't have been dead very long, because her skin was still warm. I found myself shaking uncontrollably at the implication—had I just missed her killer? Stomach heaving, I stood and stumbled to the sink for a drink of water. I reached for a glass and then drew my hand back. The whole kitchen was a crime scene and couldn't be disturbed. I should just get the hell out of here, I thought. But where was Paul? Was he dead, too?

I briefly considered checking the rest of the house, but fear instantly squashed that idea. I ran out of the house, locked myself inside the Miata, and grabbed my cell phone. As much as I'd cursed the device, I was sure glad that I had it now. I punched 9-1-1 and the Send button. An operator immediately came on the line.

"I want to report a murder," I said, choking on the words.

"Say again?"

"A murder! A woman has been strangled to death."

TEN

CONSIDERING THE CIRCUMSTANCES, I was remarkably calm—until I tried to give the operator the Crenshaws' address. My mind went completely blank, and I couldn't do anything but stammer. Thanks to the operator's insistent prodding, I managed to blurt out the house number. The fact that I'd given my old house number instead of the Crenshaws' didn't occur to me until after I'd disconnected. I didn't bother to call back since I figured a patrol car would be arriving any minute. I might not be able to talk sensibly but I could at least wave my arms and point to the right house.

Meanwhile, I focused on breathing. I'd just taken a few deep breaths when a taxicab pulled into the Crenshaws' driveway, and a young woman hopped out. She wore some kind of school uniform—a navy blue blazer and white blouse over a pleated navy skirt—and carried a bulging backpack.

I hit my forehead with the heel of my hand. Shit and

double shit. Tiffany Crenshaw. She wasn't as skinny as I remembered, but she was still as beautiful as ever. And, despite the schoolgirl attire, she had a sophisticated air about her. I hadn't seen my goddaughter in a long time, but there was no mistaking her for anyone else. With her strawberry-blond hair and emerald green eyes, Tiffany was a perfect blend of Sharon and Paul's best features. I flashed on the grisly scene in the kitchen, and my heart went out to the girl. There was no way I could let her see her mother like that. As she paid the taxi driver, I scrambled out of the Miata and sprinted across the front lawn.

"Tiffany!" I shouted.

Startled, she slung the backpack over her shoulder and turned toward me.

I approached her with outstretched arms. "It's me, Kellie," I said.

She endured my embrace as only a fourteen-year-old can and asked, "What're you doing here?"

"I was just going to ask *you* that. Your mom said you were at school in San Francisco."

"Not anymore," she said, frowning. "I quit."

"I don't understand."

"My parents need me," she said, glancing toward the house.

Now more than ever, I thought. "Then you know about your father's arrest?"

Tiffany nodded. "Like I said, my parents need me. Especially Mom. Dad hasn't been himself for quite a while." She frowned again and added, "It was his idea that I go to school in San Francisco."

My heart beat a little faster. "But, Tiffany, do you really think quitting school is going to help them?"

She tossed her head angrily. "Boarding school isn't cheap, you know." She glanced at the house again. "I gotta go," she said, dismissing me with a shift of her backpack.

"Wait," I said, putting my hand on her arm. "We need to talk."

The move startled her again. "What about?" she asked warily.

"Uh, your parents."

She shook off my hand. "Okay, but let's go inside the house."

"No!" The sudden entreaty was much louder than I'd intended, and she flinched noticeably. Damn. Now I really had alarmed her.

She backed away a few steps and asked, "Is something wrong?"

No, I thought, everything's just dandy. Your father's missing and your mother's lying on the kitchen floor with a broken neck. "Well, I, uh . . ."

She took my stammering for what it was: an ineffectual stall. "There is," she cried, turning toward the house. "There *is* something wrong!"

"Oh, Tiffany," I said, enclosing her in a tight embrace. "I can't let you go inside."

"Leave me alone!" she shouted. I struggled to hold onto her, but she was stronger than she looked. She easily wrestled out of my embrace and raced up the porch steps.

"No! Tiffany, don't!" I called, chasing after her.

Her scream was heartrending.

I rushed into the kitchen just as Tiffany fell atop her mother, wrapping her arms about the body. "No-n-o, n-o," she keened.

Her despair shook me to the core, but I summoned the strength to pull her away. "Tiffany, I know this is bad. But I'll take care of you," I said, holding her.

"We'll find your dad, and everything will be all right. We'll get through this."

She fought me, her arms flailing at the air. "My dad?" she screamed. "He's gone completely crazy! I just knew something bad was going to happen. And now it has . . . Daddy's killed Mom!"

"Oh, Tiffany, honey," I said trying to calm her. "You don't know what you're saying. You're in shock."

Whirling around, she shrieked, "Don't you understand? Daddy killed her! Daddy killed my mother!"

BY THE TIME the police finally arrived, I had coaxed Tiffany out of the kitchen and into the living room. Although she was still sobbing incoherently, she allowed me to hold her in my arms. The uniformed officers who responded to the call were a Mutt and Jeff duo with zip patience. I'd spotted their patrol car when Tiffany and I entered the living room, but the officers were nowhere to be seen. I pictured them inside my former house lambasting the perplexed owners for making a prank 9-1-1 call. I would've tracked the officers down, but I didn't want to leave Tiffany by herself. So as soon as I saw them leave the neighbors' house, I stepped onto the porch and made like a windmill to get their attention.

It worked, but the mix-up didn't do much for my credibility. They told us to stay put as they surveyed the scene in the kitchen and searched the rest of the house. Afterward, the older of the two, a short, paunchy sort with a sagging jawline, directed his rookie partner to call the medical examiner and homicide detail. Then, turning to us, he said, "I'll need a statement from each of you."

I suggested that he start with me. Gesturing to Tiffany, I added, "I don't think she's in any shape to talk right now. And I was the first one to discover the body."

He looked at Tiffany—still weeping—and agreed to my suggestion with a nod. Withdrawing a notepad and pencil from his back pocket, he said, "Let's begin with your name and correct—emphasis on correct—address."

"Why don't we move into the dining room," I said, somewhat surprised that he hadn't already insisted on it. From what Allen Kingston had told me about the interview process, the standard practice was to separate the witnesses for accuracy's sake. The dining room, adjacent to the living room, was close enough to keep an eye on Tiffany, but just far enough away that she wouldn't be able to hear us. After we'd settled ourselves at the table, I gave him a complete rundown on events from the time I entered the house to my 9–1–1 call and Tiffany's arrival. He seemed bored by the recitation and took few notes.

"Any idea who might've killed her?"

I shook my head. "None."

"What about Mr. Crenshaw? Do you know where he is?"

When I shook my head again, he didn't press the issue. Seemingly satisfied that he'd covered all the bases, he signaled that our interview had ended by flipping his notebook shut. Although I'd hardly relished the experience, I wasn't quite ready to call it quits. There was something about his perfunctory questioning technique that rubbed me the wrong way. I decided to give him something to think about. "But it's possible that Paul"—he sighed as if the weight of the world were on his shoulders—"is in the neighborhood somewhere."

"Oh, yeah?" he asked, although clearly not interested. "And just how do you figure that?"

I told him about Sharon's phone call. "When I asked her if Paul was home, she said something about him taking a walk."

He glanced at his wristwatch and frowned. "You say she called you over two hours ago?"

This guy was sharp. "Right."

"Mighty long walk."

Really sharp. "Perhaps, then, you should check the garage. See if his car is there."

"Perhaps you should save your helpful little tips for the detectives," he said sarcastically. "They'll be here any minute."

While I'd enjoyed pushing his buttons, I instantly regretted it. He struck me as the type who'd make someone pay—and I didn't want it to be Tiffany. I gestured toward her now and asked, "Do you still want to interview my goddaughter?"

Tiffany had curled into a fetal position and was crying softly. "No, the detectives can deal with her."

He trudged back into the kitchen while I rejoined Tiffany on the sofa.

"Tiffany," I said, gently rubbing her back. "It's going to be all right." I wanted to ask her more about what she'd said earlier. What had triggered the outburst about her father? Did she really think he killed her mother? Even if she was in shock, I couldn't imagine why she'd accuse her own father of such a thing. But she didn't seem responsive to my touch, so I kept my questions to myself.

After a few moments, she stirred and sat up. She stared at me with vacant, red-rimmed eyes. "I need to make a phone call," she said suddenly.

"A phone call?"

She rolled her eyes and mimicked holding a receiver to her ear. "Yeah, you know, ring-a-ding-ding. Ma Bell and company?"

The snotty attitude wasn't something I'd have expected from Tiffany. But then, it wasn't every day you came home from school to discover your mother's strangled body. She was entitled. As she disappeared into another room to make her call, I occupied myself by rehashing the brief statement I'd given the officer. Uppermost in my mind, though, was Paul and about a thousand unanswered questions. Numero uno: Where the hell was he?

Then there was Sharon's phone call. As I replayed our disjointed conversation, it occurred to me that she'd said more than what I had told the officer. She'd said that she'd found something. Something important. Was that why she had been so excited? But what could she have possibly found that had gotten her so worked up? What were her exact words? "Changes everything." That was it! She'd found something that changed everything. That's why she wanted me to come over. So she could show me what she'd found. I couldn't imagine what it was—knowing Sharon, though, it might've been absolutely nothing at all. Still, her words haunted me. Perhaps what she'd found cleared Paul of any wrongdoing. Perhaps her killer knew what she'd discovered and feared exposure. But who? Who could that be?

Right about then guilt hit me full force. God, I thought, why hadn't I canceled my class? Why hadn't I followed my instincts? She was excited, all right. But she was also upset, and I knew it. What kind of a friend was I? Why hadn't I come to her aid right away? While I pondered the imponderable, I picked up a book I found on the coffee table and began to flip idly through the pages. It was Paul's yearbook from Shoreline High School. Shoreline was a suburb of Seattle known for its quality schools and political activism. Paul often liked to say that he and Patty Murray—a former teacher and mom in tennis shoes, the state's first woman elected to the U.S. Senate—both got their start in Shoreline.

Judging from the number of photos throughout the book, Paul had been one popular boy. There were shots of him on the football field, shots with the swimming team, the chess club, the debate team, and as student body officer. It was something of a downer seeing him in these happier times, but I was drawn to the book. Continuing to flip through the pages, I recognized his pal Martin in many of the photos. Both boys were hailed as Shoreline heroes for defeating the school's main rival at a crucial football game. I remembered Martin bragging about that same game aboard *Picture Perfect*. The way he told it, though, he'd been the only hero on the field.

I couldn't help smiling at some of the silly notes and verses that his fellow students had written next to their signatures: "Yours 'til Spain fries Turkey in Greece" and "I wish you luck, I wish you joy. I wish you first a baby boy. And when his hair begins to curl, I wish you then a baby girl."

Oh, for the innocence of youth. How quickly things change.

ELEVEN

ALLEN KINGSTON AND his partner arrived shortly after the medical examiner. I was so relieved to see Kingston that I even smiled at his sidekick, the beautiful Melody Connor. Since Melody and I weren't exactly on friendly terms, that was a big concession on my part. Contrary to what some people think, our estrangement has nothing to do with the fact that she's a head-turning blonde with long, sexy legs and goo-goo eyes for Kingston. Well, maybe that's part of it. But the real trouble between us began a couple of months ago. Melody intercepted an important message that I'd sent to Kingston and tried to take down a killer by herself. I don't know why she acted on her own, but her grandstanding landed her in the hospital and nearly cost me my life.

Last I heard, the Seattle P.D. brass had put her on administrative leave pending the outcome of their investigation. So I was a little surprised to see that she'd returned to active duty. Despite my close relationship

with Kingston, he doesn't feel any obligation to keep
me informed about the goings-on within the homicide
division. And I usually don't care—except when it concerns Melody Connor. A woman who carries a gun and
looks as good as she does strikes me as rather formidable
competition. On the other hand, I'm not the competitive
type. So her teaming with Kingston again was no big
deal. Honest.

I threw the yearbook aside and stood up. "Kingston!
Am I ever glad to see you!"

He and Melody exchanged a look that told me vol-
umes about what they thought about seeing *me*. "God
dammit, Montgomery," he said, "why the hell are *you*
here?"

Not exactly the greeting I'd expected. He knew
Sharon Crenshaw was my friend and that I had to be
devastated by her death. Maybe I was asking too much
of someone as macho as Kingston, but I wanted him to
take me in his arms and hold me. Tell me everything
was going to be all right. Comfort me as I'd tried to
comfort Tiffany. The truth is, I was hurt by his abrupt
manner. Which sort of explains why I went on the defensive. "Sharon asked me to come," I said. "*That's* the
hell why."

An amused smile from Melody. "Sharon?"

"The reason why *you're* here," I said, glowering at
her. "Sharon Crenshaw is the victim." I pointed toward
the kitchen. "She's in there—along with everybody else.
Feel free to join them."

Kingston sighed. "Go on ahead, Mel. I'll be there in
a minute."

Melody shrugged and put her long legs in motion. As
she passed me, she said, "Don't keep him too long, dear.
We have work to do."

Her catty remark was difficult to ignore, but instead

of slapping the woman, I slumped onto the sofa. "The uniform already took my statement," I informed Kingston. "So there's no need to keep your partner waiting."

He sat down beside me and said, "Forget Mel. I want to know what happened here."

I shrugged. "It's really quite simple. I came. I saw. I called 9-1-1. End of story."

Kingston swore under his breath. "Montgomery, didn't you promise me just the other night that you wouldn't get involved in this thing?"

This thing? "Look, in case you've forgotten, Sharon Crenshaw was my friend. A friend that I've just found murdered. Call me crazy, but I thought you'd have at least *some* compassion for my feelings."

I must have hit a nerve. He softened his tone and said, "I'm sorry about your friend, Kellie. Maybe I did come on a little too strong." He paused and ran a hand through his thick black hair. "But dammit, woman. I meant it when I told you to stay out of the Crenshaw investigation."

I felt tears threatening and turned my head away. "I wasn't investigating anything," I said softly.

"Then what exactly *were* you doing here?"

"Just what I told you earlier. Sharon called and asked me to come over."

"That's it?"

I nodded, afraid that if I said anything more I wouldn't be able to stop the tears.

Kingston sighed again. I could tell he was gearing up for another lecture of some kind, but thanks to Tiffany, he never got the chance. With portable phone pressed tightly to her ear, she walked into the living room and curled up in a leather chair by the fireplace.

Kingston asked, "Who's that?"

Relieved to have his attention off me for a moment,

I answered, "Paul and Sharon's daughter. She's been away at school in San Francisco and came home just in time to see her mother's body. Naturally she took it pretty hard. I've been doing my best to comfort her."

Kingston took in that news as he watched Tiffany. When she disconnected and punched in a new phone number, he asked, "Who's she calling now?"

Shrugging, I said, "Talking on the phone is what teens do, Kingston. My guess is that she's calling her close friends to let them know what happened."

He stood up. "Well, the friends can wait. I'm the one who needs to know what happened."

While Kingston did his detective thing, I answered the doorbell. Officialdom had been streaming in and out the front door ever since the first uniforms arrived on the scene, but this was the first time anyone had rung the bell. When I opened the door, there stood Martin and Jason Petrowski on the porch.

"Kellie! What are you doing here?" Martin asked.

Tiffany, Kingston, and now Martin. The question was definitely wearing a little thin. I should have cards printed: *Kellie Montgomery. Have guts; will travel—to any and all murder scenes.*

"I am allowed out of the marina from time to time."

"Huh?"

"Never mind," I said, ushering them inside. "It's been a difficult morning. I take it you've heard about Sharon?"

Jason nodded. "Tiffany called me."

"I talked to her, also," Martin said. "She sounded so distressed that we thought we should come right over."

Tiffany and Kingston were deep in conversation on the other side of the room. She had her back to us, but as soon as she heard voices she turned around. Her face lit up when she spotted Jason. "Jason!" she squealed excitedly.

Jason smiled awkwardly and waved. "Hey."

I don't know whether Kingston had finished interviewing her, but she apparently thought so. Running across the room, she flung herself into Jason's arms. "I didn't think you'd ever get here!" she cried.

Jason reddened a little, but still held onto her. I noted that she accepted his comforting a lot better than she had mine. The young couple, arms intertwined, walked over to the couch and sat down.

Turning to Martin, I said, "Close friends?"

"Very close, actually," he said. "Those two have something damn special."

Whatever they had rendered them oblivious to everyone else in the room. Tiffany rested her head on Jason's shoulder as he whispered whatever it is that teens say to each other at a time like this.

Left without an interviewee, Kingston introduced himself to Martin. Flipping open his notebook, he said, "I take it you know the Crenshaws?"

Martin nodded.

"Any idea where Paul Crenshaw is?"

"No. I just came from the office, and he wasn't there—but then, he hasn't been to work since this whole mess started."

"His daughter says he murdered her mother."

Martin's eyebrows shot up. "That's shock talking. Paul didn't have anything to do with this tragedy."

Kingston eyed Tiffany and Jason. "She doesn't appear to be in shock at the moment."

"Kids." Martin shrugged. "They're more resilient than we think."

A shout from Melody in the kitchen. "Allen! You're needed in here."

Flipping his notepad shut, Kingston said to Martin, "Stick around a while. I have some more questions for you."

"Sure thing, detective."

"And you," said Kingston, frowning at me, "can leave right now."

"Already out the door," I said, returning his scowl.

Martin watched Kingston depart for the kitchen. "What that chap needs is a good stiff drink."

"Yeah, well . . . he's just doing his job."

"Give me a break," Martin said. "The guy is nothing but a hard-ass who gets off bullying people around."

"That's a rather harsh assessment."

"Just calls 'em as I sees 'em."

Kingston hadn't exactly made my heart sing today, but Martin's criticism of him hit me wrong. "You've only just met the man, Martin, but I've known him for some time. Allen Kingston is a good cop. A little uptight at times, but a good cop."

"Okay, okay," Martin said, raising his hands. "I'll take your word for it." A wicked smile played at the corners of his mouth. "Just the same, better not invite us to the same party."

I slung my handbag over my shoulder and prepared to leave. As I did, I glanced at Tiffany. Jason had diverted her attention away from the tragedy by flipping through the pages of the same yearbook I'd looked at earlier. My memory clicked in as Jason pointed out something to Tiffany. "I almost forgot to tell you," I said to Martin. "I have your ring."

"What ring?"

I described the ring I found on the sailboat after our charter trip.

"It's not mine."

"Really? Then it must be Jason's. Sharon and Paul both said it wasn't theirs."

"Oh? What did you say it looked like again?"

I quoted the inscription.

He hesitated a moment, then slapped his forehead. "Man, how could I be so dense? Yeah, that's my ring. I forgot I even had it with me."

I promised to return it to him as soon as possible, and we said our goodbyes. "I'd tell Tiffany goodbye, but she seems preoccupied at the moment."

"Don't worry," Martin said. "You can call her at our house later."

"*Your* house?"

He nodded. "She's going to stay with Jason and me for a while."

I wondered when that decision had been made but kept the question to myself and asked, "What about Paul? Won't he want his daughter staying here with him?"

"I'm not so sure that's such a good idea."

"What do you mean?"

"You heard what Tiffany told the detective about her father. She told Jason and me on the phone that she was afraid of him. Besides, where the hell is he?"

"You don't think he had anything to do with Sharon's murder, do you?"

Martin shook his head. "No, no, of course not. But I have to admit that things don't look good for him. I'm sure he'll agree that Tiffany would be better off staying with Jason and me right now. At least until things get sorted out." Martin shook his head. "It's a damn shame about Sharon. But if Tiffany had arrived home any earlier, maybe she would've been killed, too. It still might not be safe for her here—or Paul, either, for that matter."

"You're right. I hadn't even thought about that."

"Jason and I will watch out for her," he said. Then, glancing at his son, he added, "That is, if their hormones don't get in the way."

"Well, I wish you luck," I said, opening the front door. The scene that greeted me outside was your typical peaceful neighborhood run amok. All the police, paramedics, lab technicians, the medical examiner, and their attendant vehicles had drawn a crowd of onlookers. The morbidly curious included kids on bicycles, shocked neighbors, and what looked like several reporters. A TV camera crew scurried about, setting up equipment. Although I hadn't seen her, I had no doubt Danielle Korb was somewhere amongst the throng. I hurried to my car before she could spot me.

I was halfway to the curb when Kingston bounded out of the house.

"Montgomery! Wait up!"

My heart did a major flip-flop. Despite his bristly way of dealing with me, there was no sense denying that I cared for the man. Had for some time, and he knew it. I stopped in my tracks and waited. Martin had the wrong take on him. Allen Kingston wasn't the type of man to let me leave without making things right between us.

"You don't have to apologize, Allen," I said with a warm smile. "I know you were just doing your job in there."

"Damn right," he said. "*My* job. Not yours. So I'm going to say this one more time so there's no misunderstanding: Keep your nose out of this case."

"Wait a minute," I said. "*That's* why you came running out here? Not to apologize for your hard-boiled attitude? Not to comfort me for the loss of my friend? But to tell me to get out of your face?"

He nodded, a bit uncertainly.

"Well, don't you worry, Detective. Your face is the last face I want to see."

If there'd been a door handy I'd have slammed it. Stomping across the yard on soggy, rain-soaked grass didn't have the same effect, but I think he got the point.

TWELVE

THAT DID IT. The tears were back, but this time I did nothing to stop them. I just sat in the Miata and let them flow. I don't like to think of myself as a weepy female, but sometimes the circumstances call for a good cry. Losing a friend to murder and another closer friend to whatever had just happened between us called for a bunch of tears. I probably would've indulged myself a little longer, but Danielle Korb was on the loose. I saw her working her way through the crowd, thrusting her microphone at anyone willing to pose for the camera and spout off about the Crenshaws. I was afraid if I stuck around any longer she'd eventually spot the Miata and I'd be her next victim.

I wiped my tears with my jacket sleeve and put the key in the ignition. But my fingers froze while I considered a sudden idea. After taking the key out, I checked to make sure Danielle wasn't looking and then exited the Miata. I sprinted across the street to a little yellow rambler and rang the doorbell. If Emma Donnelly was surprised to see me standing on her porch when she opened the door, she didn't show it.

"Come in, dear," she said. "You're just in time for a spot of tea." Her wink told me that nothing had changed in the four years since I'd seen her. At eighty-seven, Emma Donnelly still liked a little Irish whiskey in her afternoon tea.

A small woman, she had a tiny waist and soft porcelain skin. Her thin white hair was pulled back from her face in an old-fashioned bun. Even though she used a cane, she moved with the airy grace of the dancer she'd once been.

I followed her into the kitchen and sat down at the chrome dinette. "How're you doing, Emma?" I asked guiltily. As was the case with most of my former neighbors, I hadn't bothered to stay in touch with her after moving to the marina. I didn't regret the lack of contact with the others, but Grampy's former flame deserved better. Especially since the purpose of my visit wasn't about reestablishing old friendships.

"Can't complain," she said, drawing some water for the teakettle. She placed the kettle on the gas stove, then sat down on a red upholstered chair across the table from me. "The golden years aren't all they're cracked up to be," she said, "but thanks to the good Lord and a little Irish luck, I'm still a 'kickin'. I've outlived everyone in my family, you know." She chuckled. "But your Grampy always said I was too dang ornery to die."

"Really? I thought he always said you were too dang beautiful for his old eyes."

She threw back her head and laughed, a surprisingly hearty outburst from such a fragile-looking woman. "Oh, Kellie, dear, I do believe you've inherited your grandfather's blarney."

The tea ready, she poured a healthy shot of Tullamore Dew in each of the china cups she placed on the table. Raising hers, she said, "To your grandfather. May he rest in peace—at least until I can join him and stir things up."

We chatted about old times and drank our whiskey-laced tea. Presently Emma said, "You haven't mentioned why you happened to stop by today." She nodded toward the front of the house. "But I suspect it has something to do with that circus going on outside."

"I'm sorry to be the one to tell you, but Sharon Crenshaw is dead."

Emma didn't flinch at the news. "How?"

"Strangled."

"I knew something bad had happened over there. Knew it was bound to happen eventually."

Pay dirt. Emma had a reputation as the neighborhood gossip. But it was gossip based on keen eyesight, good ears, and a nose for sniffing out the truth. I'd hoped that my visit might shed some light on what had happened across the street. Now it looked like my hunch was about to pay off. Setting my cup on the table, I asked, "What do you mean?"

"They were always fighting, and I don't just mean arguing. Screaming and carrying on something fierce." She poured another shot of whiskey into her tea. "Now, mind you, that rascally grandfather of yours and I had plenty of fights. It's an Irish birthright. But we never, ever carried on like the Crenshaws."

"I'm surprised to hear that, Emma." Disappointed was more like it. Perhaps Emma wasn't as sharp as she once was. Perhaps age had taken its toll on her powers of observation. "Emma, I've known Paul and Sharon for years, and in all that time I don't think I've ever heard a cross word from either one of them. Sharon's timidity often got on people's nerves, but Paul never seemed to mind. He was never exasperated or put off by her fears, no matter how irrational."

Emma sighed and shook her head. "Kellie, dear. I didn't say Paul and Sharon were fighting."

"Oh? Who, then?"

"Mr. Crenshaw and that daughter of theirs. What's her name?"

"Tiffany?"

"Yes, that's it. Tiffany. I realize teenagers can be difficult, especially nowadays, but from what I've heard, that little gal is quite a spitfire." She picked up on my "tell me more look" and continued. "The trouble started several months ago. I don't know what the problem was, but father and daughter did not get along one little bit. Finally things got so bad he had to ship her off to some boarding school in la-la land."

"California?"

"Right. La-la land."

"Emma," I said, "did you see Paul today?"

"I was wondering when you'd get around to that." She sipped her tea. "Except for an early-morning walk, he was there all morning. At least, his car was in the driveway."

"So he was home when Sharon arrived?"

"No, but soon thereafter."

"Do you know when he left?"

"Don't know the exact time, but it was right before you pulled up in that little red sports car. I was watering my plants in the front window and saw him jump in his car like the devil was after him. He burned rubber, I can tell you."

"Did you see anyone else go in or out of the house?"

She shook her head. "Nope. Just Sharon, Paul Crenshaw—and you."

• • •

BACK AT THE marina, I headed straight for the Topside. Before Sharon's murder, Kingston and I had made plans to meet there for dinner. I didn't expect to be meeting him for dinner or anything else in the foreseeable future but I still needed to eat. Actually, I needed to drink. Emma's spiked tea had been welcome, but it hadn't taken the edge off the day's events. I slid onto a vacant barstool to give the Topside's bartender, Austin Reynolds, a shot at relieving my misery. "I'll have a vodka Collins," I told him. "Make it a double."

Austin raised an eyebrow. "You sure, Mrs. M?" he asked. Like Janey and most of the kids who worked at the Topside, he was a university student and had been around ever since I'd moved to the marina. I wasn't much of a drinker, and he knew it.

"Bad day," I said simply.

He nodded sympathetically and moved on. Moments later, he returned with my drink and set it on the counter. "A double for the lady," he said as Rose Randall sat down on the stool next to me.

"A double?" she said. "Are we celebrating or commiserating?"

I tossed back a generous swig without answering. It stung all the way down.

She waited. When I still didn't respond, she signaled Austin for a beer. "I hope this doesn't have anything to do with your visit to Premier Escorts."

I shook my head. "No, that was uneventful. I didn't learn anything useful."

"Well, something is bothering you. Want to talk about it?"

I took another drink. "Actually, I want to forget about it."

Rose nodded and said, "Okay, but I have a feeling that whatever has you down isn't going to go away with a drink. Double or not."

"You're right," I said as Austin brought her a glass of Morelli's. "Make me another one of these, Austin."

When Austin returned with my order, I downed it as fast as the first. Rose sipped her beer without comment. I knew what she was doing. Waiting me out until the vodka loosened my tongue. It didn't take long. "I found Sharon Crenshaw's strangled body today," I said.

Rose banged her beer glass on the counter. "What?"

I told her everything, from Sharon's phone call to Tiffany's unexpected arrival on the scene.

Rose put an arm around my shoulder. "Oh, Kellie, I'm so sorry."

When my tears started, she gave me a tissue. I couldn't say anything more for a few minutes. Rose patted my back and told me to take my time. After I regained my composure I summarized my conversation with Emma Donnelly. "Emma says Paul and Tiffany had been having terrible fights. Maybe Tiffany was still reeling from being sent away to boarding school. Maybe that's why she was so ready to believe the worst about her father."

"Or she was in shock," suggested Rose.

I nodded at the possibility. "That was my first thought, too. Speaking of shock . . . Guess who showed up with Kingston?" I told her about Melody Connor's return to duty, my conversation with Kingston, and the insensitive way he dismissed me.

"Hmm. Not a very pleasant goodbye."

"I think it was good riddance."

"Oh, Kellie, you can't mean that. Kingston adores you."

I laughed in spite of myself. "He sure has a strange way of showing it."

"What can I say? Men are from Mars."

I felt a headache coming on and should've left right then, but I didn't want Rose to think I didn't appreciate her attempt to boost my spirits. "What's new with you?" I asked.

"I have a dinner date at the Broiler tonight."

"Why the frown? Don't tell me you and Bert are on the outs, too?"

She shook her head and said, "No, nothing like that. The dinner's with old man Larstad."

Lawrence Larstad hardly ever showed his face around the marina anymore. "What's the occasion?" I asked.

Rose frowned again. "Same old stuff—he's worried about all the negative publicity the marina has been getting in the media. Plus he's not happy with the plans for the marina's anniversary celebration."

"So why pick on you? I thought that shindig was the Weasel's doing."

"It is, but Larstad is convinced that the publicity surrounding the Jessup murder will adversely affect the celebration."

"Again, that's his nephew's doing. And his so-called girlfriend, Danielle Korb's."

"Well, sort of," she admitted. Sipping her beer, she added, "The thing is, I *am* on the hot seat."

"For what?"

"For hiring Paul Crenshaw in the first place."

My headache was getting worse. Rose had persuaded old man Larstad to hire Paul based on my recommendation.

"Larstad said something else today when he set up our little get-together." She eyed me carefully. "Something you're not going to like."

"Lay it on me, Rose. I've already dealt with a lot I haven't liked today."

"Wilmington has convinced his uncle that your connection to Paul Crenshaw is suspect, particularly since you conveniently set up the charter trip for him. I think he views the trip as your attempt to give Paul some sort of alibi."

"That's ridiculous."

"I agree and plan to tell him so. But, as you know, his lawyers are reviewing the marina's contract with Paul's engineering firm. I don't think I have any choice but to tell Larstad that we're suspending the charter program until things settle down."

I couldn't believe what I was hearing. I said nothing as she continued.

"I know this news comes at a bad time, Kellie."

I grimaced and rubbed my temples.

"But there is some good news," Rose said with forced cheerfulness.

"Please tell me that I've been kicked off the Weasel's planning committee."

"I'm afraid the news isn't *that* good." She laughed. "You're still on the committee, but you're also still the sailing school manager. For now, anyway."

My headache had escalated into a full-blown hammer splitting my head into two miserable parts. "Okay," I said, hoisting myself off the stool with care. "Thanks for the vote of confidence."

She grabbed my arm. "Kellie, please don't go away mad."

"I'm not mad, Rose. I'm just a little drunk." And depressed as hell, but I bid her a quick farewell before I said anything that I'd regret in the morning.

THIRTEEN

I INTENDED TO hop into bed as soon as I climbed aboard *Second Wind*. But the red light on my answering machine was blinking its little heart out, which is rather hard to ignore. I gave it a good shot, though. I took a long, hot shower; brushed my teeth; flossed and rinsed; and slipped into my jammies. When I swallowed an aspirin for my headache, it occurred to me that I'd missed lunch and dinner. There wasn't much in the fridge, but I found a jar of mayo and some pickles that I mixed with a can of tuna and spread it on two slices of stale bread. It wasn't the best sandwich I'd ever eaten, but it was better than nothing. Drinking on an empty stomach was probably what had given me a headache in the first place.

After eating, I washed a stack of dishes that had been accumulating all week and made a halfhearted stab at tidying up the cabin. The telling part is that I even changed Pan-Pan's stinky litter box—my least favorite chore of all time. Anything to keep my mind off that little red light. My concern was that the message waiting for me was from Kingston. I didn't think I could bear to hear his voice again. On the other hand, I desperately hoped that he had called. I didn't think I could take *not* hearing his voice again, either. In any case, I was afraid to play back the message tape.

When I finally screwed up the courage, the voice on the machine wasn't Kingston's. At first I wasn't sure whose voice it was. The words were slurred and garbled as if the speaker had also spent the evening drinking a little too much vodka. After several replays, I finally determined that it was Paul Crenshaw. But that was all I could determine. I had no idea what his message was about except that it had something to do with Tiffany and Jason. I started to dial his home phone number, but hesitated and then dialed *69 to verify that he'd called from home. If not, the callback feature would give me the correct number. The number that showed on the screen was unfamiliar and when I dialed, it rang and rang. I was about to hang up when a gruff, gravelly voice came on the line.

"Is Paul there?" I asked.

"Paul who?"

"Paul Crenshaw."

A muffled sound and then, "Hey, you guys! Anyone here know a dude named Paul Shaw?"

"Crenshaw. Paul Crenshaw."

Laughter in the background.

"Hello? Hello?" I shouted into the receiver.

"Yeah, I'm here."

"Who are you?"

"That's classified info. Let's just say I'm a guy who heard the phone ringing and answered it."

"Well, could you at least tell me whose phone it is?"

Laughter again. "Sure, sure. Let me see what it says here . . . okay, I got it. Property of U.S. West."

"What?"

"Look lady, I gotta go. This booth stinks like somebody puked on the floor."

Damn. A telephone booth. Where was Paul now? What was he trying to tell me? Was he in danger? The questions rattled around in my head long after I climbed into my bunk. I awoke the next morning, headache-free but still wrestling with the same questions. I shook them off as best I could and got ready for the day. I had a nine o'clock sailing class and looked forward to getting out on the water. The wind seemed a little fickle, as if it couldn't make up its mind which direction it preferred, but it was still brisk and steady enough for a good sail.

If there is one good and true thing in my life, it is sailing. It doesn't matter whether I'm by myself or with a group of students; the wind and the sea have never failed to soothe my troubled soul. I've had a love affair with sailing ever since I was a know-nothing kid in Bar Harbor, Maine. I'd hounded my grandfather for months until he agreed to let me take out his little white sloop by myself—after he was satisfied that I wouldn't capsize and drown. *Just sit in the boat, Kellie darlin'. Don't even think of taking her out until you know her as well as your own skin. Until you and the boat and the wind are one. First find the wind. Then close your eyes and imagine how your craft will behave when underway, how she will dip and soar, how the rigging will sound in the wind, how the water will gently slap against the hull, how the tiller will feel in your hand. Tack without tacking, jibe without jibing, sail without sailing.*

They call me instructor now, and I have certificates of accreditation from the American Sailing Association and the Coast Guard to prove it. But it was Grampy's hard-sought stamp of approval that still rings in my ear after all these years. *"Well done, Kellie darlin'. You're a damn fine sailor."*

My students were waiting when I arrived at the Sound Sailing classroom. A gregarious bunch in their early twenties, they were raised on MTV and every manner of instant gratification. The idea of merely sitting in a boat and sailing without sailing didn't go over well. But since I *was* the instructor, they indulged my quirky methods. They closed their eyes as I had instructed, but keeping their mouths shut while they envisioned becoming one with the boat was more than they could manage. The exercise swiftly drew to a close when they began peppering me with questions—not about sailing, but Sharon Crenshaw's murder.

"Why do you think I know anything about it?"

No one seemed eager to 'fess up until Brent, a pudgy fellow with a pock-marked face, pulled a newspaper from his backpack. "Here," he said. "You made the front page."

And indeed I had. Some photographer had managed to capture the exchange between Allen Kingston and me outside the Crenshaws' home. The black-and-white photo was sort of grainy, but it accurately portrayed the scene as I remembered it: A stern, no-nonsense Kingston waving an accusing finger at me. I quickly scanned the caption: *Police question Kellie Montgomery, a friend of Paul Crenshaw.*

"Were you really the first to find the body?" asked Brent.

I grimaced and continued to read the article that accompanied the photo. The gist of it was that Paul was a prime suspect in his wife's death and was wanted for questioning. His bail had been revoked and a new warrant issued for his arrest on the previous Jewell Jessup murder charge. Paul's lawyer, Denton Meacher, of the Truman, Scott, and Meacher Law Offices, was quoted as saying he hadn't heard from Paul, but urged his client to turn himself in to the police immediately.

"The last paragraph's a zinger," offered one of the students. "It's all about you."

I skipped to the end of the article. An unnamed source (sounding suspiciously like the Weasel) claimed that there was more to my relationship with Paul Crenshaw than that of a close friend. The article hinted that more revelations concerning our relationship would be forthcoming. I thrust the paper back at Brent and said, "Don't believe everything you read."

I cut off further discussion of the murder by suggesting that we hoist the sails and take the sloop out. We tacked and jibed across Elliott Bay for the better part of an hour and then called it a day. Since I didn't have another lesson scheduled until later in the afternoon, I closed up the school and headed back to *Second Wind.* I needed to think and didn't want any interruptions.

By the time I'd poured myself a second cup of tea, I'd come to a decision: I was going to find out who killed Sharon Crenshaw and Jewell Jessup. Kingston and the rest of the world be damned. They already thought I was involved, so I figured I had nothing to lose. Thanks to the *Seattle Times* and Todd Wilmington, my reputation was already suspect. I needed to clear my name. Besides, I told myself, I am Tiffany's godmother. Isn't that what a godparent is for? To help the child when the parents are unable to?

The phone rang, and I considered letting the machine pick up the call. Was Kingston calling? Crenshaw? The media?

None of the above. It was Cassie. "Mom, if you're there, please pick up."

My daughter had left for college just a couple of weeks before, but it seemed like forever. I jumped to grab the receiver. "Cassie, darling. How are things in New York?"

"I don't know, Mom. I'm at Sea-Tac." She filled the shocked silence that followed her announcement with, "And I'd like to see you."

"You need a ride home?"

"No, I'm not coming home. I have another plane to catch soon."

"Cassie, what's going on?"

"It's a long story."

"Are you all right? You're not sick or anything?"

"Of course not." She paused, and I heard the roar of a jet in the background. "Can you come down here, Mom? I really need to talk to you."

I hate airport reunions. The last time I met Cassie at Sea-Tac she dropped a bombshell on me that nearly destroyed our relationship, a relationship that had been on shaky ground ever since we lost Wendell. Cassie and Wendell were very close, and his death hit her hard. Coming to terms with a significant loss has no timetable, but Cassie believed the decisions I made so soon after her father's death only prolonged her sorrow. I couldn't make her understand that selling the family home (her biggest complaint) was a necessary step in my own healing process. Although she had no problem with my career change—high school science teacher to sailing school instructor—she had great difficulty accepting my preference for sailboat living versus a house in the suburbs. I sometimes think that the loss of her father and the lifestyle we had together as a family contributed to her decision to search for her biological roots.

Cassie came into our lives when she was just a few days old, but she's always known that she was adopted.

Even if Wendell and I hadn't told her, the physical differences between us would've raised a few questions in her mind. At a slender five foot ten, Cassie is a towering giant in a family of short, stocky types. Her skin is dark, while ours is light. Her hair is black and straight; ours is red or blond and curly. Her eyes are brown, and ours are blue. But physical differences aside, Wendell and I always considered Cassie our daughter. So it was a shock when she came home from college last Christmas and announced that she was going to search for her birth mother.

It took me a while to deal with the idea, but I can honestly say now that I'm okay with what she's doing and fully support her efforts to connect with her birth family. She's already located a twin sister whom we didn't even know existed. Their reunion got off to a rocky start but eventually turned out just fine. I have every hope that if and when she finds her birth mother, everything will work out just as well.

So why did I suddenly feel uneasy? Aside from the fact that she was supposed to be sitting in a classroom instead of an airport, I was certain that whatever she wanted to talk to me about wasn't something that I wanted to hear. The whole thing smacked of déjà vu.

"Mom? Are you still there?"

"Sorry about that, Cass. I drifted off for a moment."

"So, will you come to the airport? I only have an hour before my plane takes off."

"I'm on my way. Just tell me where to meet you."

FOURTEEN

WHEN CASSIE SAW me coming, she ran to greet me with a big dimpled grin and an enthusiastic hug. Passersby didn't give our embrace a second look—it was an airport, after all—but the gesture meant a great deal to me. Cassie has always been a little stingy with her hugs, especially in public, but ever since I'd agreed to support her birth mother quest, she's been almost overly affectionate.

"Thanks so much for coming, Mom. I was afraid you might not be able to get away from the marina on such short notice."

"You hit town just right. I don't have a class scheduled until later this afternoon. What I can't understand is why you're here in the first place."

Cassie patted my shoulder. "You're worried, aren't you?"

"Guilty as charged," I said, looking up at her. Although my daughter had reached her present height at

age thirteen, it still felt weird craning my neck to look
at her. "Why don't we sit down," I suggested, "and you
can tell me what this little get-together is all about."

And so we did.

"Are you sure you don't want something to drink?"
she asked, pointing to a bank of vending machines.
"They probably have your favorite, Diet Pepsi."

I shook my head.

She pulled on a strand of her long, dark hair and
twisted it around her finger. "What about a snack, then?
I know how you love salted peanuts."

"You afraid to tell me what's going on, Cassie?"

"No! What makes you think that?"

"Oh, just a wild guess."

A voice came over the loud speaker. "Mr. Nesbitt,
please pick up the white courtesy telephone." A man
with a worried look on his face—Mr. Nesbitt, I assumed—jumped to his feet and raced off.

She glanced at the telephone kiosk. "If I were afraid,
I could've just dropped this whole thing on you over the
phone."

"What thing, Cass?"

She sighed. "I'm going to Portland to see Deena. She
has a lead on the whereabouts of our mother."

"I thought this might have something to do with your
search. How'd Deena find the lead?"

"On the Internet. Isn't it amazing?"

I agreed. "So, she followed your example, huh?" Cassie had used the Internet to track her twin's adoptive
family. Their name turned up in a file that was uncovered when the attorney who handled Cassie's adoption
was murdered.

"Finding our mother's maiden name in that old file
was a big break. Even so, Deena has spent hours and
hours on the computer. And now it's finally paid off."

"How long will you be gone?" I refrained from re-minding her that school had just started.

"That's the thing. Deena thinks she may be in New Mexico. We're going down there together."

"New Mexico . . . I repeat, how long will you be gone?"

"That's hard to say. We don't know how long something like this might take. The lead is a good one, but . . ." She trailed off with a shrug.

Forget refraining. "What about college?"

"I'm dropping out."

"What?"

"Chill, Mom. It's just for the semester."

"I see. Just for the semester," I said as calmly as I could. "And what about your scholarship? You don't think dropping out—even for a semester—isn't going to affect that?"

"Well, possibly. But I'll just have to cross that bridge when I come to it."

"You've just come to it."

She gave me a puzzled look.

"You know that I support your search, Cassie. But bridges, smidges, you need that scholarship. Badly. If you drop out now and lose it, you may never be able to go back."

She swept her hair away from her face and glared at me. "It's not my fault that I need the scholarship!"

The truth stung. Wendell had made a good living as a program manager at DataTech, but the many life changes I made following his death caused a significant change in our financial picture. The only regret I've ever had is that I didn't plan better for Cassie's education. Her resentment was justified. "You're right, Cassie. I'm to blame for our current situation. Not you. But that still doesn't excuse the fact that you're putting your scholarship at risk."

"Well," she said after a moment, "I guess I'll just have to call Aunt Donna. I'm sure she'd be willing to help me."

That was a low blow, and Cassie knew it. For reasons I'll never understand, my older sister had offered Cassie ten thousand dollars to use a questionable adoption search firm to locate her birth mother. Although Donna claimed that she was just trying to help, her so-called generosity had not only almost severed my relationship with my daughter, but it also had put us both in great danger. Donna and I were still on shaky ground because of it. I felt my face flush. "Are you deliberately trying to hurt me, Cassie?"

"I'm hurt, too."

"I'm sorry about that. I really am. But there has to be another way to follow up on Deena's lead without jeopardizing your whole future."

"Finding my mother *is* my whole future. I thought you understood that."

"I do, Cass. It's just that we barely have money for college, let alone trips to New Mexico or anywhere else right now. I was under the impression that Deena's family was in the same financial boat."

Cassie stood and flung her backpack over her shoulder. "Just forget it, then. I should've known you'd react this way."

"Sit down. Your flight hasn't been called yet. We need to discuss this further."

"No, Mom, our discussion is over. I'm dropping out of school, and that's that. I'm sorry if you don't like it. Deena was right. She said I should just do it and tell you later. I didn't think that was fair, but you're the one who's being unfair."

I stood and reached for her. "Cassie, don't leave this way."

She shrugged out of my embrace. "I'm already gone."

And she was. I watched her stomp off with a sinking feeling in the pit of my stomach. Although I desperately wanted to chase after her, I knew that would only make things worse. She was too angry to listen, and I was too upset to talk. On my way out of the airport, I passed another telephone kiosk and decided that upset or not, I had to talk to Flora Hampton. I'd been the first to meet Deena's adoptive mother—at Cassie's request—and we'd since become good friends. She was still trying to come to terms with Deena and Cassie's search for their birth mother and often called me for reassurance. This time *I* needed reassurance. Perhaps Flora had a better handle on what the girls' plans were. When I called, though, I got her answering machine. Rather than leave a message, I decided to try again later.

MY AFTERNOON CLASS was a private lesson. I don't usually give private lessons, but Tom Dolan had set it up without consulting me. Tom was an excellent mechanic, but his receptionist skills left a lot to be desired. When I reminded him of my policy, he just shrugged his bony shoulders and said, "You was out, I was in. And a student's a student." He didn't have to say anything more. I'd been counting on the charter business to supplement the school's meager income, but with that income now put on indefinite hold, we needed all the sailing students we could get—private or not.

As much as I like to teach sailing, it doesn't thrill me to deal with the rich set. Since private lessons tend to be their learning method of choice, my policy tends to spare me a lot of grief. There may be some nice rich folks around, but in my experience, the size of the bank account is directly proportional to the size of the ego. While the former isn't much of a hindrance to learning, the latter almost always gets in the way. After the exchange I'd had with Cassie, I wasn't geared up to deal with anyone, let alone a rich snob. I didn't know if my student was male or female, but it didn't matter. I pictured him or her garbed in the same thick cable-knit sweater, expensive deck shoes worn fashionably (but foolishly) without socks, a brightly colored Helly Hansen jacket and pants, and just for good measure, a jaunty Tulley hat.

He introduced himself as Chris Denny. The Denny name was famous in Seattle, but the guy looked more like an old hippie than old money. He had long, shaggy gray hair that swept across his forehead and covered his eyes. His beard covered everything else. Helly Hansen-garbed he was not. Besides a sweat-stained fisherman's hat, he wore a thin, dirty white T-shirt and blue jeans under a long dark Navy peacoat that looked like a Goodwill reject. His deck shoes (with socks) were sturdy and presentable, though, which I took as a good sign. I figured Chris Denny was an eccentric, one of those millionaires who doesn't feel the need to wear his net worth on his back. He was polite and soft-spoken. Actually, he didn't say much of anything. He simply let me do the talking and nodded now and then at all the appropriate moments.

Once we were on the water, things changed dramatically. We hoisted the sails, but the wind quickly died, along with Chris Denny's interest in my lesson. We were idly drifting our way across Elliott Bay when he suddenly pulled off his beard. "Hi, Kellie," he said with a slight smile.

I sat up straight. "Paul? Is that you?"

"In the flesh."

"What's going on? Where have you been? Everybody is looking for you."

His face grew grim. "Don't you think I know that?"

"Your attorney even went on TV. He says you should turn yourself in."

"I can't."

"Why not?"

His explanation rambled, but the gist of it was that he was scared. He confirmed that he'd been on a walk when Sharon was killed. When he came home and found her, he panicked and ran, rightly thinking that the police would consider him the prime suspect. His face contorted with grief as he talked. Whatever his motives, Paul seemed genuinely devastated by Sharon's death. His gaze wandered to the Seattle skyline.

"Paul, did you know that Sharon called me the day she was killed?"

He looked back at me. "No. What did she want?"

"She said that she'd found something that she wanted to show me, something that, according to her, changed everything. Do you have any idea what she was talking about?"

"Not a clue." He was quiet a moment, then said softly, "Sharon meant the world to me. How will I ever raise Tiffany by myself?"

"Tiffany is convinced that you killed her mother," I said.

Paul looked at me and shook his head sadly. "I'm not surprised."

"You're not?"

"She hates me."

I raised an eyebrow, thinking of the fights that Emma Donnelly had overheard. "How so?"

"Because I'd forbidden her to date Jason Petrowski.

They think they're in love or some such nonsense, but she's only fourteen. What does she know about love? We went round and round about it. Tiffany can be awfully stubborn and difficult when she wants to be. Sharon was a nervous wreck. Finally, for the good of everyone concerned, I decided that she should go to boarding school. She's in San Francisco, thank God. I'd hate to have her home right now."

He paused a moment as a small gust of wind fluttered the sails. "But how do you know that she blames me for her mother's death?"

"Oh, Paul." I put a hand on his shoulder. "Tiffany came home from school."

"What?"

"It gets worse. She saw her mother's body."

The news hit him like a bullet. His pale face grew almost white as he clutched at his chest. For a terrifying moment, I thought he was having a heart attack or on the verge of passing out. But then he groaned and wrung his hands. "God, I had no idea. I should've been there for her."

"I was there. And then Martin and Jason showed up. Tiffany is staying with them for the time being."

Paul clenched and unclenched his fists. "I don't think that's a wise move."

"It's all right, Paul. Martin said he'd take good care of her."

"I know that," he said, "but Jason is another matter." He was so agitated that it took me several minutes to calm him down. I wasn't in the best frame of mind myself. Seeing Paul in such difficulty was physically painful, yet I was determined to help him as he'd once helped me. When it became obvious that Wendell's illness was terminal, many of our friends stopped calling or coming around. But not Paul. He was always there for us, doing whatever needed doing—from bolstering our spirits to taking care of household repairs. Paul Crenshaw was my strength during the darkest days of my life, and I vowed now to be strong for him. But first I had to have some answers.

When he seemed under control, I asked him where he'd been, how he'd been surviving. "The police have been scouring the city looking for you. How've you managed to avoid them?"

A slight smile. "I'm one of Seattle's homeless now. You'd be surprised how invisible that makes you. Invisible in plain sight."

I motioned to the beard he'd discarded. "In plain sight but in disguise?"

He nodded.

"What about money? How are you eating?"

"I had some cash on me when I split. But I'm learning a lot about survival on the streets, believe me."

I asked him about Tiffany. "She thinks you've gone crazy or something."

He grew quiet and covered his face with his hands.

When I realized that he was crying, I said, "Oh, Paul. I'm so sorry. How can I help?"

It took him a few minutes to compose himself. When he finally spoke, his voice was so soft, I had to strain to hear him. "Martin and Jason mean well, but Tiffany is *my* daughter. I love her with all my heart—and *I* will protect her. If you really want to help, you've got to convince Tiffany to return to San Francisco. It's where she belongs right now."

"Paul, I'll do anything you ask, but I don't think Tiffany will listen to me."

"Then talk to Herman. Tiffany's always been fond of her grandfather. If she won't go back to school, then maybe he can convince her to stay with him."

"I'll promise to talk to Herman if you'll promise to turn yourself in."

"I can't, Kellie. I told you that. At least not right now."

"But, Paul, the longer you're on the run, the worse it looks."

"I can't help that. I have to clear my name, and the only way I can do it is if I'm not sitting in the King County Jail."

"Clear your name how?"

"By proving that I've been framed. I'm convinced more than ever that someone is out to destroy me."

"Who?"

"That's the problem," he said, slamming a fist into his palm. "It could be anybody—a disgruntled employee, a nasty competitor, or even just some slick con artist. But someone has stolen my identity. At first I thought it was just a financial thing. I was having a hell of a time convincing my creditors that I wasn't the one running up all those credit card charges. But my God, Kellie, he's murdered two people now, including my wife, and tried to blame it on me." He shook his head sadly. "Sharon, my poor Sharon. You never deserved this."

The wind had died down completely by this time. I lowered the sails and started the engine. As we rounded the breakwater, I said, "I'll talk to Herman for you. But you've got to turn yourself in, Paul. As soon as possible."

He donned his beard again. "I will—just as soon as I figure out who's behind this mess."

"Promise me that you'll keep in touch. I'd like to know that you're okay and I'm sure you'll want to know about Tiffany."

He shrugged. "I'll try, Kellie. That's all I can promise right now."

We parted ways soon after we'd docked the boat. Before he left, I told him I'd have to report our meeting to the police.

"I understand, Kellie. Do whatever you have to. But please don't forget to talk to Herman. He has to get Tiffany back to San Francisco."

FIFTEEN

I CALLED ALLEN Kingston as soon as I got back to the sailing school. Reporting my conversation with Paul Crenshaw seemed like the responsible thing to do, but it sure didn't make me feel good. Even as I dialed, I questioned the wisdom of telling anyone about our meeting, especially the police. For one thing, Paul was still a friend, albeit a friend in trouble with the law. And if the press (or the Weasel) somehow found out that we'd been together, I could kiss what was left of my reputation goodbye. I had no idea whether Paul's story about being framed was true, but it was a lot more believable than thinking of him as a murderer.

There was also the matter of Abby's request to deal with. I was going to have to bite the bullet about my visit to Premier sooner or later. And since my relationship with Kingston had already been destroyed, I figured I had nothing to lose. Fortunately I didn't have to report anything at the moment. Kingston wasn't in, and I de-

clined to leave a message with Melody Connor except
to say that I'd called. Based on past experience, I wasn't
sure if she'd pass the word along, but at least I'd tried.
Whether Kingston thought it was worth returning my
call was another matter altogether.

After I hung up, I dialed Flora Hampton's number
again. Still no answer. This time I left a message, asking
her to call me as soon as possible. Cassie would be in
Portland by now. I wondered how she was doing and
what she was doing. I debated as to whether I should
call back and leave a message for her, too. Would she
judge my call as caring or interfering? In the end, I decided to wait until I'd spoken to Flora. It's a fine line
we mothers walk with our daughters.

Since I had the rest of the afternoon free, I decided
to drive over to Martin Petrowski's house and return his
ring. My plan was to kill two birds with one stone and
talk to Tiffany while I was there. According to Martin,
he was still living in his boyhood home in Shoreline. I
traveled along Aurora Avenue North, which looked like
the main shopping drag—especially if you were in the
market for trailer hitches, recreational vehicle parts,
pickup canopies, transmissions, and new and used cars.
Interspersed here and there were Sears, Fred Meyer,
Home Depot, Costco and a few specialty retail outlets,
such as Seattle's Finest Exotic Meats offering good buys
on alligator, cobra, and kangaroo.

Martin's home was located in the broad area between
Aurora Avenue North and Interstate 5. The neighborhood was a mixture of homes from the 1920s and 1930s,
and from the boom years of World War II tract expansion. Many of the homes I passed had been lovingly
maintained or restored. Others, including Martin's, had
not. Moss lay on the roof like a heavy five o'clock
shadow, and the dirty white clapboard siding desperately

needed a new paint job. But his yard was green and free of the old cars that adorned his neighbors' yards like junky costume jewelry.

Although I'd called first to make sure he and Tiffany would be home, no one answered the doorbell or my knock on the door. Either they were dodging me, or I'd messed up on our appointed meeting time. I taped a note to the front door and left before my imagination dredged up something more sinister to explain their absence.

On the way back to the marina, I stopped at Pierpont Engineering and Construction. I really didn't expect Herman Pierpont to be in the office so soon after his daughter's death, but as long as I was in the area I thought I'd check. The truth is, there was more on my mind than offering condolences and talking about Paul's concerns for Tiffany's safety. I wanted to get a bead on how the company was faring. Sharon's father owned the firm, but it was my understanding that Paul pretty much ran things. With all his problems, I had the feeling that the marina's expansion project might not be Pierpont's only contract in jeopardy right now. Nervous employees sometimes meant talkative employees. Another perspective might be helpful.

Whatever the current state of their business affairs, the firm certainly appeared to be prospering. Pierpont Engineering and Construction occupied the top two floors of the Pacific Building, one of Seattle's toniest business complexes.

As I had predicted, Herman Pierpont wasn't in the office. The firm's receptionist was a pretty little thing in a sky-blue dress who took her gatekeeping job seriously. She informed me crisply that Mr. Pierpont was not in, and no, she could not tell me when he would return. "In any event," she said with a superior air, "you'll need an appointment."

When I insisted that I was a friend of the family and my unscheduled visit was a condolence call, she turned me over to Herman's secretary, a plump grandmotherly sort named Beatrice Cooper. She smiled at me warmly. "As Ruth told you, Mr. Pierpont isn't in right now."

Ruth could've taken some charm lessons from the matronly secretary. Unlike her younger associate, Beatrice Cooper was as welcoming as a hot cup of cocoa on a winter's day. "But you can wait here for him if you'd like," she added. "He's due any time now."

"I don't have an appointment."

She dismissed the idea with a wave of her chubby, liver-spotted hand. "Oh, posh. If you were a friend of his daughter, Herman will want to see you."

"Thank you. I think I will wait for him."

After offering me a chair next to her desk, she asked if I wanted something to drink.

"Tea, if you have it, would be great."

She excused herself to fetch my drink. While she was gone, I did what anyone else would do—I looked the place over. Okay, I snooped. Besides the usual office trappings—computer terminal and filing cabinets—Beatrice's outer office functioned as a mini library. Floor-to-ceiling shelves in dark cherry lined an entire wall. Two burgundy leather wing chairs stood on either side of a low table adorned with a brass reading lamp and several popular magazines, as well as some engineering journals. Two doors on either side of Beatrice's work area proved to be Herman's and Paul's offices. No, I didn't peek behind closed doors; each man's office was clearly labeled with a brass nameplate. All things considered, it was a pleasant work environment, if you have to work indoors.

What I found most interesting, though, was Beatrice's desk. Actually her tidy work space amazed me. That's because no matter how hard I try, I've never been able to get the hang of the squeaky-clean look. Forget filing. My desk at the sailing school is a catchall for whatever I can't stuff out of sight somewhere. My idea of organization is multiple-colored Post-it notes. The only items that looked out of place on Beatrice's pristine desk were a couple of knitting needles, a ball of yarn, and the beginnings of what appeared to be a baby blanket. An ornately framed photograph of a bald-headed baby— perhaps the intended recipient of the blanket—was prominently displayed atop her desk next to a large candy dish.

I'd just helped myself to a Frango mint when she came back into the room carrying a silver tray with two china cups and saucers, a teapot, and a basket of tea bags.

"Here we go," she said pleasantly. "I'd offer you some of my home-baked cookies, but they seem to have disappeared. They don't last long around here."

"This is fine," I said, helping myself to a tea bag.

She poured hot water into our cups. "It was probably the foreman on the construction crew. He just loves my chocolate chips," she said, chuckling. "Comes in here every morning before heading out to the work site just to see what goodies I've brought in."

"Are you talking about Martin Petrowski?"

"Oh, goodness no," she said frowning. "Martin's the construction *supervisor*. He oversees all the foremen. I meant Don Williams." She sipped her tea and added, "Nice man, Don."

She seemed eager to chat, so I asked about the photo on her desk—her new grandson—and her knitting project, before easing into the real purpose of my visit. "So tell me something, Beatrice. With all the tragedy that's happened to the family lately, how are things here at the office?"

She motioned to her spotless desk. "Slow. Real slow."

"Is the firm that dependent upon Paul Crenshaw?"

The question hung in the air as she reached for her knitting. "Well," she said with a deep sigh, "the truth is, Mr. Pierpont is planning to retire at the end of the year. Paul Crenshaw was already shouldering most of the workload. Herman has never really been the same after his heart attack."

Detecting the note of sadness in her voice, I asked, "Have you been his secretary for a long time?"

"Oh, my, yes. I've been here forever."

"You must like your job."

Her knitting needles clicked softly as she replied, "Indeed I do. I probably should think about retiring, too. But I like the people here so much—we're like a big family, you know. I just can't bring myself to leave."

"Tell me about Paul."

She raised an eyebrow. "I thought you knew him."

"I do, but I've been somewhat confused by all the allegations against him."

She pointed a knitting needle at me. "Don't you believe a word of it! Paul is as nice as they come. He wouldn't murder anyone, let alone his wife."

"Obviously you think highly of him. How does he get along with his father-in-law?"

"Herman adores him. Everybody does."

"No arguments or disagreements about the business?"

"None that I know of. Paul has had some financial problems lately, but that was personal stuff. It had nothing to do with the engineering firm."

"Herman hasn't been disturbed that Paul didn't come back to work after he paid his bail?"

Beatrice stopped knitting a moment to consider.

"Well, maybe a little," she reluctantly admitted. She was clearly a big fan of Paul Crenshaw.

"From what I heard, Paul was about to file for bankruptcy. Seems to me that might've had some impact on the firm, too."

Beatrice tossed her knitting aside and leaned closer to me. "Look, I probably shouldn't be saying this, but if anyone has had a negative impact on this firm, it's that so-called friend of his."

"Who are you talking about? Whose so-called friend?"

"Paul's friend. Our construction supervisor, Martin Petrowski."

I could tell by her body language that she wanted to dish some dirt, so I obliged her. Leaning forward in my chair as she had, I said, "I take it Martin isn't your favorite member of the firm's family."

"Ha! That's putting it mildly. I don't care for him one little whit."

"Really?"

"Really. If it weren't for Paul Crenshaw, Martin Petrowski wouldn't even be working here."

"I understand that they knew each other in high school."

"Yes." She nodded. "That's when their friendship began. They both came from poor families, but Paul went on to college and made something of himself." Although we were the only people in the room, she lowered her voice a notch. "And guess what Martin did while Paul was away at college."

"What?" I whispered.

Beatrice set her knitting needles down and folded her arms across her ample chest. "Got his girlfriend pregnant, that's what."

Ah, illicit sex. Nothing like it to set tongues awagging.

And Beatrice was no exception. I didn't have to do much to draw the rest of the story out of her. Over a second cup of tea, she told me that Martin "did the right thing" and married his girlfriend, but unfortunately she died in childbirth. "I think that's why Paul has been so loyal to Martin all these years," she said. "The man is a slacker when it comes to work, but he has always been a good father to his son. Paul admires him immensely for that."

"But you don't?"

"I have to give him credit where credit is due. From what I've seen, his son has turned out real well. But . . ."

"Go on."

"Well, I just think that the handsome and charming Martin Petrowski has made a career out of sponging off Paul—or whatever woman he's with at the moment. And that doesn't sit well with me."

I decided to throw her a curveball and see what she made of it. "I'm told that this isn't the first time Paul has had trouble with the law. Something happened when he was a kid. You know anything about that?"

"Nope," she said and then launched into another ringing endorsement. "If you're his friend, you should already know this, but Paul Crenshaw is as honest as the day is long. He's a brilliant engineer, a wonderful family man, and an all-around good guy."

SIXTEEN

A FEW MINUTES later Herman Pierpont arrived, and I was ushered into his office. The last time I saw Sharon's father was at a neighborhood Fourth of July barbecue. Wendell's brain tumor hadn't been discovered yet, and the occasion was one of the last happy, carefree outings we would share together. Herman had been delightful that day. I remembered him as a robust, outgoing man who liked Cuban cigars and ribald jokes. If he teased you, he liked you. My frizzy red hair was always good for a zinger or two. That sweltering summer day, he'd dubbed me the "red-hot mama." He was sixty years old then but could've passed for fifty. A widower for several years, Herman was considered quite the catch, and more than a few ladies had tried to reel him in. So far, though, he'd eluded capture.

A heart attack followed by the death of an only child would be hard blows for anyone to take, and judging from his stooped, dispirited shuffle, Herman Pierpont was having a particularly difficult time weathering both setbacks. He looked every bit his age and then some. He was much thinner than I'd remembered, and his usually expressive face was tense and haggard. He seemed glad to see me, though, and we exchanged a warm embrace before settling ourselves on a leather couch in his office.

"I appreciate your dropping by, Kellie."

"Absolutely. But I wasn't sure whether you'd even be in the office today."

He hiked his shoulders. "Takes my mind off things."

"I understand." I silently questioned whether he was up to the effort. Herman Pierpont did not look like a well man. Normally a sharp dresser, his suit was wrinkled and hung loosely on his thin frame. The dark shadows under his eyes resembled war paint. Expressing sympathy for his tragic loss, I offered to do whatever I could to help. A cliché, perhaps, but he welcomed the sentiment. He was interested in hearing how I discovered Sharon's body, so I related the experience as delicately as I could.

"And Tiffany saw her mother like that?" he asked.

"I'm afraid so."

He dropped his head and fell silent for a moment. When he looked up again, he said, "That little girl should be with me right now."

"Paul said the very same thing."

His face registered surprise. "When'd you hear from him?"

I avoided the particulars of our meeting and said simply, "Earlier today."

"Where is he? I've been trying to reach him."

"You and the entire Seattle P.D. But he didn't exactly say where he's been."

Herman exploded off the couch. "Damn him!" The curse activated an emotional floodgate. Angrily pacing the room, he ranted for several minutes, an outpouring that seemed directed at himself rather than me. "I've loved that boy like a son. I educated him, hired him, rescued him from financial disaster, and even bailed him out of jail. And how does he repay me? By abandoning the business when I need him most. By letting some madman waltz into their home and strangle the precious life right out of my only daughter." His voice broke. "And now this . . . this selfish, irresponsible flight. He should be protecting Tiffany, not running from the police."

He was so worked up that I thought he might have another heart attack. I quickly interrupted his venting. "Paul's very concerned about Tiffany staying with the Petrowskis. He wants her to go back to school in San Francisco."

"That's the one sensible thing that boy's said in a long time. There's a killer out there somewhere. He could be after the whole family for all we know." Herman shook his head. "But Tiffany won't go. I already tried like hell to convince her."

"Paul said if that were the case, then she should stay with you."

"She won't do that, either. I love that little vixen with all my heart, but she can be damned stubborn when she makes up her mind about something." A slight smile formed at the corner of his mouth. "Takes after her grandma."

"You have to admit, there is quite a draw at the Petrowskis' house. Martin says that Tiffany and Jason are an item."

"An item? Puppy love, I call it."

"Paul says the romance caused a problem in the family."

Herman sighed. "Paul overreacted."

"According to Jason, Paul hates him."

"That's nonsense. Paul has often remarked on what a good kid Jason is. Why, he even donated blood when Jason had an emergency appendectomy."

Herman walked stiffly across the room to his desk, where he opened the lid on a cigar case. "Damn," he said, shutting the lid. "Beatrice has been at it again." He patted his chest. "Doc says I'm supposed to quit smoking, and that woman has taken it upon herself to be my conscience." He rummaged through the bottom drawer of his desk and found what appeared to be a half-smoked stogie. "My emergency kit," he explained as he lit up. "Hope you don't mind."

He plopped himself into the executive chair behind his desk. Puffing hungrily on the cigar a couple of times, he said, "As far as Jason is concerned, he can rest easy. Paul would've been against anyone dating his daughter."

Our conversation turned to Paul's more immediate problem with the police. The cigar seemed to have relaxed him a bit. Despite his earlier outburst, Herman extolled the virtues of his son-in-law and found the idea of Paul mixed up with the likes of Jewell Jessup a preposterous notion.

"Paul is convinced that someone is out to destroy him," I said. "That the murders were the work of someone else."

Herman jabbed his cigar in the air. "Well, they damn sure weren't the work of Paul. I admit I'm disappointed in him right now—we're probably going to lose the Larstad contract and a few others as well—but that doesn't mean I think he's capable of murder."

"So you think the charges against him have no merit?"

"Of course they have no merit! I don't know what all that so-called evidence is the cops say they have, but it must've been planted."

"Who do you think would do such a thing? And why?"

Herman drew again on his cigar and said, "I have no idea, but I'll tell you one thing—the cops better get to the guy before I do."

"Paul suggested that a competitor or a disgruntled employee might be out to ruin him."

He considered the idea a moment while he smoked. "Possibly. Hell, anything's possible. I'm supposed to retire soon and have been phasing myself out of the daily grind. Paul has been the driving force at the firm ever since my ticker decided to take a couple of belly flops. I haven't had much contact with the rank and file around here in a long time."

"Is there anyone else in the company who might have a better handle on things?"

"I assume you mean besides Paul?"

I nodded.

"Well, there's always Diana. She's head of Personnel."

"Do you think I could talk to her?"

Herman cocked his head at a slight angle and regarded me a moment. "Little Mama," he said, "what are you up to now?"

"Let's just say that Little Mama is on the case."

ALTHOUGH PLUMP IN the hips, Diana Sunn-Burton was an attractive woman in a taupe suit and matching silk blouse. The sign on her office door said *Director of Human Resources*, but for me she wasn't inclined toward sharing any resources, human or otherwise. This despite the fact that Herman Pierpont had personally introduced me and okayed the release of any personnel information I might request. She had greeted me warily, as if I were some kind of corporate spy, and after Herman left the room she grew even more circumspect.

"It's a matter of law," she intoned in a deep, husky voice that sounded as though she'd been smoking since she was twelve. "Confidentiality is crucial when it comes to personnel records," she continued. "And that includes *all* employees, past or present."

I acted as if I were listening intently, that her Privacy Act speech was something that I actually gave a rip about. As she droned on, I amused myself by trying to figure out how old she was. She appeared to be about my age, but it was hard to tell for sure. Makeup—which I rarely wear—always throws me off when judging a woman's age. Hers was carefully applied and gave her fair skin a youthful, rosy glow. Neither could I tell whether her silky blond hair was natural or came from a bottle. But there was one thing I *was* sure about: she was short. She tried to conceal it by wearing three-inch spike heels. Heels that caused her to wince every time she took a step.

I'd had enough of her spiel. "I understand all about the Privacy Act, Ms. Sunn-Burton. I'm just trying to help Paul."

"Hmm," she said, eyeing me a moment. She wore stylish gold-framed glasses that enhanced rather than detracted from her dark blue eyes. "How did you say you knew Paul again?"

I explained my connection to the family. "And I'm Tiffany's godmother," I said. "My purpose in coming here today is to help her, too."

I don't know whether it was my explanation or the fact that she'd been standing too long on spiked heels, but she offered me a chair and sat down at her desk. She immediately shucked the footwear. "Torture, pure and simple," she groaned, massaging her instep.

I smiled sympathetically, although I hardly ever subjected myself to such pain. I was still wearing the comfortable, all-purpose deck shoes I'd had on at the marina.

"Are you an investigator of some sort?" she asked.

I shook my head.

"Police? Lawyer?"

"No," I said, smiling. "I teach sailing at Larstad's Marina."

"Then I guess I just don't understand. How do you think you can help Paul and his daughter?"

"I'm not sure. But I want to try."

She paused as if in deep thought. After a moment she said, "You know, I've known Paul a long time, too. Ever since high school. In fact, my younger sister, Amy, married Paul's best friend."

That caused me to perk up. "Martin Petrowski?"

She nodded. "When Amy died, Paul stepped in to do whatever he could to help Martin and Jason. Martin always worked construction, but he never had anything permanent—until Paul hired him. Hired me, too. That's the kind of man Paul is. Loyal to his friends."

"And Martin? Is he loyal?"

Diana sighed and removed her glasses. "Let me guess where that question is coming from. You've been talking to Beatrice Cooper?" Before I could answer, she continued. "Bea has . . . How shall I put this? Bea has a very strong moral code. The fact that my sister and Martin had to get married . . . uh, doesn't sit well with her. And because Martin is handsome and a little flirty, Bea thinks he's some kind of sex-crazed skirt chaser." She put her glasses back on. "So don't pay any attention to what Bea says about Martin."

"She certainly thinks well of Paul."

Diana smiled. "We all do." The smile faded. "But we're awfully worried about him right now."

I leaned forward in my chair. "So help me help him."

She sighed deeply. "Just what did you have in mind?"

"I know you said that everyone at the firm loves Paul, but can you think of anyone, anyone at all, who might not?"

"Colin Dawson," she said without hesitation. "He was an engineer-in-training whom Paul fired."

I tried to keep the excitement out of my voice. "Paul thinks that a revenge-seeking ex-employee might be behind all his troubles. This Colin Dawson sounds like a possible candidate."

"Maybe," Diana said cautiously.

"Why was he fired?"

"He was accused of giving confidential client information to our firm's major competitor, Emerald City A and E."

"When did this happen?"

"A few months ago." She gestured toward the computer terminal on her desk. "I could look up the exact date."

"That'd be great."

It took her several frustrating minutes before she could access Dawson's records. "We got this new computer system a while back, and I still haven't got the hang of it," she complained. Moving the screen's cursor via the mouse, she found the icon she was looking for. "Here," she said, clicking the mouse. "Here we go." After giving me the date Colin Dawson left the company, she said, "You know, you may be on to something. As I recall, Paul's financial problems all started about this same time."

"Do you have Dawson's address?"

She moved her hand away from the mouse. "Uh, that's confidential information."

"Come on, Diana. This is important. Paul's future may depend upon it."

"You're going to go see him, aren't you?" she asked. "You're going to talk to Colin Dawson."

I nodded.

She hesitated a moment and then copied his address on a slip of paper. Pushing the note across her desk, she said, "Okay, here it is. But I should warn you. Colin has a terrific temper."

SEVENTEEN

I ATE A late lunch at a downtown café and then checked my voice mail for messages. No call from Flora Hampton. No call from Cassie, but I really didn't expect one. Still, I felt disappointed. No call from Allen Kingston, either. I didn't know whether to feel relieved or disappointed but I tried not to dwell on it. The only call had been from the Weasel with an irritating reminder about the planning meeting scheduled for later this afternoon. No disappointment there—just disgust. After I paid my check, I hopped in the Miata and drove straight to Colin Dawson's apartment building.

I'd never been to Tuscany Towers but I'd heard a lot about it. A relatively new addition to the Seattle skyline, the developers had touted the architecturally eclectic building as an "upscale living experience for entrepreneurs and other young professionals." In other words, a meet-and-greet type of place with sky-high rents. I was rather looking forward to a look-see at what the *Wall*

Street Journal had dubbed "the newest trend in urban living for young business lions." Unfortunately the one I hunted had abandoned his lair. Fortunately the on-site manager—a designer-clad young lioness barely old enough to vote—gave me Colin Dawson's forwarding address.

The engineer-in-training's new digs were a far cry from the splendor he'd been used to at Tuscany Towers. He lived on the first floor of the Cambridge, a dilapidated hotel on First Avenue that had somehow missed the downtown renovation process begun in the 1980s. In saltier times, First Avenue had been known as "Flesh Avenue" and housed strip joints, funky bars, and a host of marginal businesses. The Cambridge's former neighbors were all but gone now, replaced by three hundred shops and watched over by uniformed patrol guards funded by the First and Second Avenue business improvement district. Dawson's apartment building was a little oasis of decay that no doubt gave the improvement folks apoplexy. It gave me the creeps. I grasped my shoulder bag tighter and entered the building before I changed my mind.

Nobody was around. Unable to decide whether that was a good thing or a bad thing, I paused in the dimly lit hallway to get my bearings. Definitely not a good thing. The whole place reeked of urine, mold, and broken dreams. I struggled with nausea as I navigated the litter-strewn hallway to Apartment 106. An elderly woman with short-cropped blue hair answered my knock.

"Yes?" she asked, eyeing me through a narrow slit in the chain-locked door. A deep scowl etched its way across her wrinkled forehead as she waited for me to state my business.

"Is this the apartment of Colin Dawson?"

A brief nod.

"Is he here?"

The scowl deepened. "Who wants to know?"

"Kellie Montgomery. I was sent by Pierpont Engineering." Not precisely true, but the ruse got me invited inside.

Although the apartment smelled like stale cigarettes and fish cooking in oil, it was still better than the stench in the hallway. The woman introduced herself as Colin's grandmother, Hannah, and told me to sit down while she fetched her husband. "He'll want to hear what you have to say," she said.

"It's Colin that I really wanted to talk to," I said. "Is he home?"

The question went unanswered as she scurried out of the room. I looked at the ratty pea-green sofa coated with cat fur, and decided to remain standing. The carpet beneath my feet was thin and cheap and much too large for the tiny room. When Hannah returned, she introduced the cadaverous little man with her as Pete Dawson, Colin's grandfather. He held a pack of Marlboros in one hand and pulled a cart toting an oxygen tank with the other. I mentally shook my head at the incongruous sight and suddenly thought of my sister, Mary Kathleen. She'd been a heavy smoker until she developed a serious case of asthma. Although she's been cigarette-free for several months now, it's still a daily struggle. Colin's grandfather, though, appeared to be losing the struggle with the weed.

The couple sat side by side on the sofa while I settled for a plaid overstuffed rocker that seemed relatively free of cat fur.

Colin's grandparents looked at me expectantly. "Well?" said Pete, setting his cigarettes on the coffee table.

"Is Colin home?" I asked.

Hannah and Pete exchanged a nervous glance as Pete started coughing. He reached for the breathing apparatus on his tank, but the coughing spasms doubled him over. Hannah came to his rescue and gave him his oxygen fix. Afterwards she said, "I'm sorry. Now what were you saying?"

I stood. "Maybe this isn't a good time." I threw my handbag strap over my shoulder. "If Colin isn't home, I could come back later."

Hannah pleaded, "No, no. Please sit down. We need to talk to you." She looked at her husband, who nodded silently. The desperation in their tired eyes got to me. I sat down again.

"Colin isn't here right now, but you can tell us why Pierpont sent you."

I probably should've just 'fessed up at that point but I hated to disappoint the old couple. And they looked . . . well, eager to talk. I thought that if nothing else, they could give me a little background on their grandson. So I rationalized myself into another slight fib. "Well," I began, "I'm investigating your grandson's dismissal from the firm."

Pete suddenly straightened his shoulders. Tearing the breathing apparatus away from his face, he said, "Hot damn, it's about time!"

Smiling broadly, Hannah added, "I knew it! I just knew that Colin would get his job back and everything would—"

Oops. I raised my hands and said, "Wait a minute. I didn't say he had his job back. I'm just trying to understand why he was fired. As it was explained to me, Colin released confidential information to Pierpont's major competitor."

Hannah's smile faded. "That's a lie. Colin never did

any such thing. He's a good boy." She glanced at the room's sparse and shoddy furnishings. "Before they let him go for no good reason, he had a great place in that fancy new tower building. Now he's bunking here with us." She sighed. "He was going to move us out of this dump before he got into all that trouble. We'd picked out a real nice little place over in Ballard. It was just for seniors. Ballard Retirement Villa it was called. Colin said they even provided the dinner meal as part of the rent. Can you imagine?"

Pete turned off the oxygen and lit a cigarette. Through a haze of smoke, he said, "Is that what they told you? That Colin sold out his own firm?"

"Something like that."

He shook his head. "It was all her fault, you know. Colin would still have his job, and we'd be sitting pretty in a goddamn villa if it hadn't been for that woman. She was always riding Colin's butt. He put up with it as long as he could. When he finally told her to get lost, she canned him."

"What woman are you talking about?"

"We don't know her name," said Hannah. "Colin just calls her 'that bitch in Personnel.' "

"She was a bitch, all right," agreed Pete. "Colin hasn't been able to find another job since. Blackballed right out of the industry, is the way he put it."

The rest of our conversation ran in much the same vein: a rage against Diana and the suffering she'd unfairly caused their grandson. I ended the visit by giving them my business card for *Sound Sailing*. They glanced at the sailboat logo but didn't seem to question why a sailing instructor was investigating their grandson's dismissal. "Please tell Colin I was here," I said, "and have him call me. I'd like to hear his side of the story."

"We can do that," his grandmother said as she escorted me to the door. "But if you want to talk to him in person, try Joe's Pub."

"Joe's Pub?"

"Colin's favorite hangout. You can't miss it. It's just down the street a couple of blocks."

MY FAULT. I should've asked where he was in the first place. Joe's Pub & Ale House was a trendy bar catering to the yuppie crowd. I figured Colin Dawson probably hung out there to network. I was wrong. He hung out there to get drunk. At least that's the way I found him— hunched over a drink and babbling incoherently. I'd rushed out of the Dawsons' apartment without asking what their grandson looked like, but the bartender knew him. Pointing to the end of the crowded counter, he confirmed that the pudgy, sandy-haired fellow straddling the last stool was Dawson. He looked about twenty-five years old. "That's him. That's cryin' Colin."

"Crying?"

"As in 'cryin' in his beer.' Dawson's an expert at it."

I ordered a Diet Pepsi and carried the can with me. Settling onto the stool next to Dawson, I sipped my drink and caught him giving me a sideways glance.

"Pepsi," he said, shaking his head. "Why don't you let me buy you something with a little more kick?"

Was that a pickup line? If so, the guy must be drunker than I thought. "I'll pass," I said, smiling, "but you could give me some information."

"Huh?"

I held out my hand. "The name's Kellie."

He wiped his hand on his jeans and shook my hand. "Call me Bud."

"Bud?"

"Bud Dawson." He raised his bottle and motioned for

the bartender. "The Budweiser man," he said, laughing.

I shrugged my shoulders. Okay, whatever. "But you used to be a Pierpont man, right?"

He focused his bleary eyes on me. "Do I know you? Don't tell me you work at Pierpont."

I handed him one of my business cards. "No, I work at Larstad's Marina."

He tucked the card inside his shirt pocket as the bartender set another bottle of Budweiser in front of him. "Good," he said, gulping his drink. "I was afraid that I'd have to vacate the premises." He looked me over. "And I sort of like the neighborhood."

"I take it you don't think much of Pierpont's employees?"

"Aw, they're all right, I guess. Except for Ms. Big Mouth."

"Let me guess. You're referring to Diana Sunn-Burton."

He set his bottle on the counter and swiveled toward me. "You do work there!"

"Honest, I don't. But I heard about your departure."

"My departure?" He snorted. "I was fired. Canned. Axed. Sacked. Booted out the door. *Sayonara*, goodbye and good riddance."

"Willing to talk about it?"

He was more than willing. Trouble is, I didn't learn anything useful. Like his grandparents, he claimed that he was unjustly accused. Snatches of the temper Diana had warned me about surfaced from time to time, but never became worrisome. His ramblings, increasingly incoherent, finally stopped altogether when he plopped his head on the bar. Out cold.

As I prepared to leave, the bartender stopped me. "I heard you pumping Dawson about his job at Pierpont."

"So?"

"So, I don't know what your angle is, but Dawson has a legitimate gripe."

"How do you know?"

"Hey," he said, grinning, "I'm a bartender. I know all."

"Then tell me."

He leaned across the counter and lowered his voice. "It'll cost you."

Having been down this route on another case, I opened my handbag and pulled out a ten spot.

He snapped it out of my hand. "Dawson is convinced that someone at that engineering firm doctored his computer records."

"Doctored how?"

"That's the problem. He can't figure it out. But he's trying to prove his innocence."

I glanced at Dawson, still comatose on the counter. "How? Like you said earlier, he's an expert at crying in his beer."

"There are other experts around."

"Meaning?"

He held out his hand, palm up. I wasn't sure where this conversation was leading, but I slapped another ten-dollar bill on the counter.

The bartender scooped it up and said, "Dawson had a stash saved up. After he got fired he used the dough to hire some computer geek. Says the guy has uncovered some interesting shit about the goings-on at Pierpont."

"This computer geek have a name?"

He held out his palm again.

"I'm all out of cash."

"No problem," he said. "I take Mastercard, Visa, and American Express."

EIGHTEEN

THE PLANNING COMMITTEE for the marina's fif-teenth anniversary celebration met in a small conference room on the main floor of the administration building. Todd Wilmington had cajoled over a dozen hapless souls into serving on the committee, and they were all present and accounted for when I arrived—nearly half an hour late. Any hope I'd had of slipping into the room unnoticed died as soon as the Weasel saw me. He interrupted the financial report he was delivering to denounce my "lack of courtesy and complete disregard for those who managed to get to the meeting on time."

I weighed the pros and cons of telling him what I thought *he* lacked and decided that keeping my job at the marina was a higher priority than dressing down the Weasel in public, no matter how good it would've felt. So I clamped my jaws together and sat down—as far away from him as I could get without leaving the room. But it wasn't far enough. He kept up the jabs until someone with a little more clout (or guts) suggested that he get on with the prepared agenda. I nodded appreciatively to my benefactor and then, to ensure my continued silence, I snatched a cookie from the refreshment platter and stuffed it in my mouth.

It was a long and boring meeting, the details of which I really can't recall except that the Weasel assigned me the responsibility of coordinating the kids' dinghy races. I could tell that he thought the job was a put-down, but I was okay with it. The races would be a lot of fun, especially since I knew the Weasel wouldn't be hovering around trying to run things like he usually did. Ordinarily the fact that he didn't know anything about dinghy races wouldn't have stopped him from getting in my face. What would spare me this time were the intended participants in the races. He hated kids, or as he called them, "the little monsters." I won't say what they called him.

After the assignments were agreed upon, Wilmington still droned on for the better part of an hour. To avoid nodding off, I amused myself by watching Bill Starkey. What the Weasel's handsome friend was doing at our meeting was a mystery, but I didn't care. Anyone that sexy could hang out wherever he wanted. For a few fanciful moments, I considered what it would be like to hang out with him—minus a few articles of clothing. I decided that I'd rather hang out with Allen Kingston. Unfortunately that possibility seemed like a mere fantasy also.

But I was curious about Starkey. Maybe, I told myself, I'd stick around after the meeting and chat with the guy. See what kind of yacht he owned—I figured it must be something if the Weasel was still palling around with him. But as soon as the Weasel finally brought the session to an end, I couldn't even get close to Bill Starkey, let alone talk to him. Every woman at the meeting had suddenly felt the need to introduce herself and welcome him to Larstad's Marina. I put my curiosity on hold and left.

Outside, I paused a moment to take in the sights and sounds of the marina. This was my favorite time of the day—twilight, that brief period when the hustle and bustle winds down and everything takes on a softer, gentler look. Most of the day-shift employees had already gone home, and the night crew was just beginning to straggle in. Because of the unseasonably warm day, there were still some boats out on Elliott Bay. I caught sight of a little sloop dipping and soaring in the gentle wind, as free and unfettered as a bird on a thermal and decided that was exactly what I wanted to be doing.

As I approached *Second Wind's* slip, I saw Allen Kingston leaning against the dock box. I don't think my heart actually skipped a beat at the sight of him, but it was definitely beating faster. He was casually dressed in jeans and a white polo shirt with a hunter-green sweater wrapped loosely about his shoulders. Very preppy—and very un-Kingstonlike. "Hey, Montgomery," he said, "it's about time you showed up."

I swallowed nervously. "You got my message, then?"

"What message?"

"I called earlier today and . . . Oh, never mind. Why are you here?"

He turned slightly and reached behind his back to retrieve a wicker picnic basket and a bottle of wine that he'd stashed atop the dock box. "I came bearing gifts," he said, grinning.

"You know what they say about that, don't you?"

"No, what do they say?"

"Beware of Greeks bearing gifts."

Still grinning, he said, "Then you're safe. I'm Sno-

qualmie with a little French thrown in for good measure."

"French?" I knew that he was American Indian, that
he even spoke a little of his native Lushshootseed language, but this French business was a new one.

He shrugged. "On my father's side."

"Kingston doesn't sound like a French name."

He shrugged again. *"Je ne sais pas.* French, English,
Indian—I'm a regular melting pot. Now, we can stand
around yakking about my heritage if you want to, but
the sun will be going down soon," he said, gesturing
west toward the Olympic Mountains.

"So?"

"So, let's get out on the water before we miss the
sunset altogether." He held up the basket and the wine
bottle. "I figured that if I provided the food and drink,
the least you could do was provide the transportation."

Although he hadn't apologized or made any reference
to the circumstances surrounding our last meeting, I
knew that he was trying to make amends. Kingston's
suggestion that we go sailing was a real act of contrition,
especially since he wasn't particularly fond of the water.
He wasn't particularly fond of cats, either, but he en-
sured that Pan-Pan's little life jacket was snugly secured
before we headed out. Then he made like a Sea Scout
and untied the mooring lines, pulled in the fenders, and
did whatever else I asked of him as we got *Second Wind*
underway. Once we were clear of the marina's rocky
breakwater, he took over the helm and steered the boat
into the wind so that I could raise the mainsail and jib.

After the sails were up, I joined him at the helm. "Do
you have a particular destination in mind?" I asked.

He smiled and looked to starboard. The setting sun
had turned the sky a vibrant red. "Someplace close," he

said. "This Technicolor spectacular isn't gonna last much longer."

"I know just the spot."

A few minutes later, we dropped a hook at Rocky Point, a little cove adjacent to the marina. The wind had died down by then, but the air was still chilly. Kingston put on his sweater and cuddled up next to me on the bow of the boat. As the sun finished its downward trek across the horizon, he uncorked the wine and poured us both a glass.

"Here's to the red sky at night—sailors' delight," he said, raising his glass.

I raised my glass to his. "Do you know the rest of the saying?"

Grinning, he nodded and said, "Red sky at morning— sailors take warning."

"I'm impressed."

"Here's one for you," he said. "Halo around the moon. What does it mean?"

"Easy. Rain or snow is coming."

"And the larger the halo, the sooner it will fall."

"Now I'm really impressed, Kingston. Where'd you learn all that sailor lore?"

"Indian lore—on my mother's side." After a moment he set his wineglass on the deck and looked directly into my eyes. "I'm real sorry about the other day, Kellie. I shouldn't have come down so hard on you. I've been stewing about it ever since."

I was touched by his apology. This was major stuff coming from Kingston. I set my wineglass next to his. "It's all right," I assured him. "I shouldn't have reacted the way I did."

"No, you had every right to get upset. You'd just lost a good friend, and I was callous and uncaring."

"Jeez, Kingston," I said, trying to lighten the mood.

"Keep this up, and I might think you're a sensitive kind of guy."

He took my hands in his. "I know it probably doesn't seem that way, but I *am* a sensitive guy."

"That's good to know, because I have something to tell you that is sort of sensitive."

"Personal or professional?" he asked.

"Both." I started with my visit to Premier Escorts. Predictably, Kingston made some noise about it, but didn't cut me off either. After he'd heard me out, he even agreed to contact one of his buddies in the vice unit about Abby.

"Al's a great guy," he said. "He'll do what he can for her."

So far so good, I thought. The next part wasn't so easy. I took a deep breath and said, "I saw Paul Crenshaw yesterday."

Eyebrows raised half a mile. "What?"

"Now, don't get excited."

"I'm not excited," he said, releasing my hands.

My turn to raise the eyebrows. "Hmm, I see. Just sensitive?"

"Okay, okay," he said, "you made me. But tell me this: Why? Why did you go behind my back on the Crenshaw case again?"

"I didn't! Paul contacted *me*. I didn't even recognize him at first. He was in disguise, dressed up like an old hippie in a gray beard and wig."

Kingston looked at me without saying anything. After a moment, he asked, "What did he want?"

"Someone to listen to him. He's been through an awful lot lately and needed a friend."

"Let me guess," Kingston said without bothering to hide the sarcastic tone. "He talked about his innocence. How he's been unjustly accused of two murders. How he's on the run because he's been framed."

"As a matter of fact, he does think he's been framed."

Kingston threw his hands in the air. "Of course. It's O. J. all over again. No bloody glove, but the police made do with planting his fingerprints."

"Don't be ridiculous," I said, frowning. "Paul hasn't accused the police of any such thing. He thinks a disgruntled employee or a competitor might be behind his troubles."

"How does he figure that?"

I sighed and tried to gather my thoughts. It was still a little early, but I searched the sky for the moon. Didn't find it. "Listen. All I know for sure is that he's very worried about his daughter Tiffany. He thinks she may be in danger."

"What kind of danger?"

"He didn't get into specifics, but someone did kill his wife. His daughter could be next."

"I know how he feels."

"What do you mean?"

Kingston hesitated and then reached for my hands again. "I'm very worried about you."

"Me?"

"Yes, you. The more you get involved in this case, the more you put yourself at risk."

When he paused to take a deep breath, I opened my mouth to speak, but he covered my lips with his fingertip. "I'm not finished, Kellie."

His expression was so dead-on serious that I didn't protest.

"I haven't talked about Bobbie much," he continued, "but do you remember how she was killed?"

I nodded, remembering very clearly how he'd lost his young wife. It had happened over twenty years ago. A rookie cop, she was three months pregnant with their first child when she was killed in the line of duty.

"Bobbie was a trained professional," Kingston said, "armed and able to defend herself." He was quiet a moment. "But she still caught a bullet. You know what it's like to lose someone you love. Your life is never the same." His eyes bore into mine. "When you got shot last year, I thought it was happening all over again. I thought . . . Well, I thought I'd lost you, too."

He noted my startled expression. "Don't you realize that I care about you?" he asked. Without waiting for me to answer, he ran his hand through his thick unruly hair and continued. "Don't you realize that I . . . uh . . . I . . ."

"Kingston, what exactly are you trying to—"

"Oh, hell," he said, pulling me toward him. "I love you, Montgomery. I love you!"

The kiss was long and tender.

NINETEEN

I LOVE YOU. Three little words. Three little words that are often the most difficult words in the English language to say. Yet Allen Kingston had said them to me—and more than once. I was stunned. Overwhelmed. Completely undone by the revelation—and the passion that his kiss aroused in me. It wasn't the first time our lips had touched or even the first time we'd shared the intimacy that inevitably follows such an intense moment. But everything about that night—the wine, the sunset, the kiss, the embrace, and yes, even the sex—was different. Our entire relationship changed the instant he uttered those three little words.

The rest of the evening was a blur. I know that we devoured all the food he'd packed in the picnic basket, but I haven't a clue as to what we ate. I ached to tell Kingston how I felt about him. I even came close a few times, but for some reason I just couldn't get the words out. My thoughts were in such a jumble that Kingston pretty much handled the short trip back to the marina. Sensing my internal struggle, he took me in his arms and kissed me again. "It's okay, Montgomery," he said. "It's okay."

Okay that I couldn't share what was in my heart? Okay that I couldn't tell him that I loved him, too? As he held me, I searched the sky for the moon again. The halo around it was big and bold. Change was in the air, but I couldn't accept it. "Give me some time, Allen. I just need some time."

"Sure," he said. Then, flashing a big grin, he added, "But remember. Time and tide wait for no man—or woman."

THE NEXT MORNING I was awakened out of a deep, dreamless sleep by a phone call from Flora Hampton. I'd tried calling her after Kingston left, but she hadn't answered again. "Is everything all right?" I asked. Always the first question when you get an early-morning phone call—especially when you've been trying unsuccessfully to reach someone.

"I guess."

"What's going on, Flora?"

"I tried my darndest to stop 'em, but they took off this morning for New Mexico."

"How'd they get the money for airline tickets?"

"They're not flying. Deena cashed in the savings that were supposed to go for her tuition at the art institute and bought a used car."

"They're *driving* to New Mexico?" I didn't have to complete the rest of the question for Flora: two girls alone on the road?

"I know what you're thinking and I agree. It's just asking for trouble. That car they're driving is nothing but a rattletrap. They'll be lucky if it holds together long enough to get them out of Oregon."

Great. That made me feel *much* better. The rest of our conversation was spent commiserating with each other on how badly we'd handled the situation. Hindsight. Monday-morning quarterbacking. We were both shouldering a lot of guilt, but we promised to keep in touch. Perhaps one of us would hear from the girls soon.

I'd no sooner hung up the phone when it rang again. This time the call was from Martin Petrowski.

"Got your note. Sorry we missed you."

He didn't offer any explanation, and I didn't press the matter. Instead, I asked about Tiffany.

"Tiffany's fine. Just fine. No need to worry about her." Then, switching gears a little too quickly, he asked, "Say, Kellie, have you had breakfast yet?"

"Uh, no."

"How about meeting me for breakfast at the Topside in an hour? My treat."

"Well . . ."

"I have something important to discuss with you."

"Does this concern Paul?"

"Indirectly, but I don't want to get into it on the phone. How about it? Will you meet me at the Topside?"

IF YOU WANT a good, hearty breakfast, the kind your mom used to make before cholesterol was out, health clubs were in, and grazing replaced eating, the you head for the Topside. Although primarily a beer and pizza joint, the cook had added a breakfast menu that was to die for. Everybody in Seattle knew this, which wouldn't be so bad, except that the Topside didn't take reservations. Meaning you could die of starvation while waiting for a table, especially on the weekends. This was only a Wednesday morning, but I didn't want to take any chances. As soon as I hung up the phone, I scrambled out of bed, rushed through the daily hygiene thing, and made it to the restaurant before a line could start forming. I was already seated at a window table, drooling over the menu, when Martin arrived.

"Sorry I'm late," he said. "Traffic was a bear this morning."

"This *is* Seattle."

"Touché. Guess you don't have to worry about gridlock."

"One of the advantages of living where you work."

"Plus you can walk to the best breakfast spot in town," he said, retrieving the booklike menu our waitress placed in front of him. "Quite a selection here. What do you recommend?"

I gave him a rundown on my personal favorites, and we ordered. After our waitress left, I handed him his ring. "Here," I said. "I want to make sure I give you this before I forget it."

"Oh, yeah, thanks. I'd forgotten all about it." He looked at the inscription briefly and then slipped the ring on his little finger. It was too loose. "Reason I lost the thing in the first place," he explained with a shrug. After removing the ring, he put it in his pants pocket. "That was some sailboat trip we had," he said. "Who'd have thought our little outing would end up with Paul running from two murder raps?"

"It's unbelievable, all right. But no more so than Sharon's death."

"Ironic, wasn't it?"

"How so?"

"Sharon was always freaked out about one damn thing or another. Most of the time she wouldn't even leave the house. Paul had to beg her to go on that sailing trip.

She was convinced that she'd fall overboard and drown. Or get hit by a car on the way to the marina. The only place she really felt safe was in her own home. And wouldn't you know, that turned out to be the most dangerous place of all."

"Any theories as to why she was killed?"

"It had to have been a burglar. Probably didn't think anyone was home."

"But she was strangled just like Jewell Jessup."

He shrugged. "From what I heard on the news, Jewell wasn't even her real name. And that sleazy outfit she worked for was nothing but a front for a prostitution ring. I'd hardly put Sharon in the same category as a twenty-two-year-old hooker."

"You missed my point. What I was getting at was the murder scene. They were both strangled—with the same type of designer scarf. From what I saw that day and verified by what I've since read in the newspapers, there weren't any signs of a break-in. Nor was anything stolen."

"What can I say? Maybe the guy wheedled his way into the house on some pretext or another. Sharon could be real gullible at times. He probably didn't get a chance to steal anything."

"So he gets into the house somehow, strangles Sharon, and then what? Panics and runs?"

"Possibly. It's a whole lot more believable than Paul suddenly going off the deep end and killing her."

"You and Paul are pretty close. Have you heard from him at all?"

"Not a word. But I'm not surprised. We've been friends ever since high school, but lately we've . . . well, let's just say things haven't been right between us for quite a while."

"You both seemed to get along okay on the sailboat trip."

"True, but it wasn't like the old days. And you have to admit there was a lot of tension on the boat."

"Yes, but I thought the tension had more to do with Jason. Everything was fine until we picked him up in La Conner."

"That was my fault."

"What do you mean?"

"Inviting Jason on the trip. He doesn't care much for Paul."

"Because of Tiffany?"

Martin nodded. "He blames Paul for trying to break them up. Tiffany going off to school in San Francisco really upset him."

Our conversation came to a momentary pause when our waitress arrived with our breakfast. "Here you go, folks," Janey said. "Pecan waffle with marionberries for Mrs. M. and scrambled eggs with honey-baked ham and country potatoes for the gentleman. Enjoy!"

We dug in.

"I don't know about you," Martin said, waving his fork at his plate, "but I'm loving every bite of this."

I smiled and took a bite of waffle. "So tell me, Martin, why did you invite Jason along on the trip, knowing how he felt about Paul?"

"Looking back on it now, I realize it was a big mistake. You know, I'm just as bad as Sharon was when it comes to being out on the water. I can't swim. Actually, I'd have to say that I'm probably worse than Sharon— I'm deathly afraid of the water."

"But she said chartering the sailboat was your idea!"

"Right. I just thought that the trip might help mend things between Jason and Paul. He's been under so much pressure—all that messed-up credit stuff was driving him bananas. Dealing with his daughter's budding sexuality seemed to be more than he could handle. I guess it was unrealistic of me to think that a little sailing could set things right."

"Paul seems to think that he's been framed—for the murders and for his financial problems."

"I want to support Paul, I truly do. He's always been there for me. But I don't think he's thinking too clearly right now. A frame-up? Naw, he just couldn't say no to Sharon."

"Meaning?"

"Meaning Sharon liked to spend money like there was no tomorrow. You saw their house. All that remodeling was her idea. She really wanted to move to Hunts Point, but there was no way Paul could afford to live in that stratosphere. He makes good money, but Herman still owns the firm. Anyway, Paul just couldn't say no to Sharon. All those credit cards he complains about—my guess is that Sharon ran up the bills. She thought the shopping channel was created specifically for her benefit."

There was no denying Sharon had a taste for fine clothes and furnishings. "So you're saying Paul spoiled Sharon?"

"Indulged her every whim."

"What about the yacht and Jewell Jessup?"

"That's a puzzler, all right. I could see him buying a yacht, but there's just no way Paul would've been mixed up with a hooker. He's too much of a straight shooter. Marriage and family are very important to him." He looked out the window at the rain that had started to fall. "But . . ."

"But what?"

He wiped his mouth and tossed his napkin on the table. "Nothing. I shouldn't even bring it up."

"Come on, Martin. If there's something I should know about Paul, please tell me."

He eyed me carefully for a moment and then lowered his voice. "Please don't take this wrong, but I think Paul's problems have been almost too much for the guy to handle."

"In what way?"

"Remember how he reacted at the Friday Harbor sheriff's office?"

I nodded, remembering all too well Paul's violent scuffle with the police.

"That's not the first time he's gone ballistic."

I waited, but he must have thought better of disclosing anything further. I thought about the incident that sent Paul to juvenile hall. "Are you referring to something that happened when he was in high school?"

He hesitated and then nodded. "But I don't want to make a big deal out of it. We were all a little crazy back then." He chuckled. "I haven't always been the even-keeled guy you see before you."

He meant it as a joke, but the remark made me think. How would someone describe me? I've been known to have my own brushes with anger, spouting off and regretting it later. I'd sure hate those episodes to be used against me in a murder case. The fact is, we all have our moments.

Janey came to take our plates and refill our tea and coffee. After she left, Martin said, "What I really wanted to talk to you about this morning is Tiffany." He took a sip of his coffee and added, "I wasn't totally truthful when you asked about her on the phone."

I sat forward in my chair. "What's wrong?"

"She's depressed."

"I'd be surprised if she wasn't depressed."

"Herman keeps calling to beg her to stay with him,

but she won't leave our house. Refuses to return to school, too."

"How can I help?"

"I was hoping you'd ask that," he said, smiling for the first time. "Despite everything that happened in the San Juans, Jason says he had a ball sailing with you. He thinks that a day's outing on your boat might be what Tiffany needs. Lift her spirits, that type of thing."

I considered this for a moment. "What does Tiffany think of the idea? Is she up for it?"

"Let's put it this way. If Jason thought she should fly to the moon, that little gal would hitch a ride on the next shuttle."

"Then it's a date. I think Jason might be right. Sailing always lifts my spirits. Maybe it will work for Tiffany, too."

TWENTY

"ARE YOU MAURY Kranich?"

"Yo!"

He stood in the doorway and waited for me to continue. "I'm Kellie Montgomery," I said, offering the young man my business card. "We talked on the phone."

Maury Kranich was the owner of MM&I, a computer-recycling company headquartered in an unassuming, no-account building on Second Avenue near the Pike Place Market. He was also the "computer geek" that the bartender said Colin Dawson had hired to help him get his job back at Pierpont Engineering. I'd called him right after my breakfast meeting with Martin ended.

"Oh, yeah," he said, hastily shaking my hand. "I forgot all about you coming over." His honesty was refreshing, which is more than I could say about his appearance. Twenty-something Maury Kranich had the unkempt, dirty-laundry-basket look down pat—several days' stubble on his round face, greasy hair pulled into a loose ponytail, ragged cutoff jeans, a wrinkled Grateful Dead T-shirt, and shabby sandals straight out of the sixties. His toes were almost as hairy as his legs. He had a nice smile, though, which he turned on like a lightbulb. "Come on in," he said, ushering me inside.

The building's vast interior looked like a cross between a garage sale and a computer museum. A series of long tables stretched from one end of the large room to the other and were laid out with boxes of disassembled hard drives and cartons of floppy disks. Row upon row of monitors and computers were stacked like bricks throughout. Kranich unloaded a pile of whatnot from two metal chairs and invited me to sit down. "Sorry about the mess around here," he said. "Things have been so hectic that I haven't been home in two days."

"Business must be very good."

He yawned and stretched his hairy arms over his head. "Well, this is a one-man operation. MM&I stands for Me, Myself, and I," he said, chuckling. "You know how you can tell you work in the new millennium?"

"How?"

"You think a half day means leaving at five o'clock."

"I appreciate you taking the time to meet with me."

"No problem," he said. "I needed a little break." He flashed another friendly smile. "What exactly can I do for you, Ms. Montgomery."

"Call me Kellie," I said, returning his smile. "As I said on the phone, I'm investigating Colin Dawson's dismissal from Pierpont Engineering."

Kranich fingered the business card I'd given him. "Your card says you're a sailing instructor."

"That's right. I am."

"I don't get it. What's your connection to Pierpont?"

"I do some investigating from time to time."

"Yeah? Cool." He looked at my card again. "Sailing instructor. What a great cover!"

He'd read more into my answer than I'd intended, but that was okay as long as it got me what I wanted. "I understand you're investigating Colin's dismissal also."

He shrugged. "It's a paying gig."

"You're a software programmer, right?"

"Bachelor's in computer engineering, so my degree says. Four years at U.C. Berkeley thanks to a scholarship and a slew of hefty loans." He shook his ponytailed head. "Man, I'll still be paying off that mountainous debt when my own kids head for college."

"So, this work you're doing for Colin . . . it involves computer programming?"

"I prefer to call it electronic sleuthing." He gestured toward the long rows of tables and equipment. "But basically I'm in the junk business. I buy up old computers, then recycle and resell them."

"I guess I'm confused. How does recycling computers relate to Colin Dawson's dismissal?"

He heaved a sigh and stretched again. "I need a Dr Pepper," he said. "You want one?"

"Sure."

Reaching underneath a nearby table, he pulled two soda cans from a Styrofoam cooler. "Almost out of ice, but they're still cold," he said, handing me one. He popped the top on his can and swallowed heartily. "The deal is this: Colin is convinced that someone tampered with his computer records at Pierpont. It was that tampering that led to his firing. He asked me to find out how it happened."

"And have you?"

He eyed me a moment. "How much do you know about computers?"

"I can spell Macintosh and Compaq. Does that

count?" He didn't laugh at my little joke, so I continued. "I have a laptop that I use primarily for record-keeping purposes and E-mail but I wouldn't say I'm technically savvy."

"Okay, then I'll try to make this as simple as possible."

Old dim bulb smiled her appreciation. "Thank you."

He leaned his forearms on his knees and said, "I believe that Colin's firing stemmed not from anything he did but because Pierpont Engineering purchased a new computer system."

"You've already lost me."

"When a company gets a new computer system, they often sell their old PCs to a computer-recycling outfit like mine. The recycler reformats and cleans the hard drives and then resells them to other clients."

"Is that what Pierpont did?"

He nodded. "They sold their old PCs to an outfit on the Eastside—Shelton RE-PC."

"And?"

"And one of the Shelton employees didn't wipe Pierpont's hard drives clean before selling them to Emerald City Engineering."

I thought about what he said as I sipped my soda. "So all of Pierpont's data now belongs to Emerald."

"Exactly," said Kranich. "And what a coincidence— Emerald is Pierpont's biggest competitor. The confidential information that Dawson was accused of disclosing to Emerald was on the hard drives they purchased from Shelton RE-PC."

"Can you prove all this?"

"A buddy of mine works at Shelton. He's the one who told me about Terry Lindstrom."

"Who?"

"The guy in charge of wiping the hard drives that

came from Pierpont. Right now Lindstrom's about to get his ass fired, too. Shelton management believes he's been blackmailing clients by threatening to disclose and disseminate the information on the uncleaned hard drives to their clients' competitors unless they pay him. And I mean pay him well."

I tried to digest and store all this. "Did Lindstrom approach Pierpont with a similar scheme?"

"That I don't know yet. I'm still working on it."

We drank our sodas in silence for a few moments. "Well, Maury, I should let you get back to work," I said, standing. "You've been a big help."

He drained the last of his Dr Pepper and stood also. "No problem," he said. "You know, when he isn't drinking, Dawson is an all right dude. I hope he gets his job back."

As he walked me to the door, I said, "I do have one more question before I go."

"Shoot."

"How hard is it to steal someone's identity using a computer?"

Kranich grinned broadly. "Want a little demonstration?"

I nodded.

He retrieved the business card that I'd given him from his jeans pocket. "All I know about you right now is what I see on this card: your name, occupation, place of business, and phone number. Give me a couple of hours, and I think you'll be surprised at what else I know about you."

THEORETICALLY THIS WAS my day off. All that meant was that I didn't have any classes scheduled. What I did have was a pile of paperwork waiting for me back at the sailing school. If there's anything I hate worse, it's sitting behind a desk shuffling paper from one stack to another. Which probably explains why my desk was buried at this very moment. My first impulse was to stroll down the street to Elliott Bay Books. I pictured myself idly whiling away the afternoon as I meandered through the cavernous bookstore, stopping now and then to peruse whatever reading material happened to catch my fancy.

But it was raining when I left Kranich's office, and the Miata's top was down. By the time I'd hustled back to where I'd parked the car and saved it from becoming a duck pond, I'd scrapped the leisurely afternoon idea. Guilty conscience strikes again. I drove straight to the marina and the paperwork I loathed.

I lasted an hour. Less than an hour, if you discount all the time I wasted staring out the window at the rain. Fascinating stuff, rain. Let's face it, I don't shuffle paper well. What I do well is daydream. I thought about Allen Kingston for a good while. When that fantasy got a little too hot, I forced myself to think about something else. Anything else. Like having another chat with Diana Sunn-Burton. I had a hunch that there was a lot more that that woman knew. And there was only one way to find out.

A call to her direct line at Pierpont Engineering rewarded me with her voice mail. I hung up without leaving a message and called Beatrice, who told me that Diana had already left for the day. Something about a dental appointment.

With a little gentle prompting, Beatrice gave me her home telephone number. "It's unlisted," Beatrice whispered cautiously. "Please don't tell Diana I gave it to you, or she'll rake me over the coals. She's such a stickler about confidentiality." Promising not to rat on her, I jotted down the number and ended the call.

Diana answered on the second ring. Her husky voice sounded odd. "Diana? Is that you?"

"Yesh."

"This is Kellie Montgomery. Anything wrong?"

"No, jus got back from the dentist. Can't talk right yet."

I sympathized with her plight and then asked if I could drop by to see her. "I need to talk to you about Paul," I said.

Long pause. I thought she was trying to think of a polite way to refuse, but I was wrong. "All right." She sighed. "Come on over."

Beatrice shouldn't have worried. Diana raised no ticklish questions about how I'd learned her telephone number. She simply gave me her address, a town house on the Eastside, and told me how to get there. Her directions were easy to follow, but the rain had turned nasty by then, making driving a real problem. You'd think Seattleites would have this rain and driving thing figured out by now. Even on a good day, getting across Lake Washington via either of the two bridges that connect Seattle to the Eastside can be a slow, rage-inducing process. Today's pace gave new meaning to the term "glacial."

By the time I finally arrived at Diana's doorstep, it was almost four o'clock. Her town house was located in a woodsy development on the eastern edge of Bellevue. When she answered the door, she apologized for the way she looked. She wore gray sweats and tennis shoes, which looked just fine to me. Casual is good. But it was her left cheek, swollen and a little bruised, that wasn't so good.

"Just call me chipmunk," she said with a grimace.

"Does it hurt?" I asked as she ushered me inside. Ask a stupid question and get a stupid answer.

She rolled her eyes. "Does an outhouse stink?"

"Sorry."

"Never mind," she said. "I have just the cure." With that, she led me into a small kitchen with a large, well-stocked wine rack on the counter. She uncorked a bottle of Merlot and poured us each a glass.

"Great place you've got here," I said.

"You think?" she asked, clearly pleased.

"Absolutely." The pink carpeting and flowery wall-paper were a little too frilly for my taste, but it looked good. "How do you like commuting into the city every day?"

"Hate it."

I asked her why she put up with it, but she just shrugged her shoulders and sipped her wine. Since I really didn't care anyway, I changed the subject. "I talked to Colin Dawson yesterday."

"I thought that was the reason you showed up here today. Learn anything useful?"

I summarized my conversation with him, omitting his opinion of her. "The bartender actually told me more than Colin did," I said.

She rubbed her finger along the rim of her glass. "Oh?"

"I don't know all the details, but Dawson thinks that he got screwed when your firm changed computer systems."

She downed the last of her wine and poured another glass. "That's ridiculous," she said. "Dawson is grasping at straws."

"Some people think Paul is doing the same thing."

"What do you mean?"

"That's he's lying—or grasping at straws when he claims that someone framed him."

"Ha!"

"I take it you believe Paul."

"You take it right, girl," she said emphatically.

Noticing that her glass was empty again, I refilled it. She didn't refuse the wine or notice that I'd stopped drinking after the first glass. She was getting tipsy and talkative, but who was I to judge? Especially if it helped me gain her confidence. I'd been skirting around the real reason for my visit long enough.

"So, Diana," I said. "Tell me about you and Paul."

TWENTY-ONE

SHE CONFESSED EVERYTHING. It happened suddenly, right after she rummaged through her closet and plopped her high school yearbook in my hands. "I was in love with him," she said, lightly brushing his photo with her fingertip. She swallowed a sip of wine. "But . . ."

"But what?"

"He only had eyes for Amy. Called her his little ray of sunshine."

"Your younger sister?"

"That's right," she said. "My beautiful younger sister." She quickly flipped through several pages. "Here. Here she is."

"She *was* beautiful, Diana. But I thought she dated Martin."

"Yes. And Paul respected that. That's why he never told Amy how he felt about her."

"But he told you?"

She nodded. "Paul and I were buds. Take a look at this." She flipped through the yearbook again. "This was me back then. What a loser. No wonder he fell for Amy instead."

Diana wasn't as beautiful as her sister had been, but she wasn't ugly, either. "I think you're being too hard on yourself," I offered.

"Think what you will. The bottom line is I loved Paul. Paul loved Amy."

"And Amy loved Martin?"

"She married him, didn't she?"

"How did Paul take that?" I asked.

Diana drained the last of the Merlot and said, "He was devastated when he found out Amy was pregnant. But her marriage to Martin just about crushed him."

"Did Amy know how Paul felt about her?"

She shook her head. "Amy didn't know anything. She was so naïve. Getting pregnant scared her shitless."

"And killed her, too."

Diana was quiet a moment. "Yeah, it killed her. And just about killed Paul, too. He went off to college right after the funeral. Never heard boo from him until he came home married to Sharon Pierpont."

"Do you know anything about his juvenile record?"

"Oh, God. That was bad."

"What happened?"

Diana was more than a little tipsy by this point. She slurred her words, but the story she told was clear enough. "Paul and Marty had another close pal back then. Chip was on the football team with them. He wasn't as good a player, but he did all right for himself. Anyway, one night they were joking around, and things sort of got out of hand. Chip said something about Amy being "knocked up," and Paul just lost it. He beat Chip to a bloody pulp.

"He was sent to some juvenile detention facility for the rest of our senior year—until he turned eighteen, I think. When he lost his scholarship, everyone thought he'd wind up digging ditches or something. But Paul was determined to become an engineer. He worked full-time his entire freshman year. I don't know how he found time to fall in love with Sharon, but he did. Her father paid for the rest of his education."

"How do you feel about Paul now?"

"If you're asking whether I'm still in love with him, the answer is no. We're buds, just like in high school."

THE PHONE LINE dedicated to the fax machine rang as soon as I walked into my office at Sound Sailing. After the whirring and buzzing stopped, I retrieved a hand-written note from Maury Kranich. "Hey," the note began. "I was wrong. Your data only took me an hour to assemble. Took me longer to get my fax to work." As I scanned the rest of the page, I found the basic facts of my life listed in big bold print: birth date, Social Security number, driver's license number, mother's maiden name, Wendell's name and death date, and a record of all property I'd owned, including the sale price of our former home in Greenwood. If that wasn't enough, Kranich added a postscript. "If I were the unscrupulous kind, I could also find your medical and financial records. For the right amount of cash, of course."

I picked up the phone and called him. "You got all this stuff about me off the Internet?"

"Yep. A whole new identity is just a keystroke away. Scary, huh?"

"I thought there were laws against this type of thing. The Privacy Act and all that."

"There really isn't such a thing as privacy anymore.

And the laws we have now are basically unenforceable."

"Makes me feel really vulnerable."

"Reality bites. But you don't have to use a computer to steal someone's identity."

"How so?"

"My girlfriend—who should've known better—got hit last year. And it didn't take a computer to turn her life upside-down."

"What happened?"

"Jill went to work out at some health club and locked her briefcase in the trunk of her car. When she returned, her trunk had been jimmied, and her briefcase was gone. With it went her good name and credit. A ring of so-phisticated and ambitious thieves used her driver's li-cense, Social Security number, and credit cards to forge a new identity for a woman who then masqueraded as Jill. She went on a massive shopping spree that de-stroyed Jill's credit."

"Unbelievable."

"Believe it. The impostor even rented an apartment in Jill's name. All that stuff happened a year ago, and she's still trying to get things sorted out."

"Isn't there anything we can do to protect ourselves?" I asked.

"Sure," Kranich replied. "In the paper world, you tear up your credit card receipts and keep your ATM card separate from your personal identification number. But protecting yourself in the digital world takes a little more vigilance."

"Such as?"

"Such as not sending any financial data, including your Social Security number, via E-mail unless it's en-crypted. And if you make purchases or financial trans-actions on the Internet, make sure they're encrypted. Most people check their bank and credit card statements monthly, but you should also check your credit report once a year. If credit accounts have been opened in your name, you'll find them there."

"Good advice."

"Here's some more," Kranich said. "Guard your Social Security number with your life. Anyone who is required to report your income to the IRS has a legitimate need for your SSN. Beyond that, don't give it out. Don't have it printed on your checks or even carry the card with you."

"But you still got my number on the Internet."

He laughed. "Yeah, it's out there. But you don't have to make it any easier than it already is. Think about this," he added. "I bet your bank has Touch-Tone phone access to your bank account balance."

"You're right," I said, shuddering at what that implied. "They use the last four digits of my Social Security number as the password."

"Bingo. And I have your SSN now."

"Well, I hate to disappoint you, Maury, but my bank balance wouldn't be worth any thief's efforts. It's been stuck at nearly zero for years now."

The phone rang as soon as I replaced the receiver.

"Hi, Kellie, this is Abby. Remember me?"

"Of course I do. How're you doing?"

"Pretty good. I just wanted to thank you for giving my phone number to your friend. I just got back from a meeting with Al. That matter we talked about looks like a go."

She was being circumspect, but I got the picture: Kingston had come through as promised and called his pal in vice; Abby was now a double agent, so to speak. "Great!" I said. "I hope things work out for you." It took a lot of courage to do what she was doing, and I told her so.

"I just hope I can pull it off." She lowered her voice a notch and added, "There's something else you might like to know. I found the book."

My conversation with Kranich had me spooked about security, so I didn't mention Jewell Jessup's name. "Are you talking about your college friend's business records?"

"Exactly. We shared a locker at the Washington Athletic Club. I hadn't been over there since she was . . . you know, since she left. Anyway, there was a notation in the book for a 'P.C.' followed by 'twelve-m' and the code name 'Sunshine.' "

Sunshine. The name of the yacht. Paul's pet name for Amy. Coincidence or deliberate? "What does twelve-m mean?"

"Remember when I said that P.C. was probably a regular? Twelve-m confirms it."

"How so?"

"Twelve-m means that P.C. was seeing my friend for at least twelve months. A whole year is a long time in this business."

Was my friendship with Paul blinding me to the evidence? Had Paul been seeing Jewell after all? For an entire year? Or was the overwhelming evidence just too pat? Had the frame started long before his credit problems or the murders? I shook off the unanswered questions and said, "Abby, you need to give the book to Al. He'll know what to do with it."

"Already have," she said.

THE NEXT DAY, I looked up the address for Shelton RE-PC and went to see Terry Lindstrom. Contrary to what Maury had said, Lindstrom was not only still working at Shelton, he was the company's "main man" to see if you had a computer system to sell. I had called in advance with a cover story—the marina was thinking of updating its computers, and I had a few questions about the recycling process before we went forward. I don't usually twist the truth that much, but I didn't think I'd get anywhere near Terry Lindstrom otherwise. The ruse worked like a charm, and I was granted an early-morning appointment, which suited me just fine as I had another stop to make before my real job started.

Shelton RE-PC wasn't all that different from Maury's one-man show. It was housed in a larger building in a slightly spiffier part of town, but the interior arrangement was almost identical to the way Maury had set up his operation. Long rows of tables stockpiled with computers, terminals, and various peripherals dominated the warehouselike workroom. I counted at least six employees. Like Maury, they were a weary, ragtag bunch in their early twenties. There wasn't a receptionist, so I flagged down a kid carrying a cardboard box of used mice (the kind without whiskers), and asked where I could find Lindstrom.

He had fashioned a little office for himself in a corner of the vast room by stacking empty packing cartons around his desk. The partitionlike boxes, while probably not acoustically effective, did shield him from the rest of the goings-on in the room. His desk was a battered wooden door propped up by two sawhorses but his computer equipment, including an ergonomic keyboard, appeared to be state-of-the-art. A little older than the rest of the employees—but not by much—Lindstrom had carrot-red hair that was frizzier than mine and a thin face chock-full of freckles. Besides a Mariners baseball hat, his working attire was the standard issue: jeans, T-shirt, and sandals.

I introduced myself and began lying. Did a bang-up

job of it, too, judging by Lindstrom's animated response. With an implied hot contract from Larstad Marina in the works, he offered me a chair, rattling on enthusiastically about the computer recycling business in general and Shelton RE-PC in particular. I nodded in all the right places and asked a question now and then that he answered politely, even though I was pretty sure he'd pegged me as a computer illiterate. His attitude changed dramatically when I brought up the subject of confidentiality.

He cocked his head and stared at me as if I'd said a dirty word. "We run a secure operation here," he said. "Why do you ask?"

"I've heard things."

"What things?"

"Something about selling data that was supposed to have been wiped clean from the hard disks."

"Here we go again," he said. "That rumor has been floating around town ever since Maury Kranich started it."

"Why would he start a rumor like that?"

Lindstrom gestured to the vast interior of Shelton RE-PC. "Why do you think? This place might not look like much, but we're thriving. We keep our overhead down and we hire the best techies in the business. Kranich is a one-man band that is barely making it."

"He seemed busy to me."

"Busy at what? How much are the contracts paying him? He's got a reputation as a good programmer, but he's not very astute when it comes to securing high-paying contracts. We are."

"So you're saying he's jealous of your success?"

Lindstrom shrugged. "Something like that. Why else would he bother cutting me down with unfounded rumors?"

"Okay, maybe you're right. But I happen to know that some data from Pierpont Engineering somehow ended up with their major competitor right after they changed computer systems. In fact, right after their hard disks were cleaned by you."

"Man, oh man. I can't believe this," he said, doffing his Mariners hat and running both hands through his hair.

"The Pierpont employee who got fired couldn't believe it, either."

"Fired? She was fired?"

I raised an eyebrow. "She?"

"The Pierpont employee! Diana Sunn-Burton." He was clearly agitated now.

I waited for him to continue.

"I just sold her the data she asked for. There wasn't anything illegal or wrong with what I did."

"I think you've lost me. You sold her data?"

"Look, I don't know what Kranich told you, but the Pierpont deal had nothing to do with a breach of confidentiality. Ms. Sunn-Burton came here to check out how we did things—much like you're doing. I showed her our operation, and she seemed satisfied. But then a curious thing happened."

"What was that?"

"She wanted to know if she could have the data off the hard disks before we cleaned them. I didn't see any harm in it, so I said yes. It was Pierpont's data after all, and she is their personnel director."

"So you had no dealings with Emerald City A & E?"

"Emerald City what?"

"It's an architecture and engineering firm."

Lindstrom snapped his fingers. "Oh, I get it now. That's the major competitor you were talking about."

I tried to gauge his reaction. If he was lying, he was better at it than I. "You know nothing about selling them data?"

He stood up. "Get real," he said. "I don't sell out our clients. Pierpont or anyone else."

Our meeting ended on that indignant note. I told him that I'd get back to him regarding the marina's computer system. He said he wouldn't hold his breath.

TWENTY-TWO

EMERALD CITY A & E was my next stop. I had no plan, no story to finagle an appointment, and, worse yet, no agenda in mind if I managed to persuade someone to talk with me. What I did have were lots of questions. Ever since Colin Dawson's name had surfaced, I'd felt that Paul's frame-up claim might have some merit. But the more I probed, the more confused I became.

I was still puzzling over the significance of the twelve-m notation in Jewell Jessup's little black book, but uppermost in my mind was what to make of Dawson's firing. Had he disclosed confidential information to Emerald City A & E? Or were Terry Lindstrom and his company somehow involved? Maury Kranich surely seemed to think so. Unfounded rumor or not, I hadn't expected Lindstrom to admit to any wrongdoing. Nor did he. But he seemed genuinely surprised that his actions had resulted in a firing at Pierpont. But so what? How did any of that relate to a frame-up or murder?

Most troubling of all—how did Diana Sunn-Burton figure into all of this? Why would she have paid Lindstrom to retrieve Pierpont's data from the hard disks? And how did Emerald City come to possess that data if, in fact, they did? Well, Kellie, I thought, there was only one way to find out—ask. Just whom I would ask was not entirely clear to me. As usual, I was winging it and hoping for the best.

Emerald City A & E occupied the entire fiftieth floor of the Columbia Center, a monstrous skyscraper in the heart of the business district. Exiting the elevator, I paused in the broad and airy lobby to get my bearings. And gawk. The entry was elegantly gawkable in green and black marble, plush carpeting, ornate Chinese vases, and wall hangings from some ancient dynasty. The whole place had a hushed, museumlike quality. I mentally kicked myself for not wearing a dress. The fashionably attired receptionist sized me up quickly and, judging by her icy stare, found me wanting. I unzipped my windbreaker and walked over to the expansive counter in front of her desk with a confident, purposeful stride. Kind of hard to pull off when you don't know what the hell you're doing.

"Yes?" she said as I approached. "May I help you?" Her words were friendly, but her body language was as cold as the north side of a tombstone in winter.

As I scrambled to think of something brilliant to say, I felt a hand on my elbow. Then a familiar voice. "Kellie! What a surprise!"

I turned and found myself looking into the sexy eyes of Mr. Bill Starkey. *He* was surprised? The Weasel's rich pal was the last person I expected to run into. He wore a navy blue pinstriped suit that fit him well. Very well. I tried not to drool. "Uh, hello Bill. What are you doing here?"

Starkey laughed. His mellow guffaw sounded almost musical. The receptionist suddenly warmed up and laughed, too. Tittered, actually. "Mr. Starkey is our head engineer," she informed me, gazing adoringly at her boss.

"You . . . you work at Emerald City?" I asked.

"That's what they pay me for," he said, "but it's more like fun than work." He winked at the receptionist. "Any messages, Susan?"

She handed him a stack of little pink notes. "Glad to have you back in the office, sir. We've missed you."

Starkey gave her a two-fingered salute and then turned to me. "So, Ms. Montgomery, now that we've established why *I'm* here, what about you?"

I figured I had two choices: I could admit I was on a fishing expedition or I could fib a little. I've never liked fishing. "I need some advice," I said. "Engineering advice."

"Then you've come to the right place," he said. "Follow me." He led me down a long hallway adorned with black and white photographs of buildings in various stages of construction. "We call this hallway memory lane," he said, gesturing at the display. "Emerald City Architecture and Engineering has been in business since the 1930s. Back then it was called Starkey and Sons."

He ushered me into his office, or more accurately, his executive suite. It was larger than most apartments. Two of the walls were floor-to-ceiling glass with killer views of downtown Seattle and Elliott Bay. The other walls were paneled in dark cherry and decorated with framed photographs similar to those we'd passed in the hall. A drawing board with a plethora of blueprints spread across it sat in one corner of the room. Additional blueprints, rolled up and bound with rubber bands, were stacked on the floor.

Behind his expansive cherry desk was a matching credenza on which sat a collection of Chinese artifacts interspersed with more framed photographs. Unlike the others, most of these photos were in color and appeared to be family members engaged in very active, Kennedyish sports—skiing, tag football, tennis, and whitewater rafting. The women crowding around him at the marina would be pleased—none of the shots suggested a wife or little kiddies.

Starkey tossed the message slips on his desk and invited me to sit in a tapestry-covered chair near the windows. The chair was part of a grouping that included a matching chair, small sofa, and coffee table.

"When I took over," Starkey said, "I changed the company name." He lowered himself into the chair opposite mine and chatted amiably about the firm and its history for a few more minutes. "But enough about Emerald," he said slapping his knees. "You said you needed some advice?"

I smiled awkwardly. "Well, before I get into all that, there is something else on my mind."

"Oh?" His shoulders were marine-straight but he leaned forward slightly. "Go on," he said with an encouraging nod. A nod that said whatever I had on my mind interested him mightily.

"I was just wondering how you happen to know the Wea—I mean, Todd Wilmington?"

Starkey unbuttoned his suit jacket and loosened his tie. Then he extended his long legs in front of him and crossed his ankles. It was a relaxed, easygoing pose that belied the nervous twitch at the corner of his mouth. "Todd and I belong to the same golf club," he said with a dismissive shrug. "But I suppose that question has more to do with our relationship at Larstad's Marina. I take it you've heard the news?"

"What news?"

"I just got back from the marina. Emerald City A & E has been awarded the expansion project." He noted my shocked expression. "Don't tell me you didn't know that was in the works. Why do you think I've been hanging out there so much lately? It certainly wasn't because I enjoyed Wilmington's company."

"But," I stammered, "Pierpont Engineering has that contract."

"Not anymore. Lawrence Larstad's attorneys found a loophole. It's a good thing, too. With Pierpont's chief engineer missing and facing a double murder charge, the marina's project was bound to suffer."

"So let me get this straight," I said, struggling to rein in my growing anger. "Emerald City got the expansion contract because of your friendship with Todd Wilmington?" Never mind that my friendship with Paul Crenshaw had been a factor in Pierpont's selection.

Starkey's jaw clenched noticeably. "No," he said, "we got the contract because we're the top architectural and engineering firm in Seattle."

"I see."

"You don't sound convinced."

His office alone was convincing. "Well, I admit your firm is successful, but . . ."

"Go on."

"I don't know how to say it tactfully."

"Don't worry about tact. I'm a big boy. What are you trying to say?"

"I've heard that confidential data belonging to Pierpont Engineering somehow made its way to Emerald City."

"Preposterous!"

"I didn't expect you to say otherwise. But I have reason to believe that there might be some truth to the tale.

Pierpont even fired one of their engineers over it."

"Look, don't get me wrong. I don't mean to come off as an arrogant know-it-all. Paul Crenshaw's firm is a great outfit. And Paul is a great guy. Hell, I've known him since high school. He would've done an outstanding job at the marina. It's just that Lawrence Larstad didn't want to deal with a firm in trouble. I know nothing about any confidential data from Pierpont. We won the Larstad contract fair and square."

I sat up in my chair. "Wait a minute. Did you say you went to school with Paul?"

Starkey's expression grew nostalgic. "That's right. Old Shoreline High. Paul, and Marty, and the whole gang."

"Did you know someone back then named Chip?"

He burst out laughing. "Chip? Oh, yeah, I knew that little smart-ass real well."

"Good," I said, "then maybe you can verify a story I heard recently."

"What story was that?" Starkey asked.

"That Paul has a juvenile record because he assaulted this Chip fellow."

Starkey turned his face slightly and pointed to the thin white scar running along his jawline. "See this? It's the only scar that's visible now. The plastic surgeon could've taken care of it, too, but I wanted to keep it as a reminder of what a jerk I'd been."

I was stunned. "*You're* Chip?"

"Guilty," he said sheepishly. "We all had nicknames back then—Mooney, Jughead, Ratface, Noodles. I was known as Chip-on-His-Shoulder-Starkey. It fit, too. I was always angry about one damn thing or another. That beating nearly killed me, but it did some good, too. It beat some sense into me. I came out of surgery completely changed."

"What about Paul? Do you think he's changed, too? Or is he still capable of violence? Possibly murder?"

Starkey raised his hands in the air. "Whoa. I know where you're going with this, but you're on the wrong track."

"I'm listening."

"The Paul Crenshaw I knew in high school was a decent, caring person. I respected him then and I respect him now."

"Even though he nearly killed you?"

"Who said that?"

"You did. Just a minute ago."

He shook his head. "Paul never touched me. He took the rap, but he never fought with me—or anyone else."

"Then who . . . ?"

Starkey rubbed a finger across his jaw. "Who gave me this scar?"

I nodded.

"Marty Petrowski. Marty gave me the beating that changed my life forever—and Paul's, too."

I MUMBLED SOMETHING about having to get back to the marina and cut our meeting short. But I felt like driving straight to Martin Petrowski's. As far as I was concerned, the man had some explaining to do. If Martin truly believed in Paul's innocence, why infer he was capable of violence? And why did he let Paul take the rap for him? Then there was Martin's girlfriend who later became his wife, Amy. Did Martin know Paul loved her? Did he know that Paul called Amy his "Sunshine"? Yes, I thought, I definitely needed to talk to Martin Petrowski. But our talk would have to wait. There was one little matter I had to deal with first—my job.

My students today were an advanced group, which was a good thing considering the "heavy weather" conditions on Elliott Bay. Simply put, heavy weather or heavy air is any wind and wave condition that is so strong and forceful that the sailor is challenged (to some level or another) by its intensity. Sailors measure wind velocity in units called knots and can estimate the speed of the wind by looking at the water's surface. I always recommend that beginners head for shore when whitecaps (foamy wave crests) become commonplace, or at about fifteen knots. But fifteen knots of wind is just when sailing starts to get fun. As Grampy always said, a little spray in the face never hurt anyone.

I had four students—all in their early twenties and naturally-born speed freaks. They were eager to get out on the water, but I made them sit through a little preparatory talk first. "In sailing, just like in life," I told them, "knowing your limits is important. This means being able to assess not only the wind and wave conditions, but also the condition of the boat and crew and whether you feel capable." I then told them about all the things that could go wrong, including—depending on the type of boat—the possibility of capsizing.

"What are you trying to do, Kellie? Scare us?" This from Ryan Andrews, an avid skier who'd won plenty of races on the slopes. He had set his sights on eventually doing some sailboat racing.

"No, I just want to make sure you understand what's involved in heavy-weather sailing."

"What's to understand?" he said with a grin. "The faster it blows, the faster we go."

"Maybe, but consider this: The force of the wind increases by the square of the velocity, which means that at fourteen knots, the wind force on your rigging and sails is double the load on the boat at ten knots. And that's before you add in the effect of the waves. Sailboats and their component parts can only stand so much load before they begin to break. Anything you can do to reduce the forces on the boat in extreme conditions can make a big difference." I followed that little lecture with a discussion on ways to reduce sail power, including dropping a sail, reefing, switching to a smaller sail, and using an engine.

Once we were actually out on the water, we practiced some of the techniques I'd talked about. The group performed real well in the windy conditions, but I can't say the same for me. Don't get me wrong. I walked and talked the part of the able sailing instructor, but my heart wasn't in it. Or my brain. That became patently obvious when I almost failed to catch a potentially disastrous situation when Ryan was at the helm.

We had been sailing on a broad reach with the wind almost directly behind us. I was so preoccupied with my own thoughts that I didn't notice that Ryan had allowed the boat to turn slightly downwind. Now the wind was directly astern of us. It was an important difference, because if he allowed the boat to turn any further to port, we could experience an accidental jibe—a violent swinging of the boom to the other, or starboard side of the boat. In these weather conditions, that kind of action could damage the rigging or even dismast us. Not to mention knock someone overboard.

"Ryan!" I yelled. "Come to starboard!" He ignored my command, and I grabbed the wheel away from him. Another lesson about accidental jibes followed.

Once we were on course again, it occurred to me that the Crenshaw case was fast becoming an obsession, overriding everything else in my life. My job, my daughter, and even my relationship with Allen Kingston had taken a backseat to solving the murders. But, as Kingston had reminded me so many times, a murder investigation wasn't for amateurs. I was touched by his concern for my safety, but the only danger I'd encountered on this case was a headache.

When the class ended at four o'clock, my temples were throbbing without mercy. I couldn't wait for the last of my students to leave so I could call it a day. As they gathered their belongings, I downed some aspirin and then followed them out the door. I'd just locked it when Jason and Tiffany arrived. They were both dressed in jeans, windbreakers, and deck shoes.

"Hey, Kellie!" called Jason. "You didn't forget about us, did you?"

As a matter of fact . . . "No, of course not," I fibbed. "I thought you might enjoy taking *Second Wind* out this afternoon." Although I didn't say it, I figured the larger vessel would be safer, considering their skill level and the strong winds.

"You mean the Hinckley?" Jason asked excitedly. I'd told him all about my sloop when we were in the San Juans and I knew he was dying to see her.

"Yep. Unless, of course, you'd rather try one of the crafts in the school's fleet," I teased. "We've got some real nice J-twenty-twos and Catalinas—"

"No, no. The Hinckley would be great!" he said, grinning. "Wouldn't it, Tiff?"

She gave a halfhearted shrug. "Whatever."

Jason's eyes met mine. "Tiff didn't want to come," he explained.

Great. A headache *and* a reluctant sailor. Martin had said Tiffany was depressed, but she struck me as being just plain bored. Her attitude irritated me until I reminded myself what a severe trauma she'd been through. Witnessing your mother's strangled body was one thing, but believing your father was responsible for the murder was something else again. Who was I to judge her behavior? That she could even function at all was something of a miracle under the circumstances.

I forced a grin on my face and put my arm around Tiffany's shoulder. "Don't worry," I told her. "You're going to love sailing with me."

"Whatever."

So began our outing.

TWENTY-THREE

AS SOON AS we were aboard, I grabbed the aspirin bottle and fortified myself for a rough ride. Then I gave the kids a tour of *Second Wind*. Since our outing wasn't a lesson per se, I dispensed with my usual chat about boating terminology and gave them a little background on the Hinckley. Most American sailors are familiar with the name, although it connotes different things to different people. For some, it means big bucks and East Coast blue-blood snobbery. For those familiar with the company's work, it more likely means fabled craftsmanship such as mirrorlike varnish, custom stainless steel castings, the trademark dustbin in the cabin sole, and "frameless" portlights. For me, it meant scraping together enough cash to purchase a 1960s model that had been seriously neglected by its owner. I got a good bargain, but there was another price tag—lots of elbow grease to restore it to its former glory.

Jason seemed interested in what I had to say, but Tiffany was more taken with Pan-Pan. She played with the cat while Jason peppered me with questions. "I heard that the first Hinckley was a powerboat," he said.

"Very good, Jason," I said, genuinely impressed. "Not many people know that. "Henry R. Hinckley started the company that bears his name on graduation from Cornell University. His first boat, launched in 1934, was a twenty-six-foot lobster-type powerboat, but he soon moved to sail, and the rest is history."

I could tell Tiffany was bored out of her mind, so I suggested we get underway. I had Jason help me with the presail checklist, and then we donned our life jackets and untied the lines. Once we had cleared the breakwater and hoisted the sails, Tiffany's interest picked up. She had been amused when I insisted that Pan-Pan wear a life jacket like the rest of us, but she quickly understood the need when the strong wind came ripping out of the north. *Second Wind* shot across Elliott Bay at such a rapid clip that I had to reef the sails a notch to keep us under control. I thought Tiffany would be frightened when the sloop heeled so much that the port side rails almost touched the water. But as soon as I altered our course by bearing away from the wind and letting out the sheets, Tiffany shouted, "Hey, let's do that again!" I realized then that my headache had disappeared.

By the time our outing ended, Tiffany had not only volunteered for a turn at the helm, she was tacking and jibing with an enthusiasm equal to that of Jason. Although not as naturally skilled as Jason, the girl had a need for speed, and fortunately the wind accommodated her. At one point the gusts became so strong that I lowered the jib, which caused her to complain mightily. But she was all smiles when we finally lowered the mainsail and headed back to the marina. "That was great, Kellie," she gushed. "Can we go again sometime?"

"Sure," I said. "Just let me know when." After we'd secured the boat in her slip, I told her about the dinghy races that were planned for the marina's anniversary celebration. "Maybe you and Jason would like to compete," I suggested. "We'll have a teen division."

Her eyes lit up. "Could we? I mean, I don't know that much about sailing."

"Hey, you were super today," Jason said.

"He's right," I said. "And if you like, I could give you both some pointers and a little practice run before the event."

They both jumped at the idea. Their gung-ho attitude gave me a needed energy boost, and I found myself asking them to stick around for a while longer. If Tiffany was suffering from depression, boredom, or whatever, it surely didn't seem like it now. I was pleased to have had a hand in raising her spirits—however long it lasted. We went inside the cabin for a cup of hot chocolate. At first our conversation centered on the dinghy races, but eventually the topic turned to the couple's relationship. "We love each other," admitted Jason as he put a protective arm around Tiffany. "But it's such a downer."

I nodded. No one had to verbalize what Jason meant. Paul's attempt to squelch their blossoming love by sending Tiffany to boarding school was clearly the underlying reason for Jason's remark.

"We're going to get married as soon as I turn eighteen," Tiffany said. "No one can stop us then."

Jason grimaced and added, "Unless your dad kills me."

"Don't even joke about something like that," I said.

"It's not a joke," Tiffany said. "Dad killed my mom. What makes you think he won't kill Jason?"

I eyed them carefully. "Do you seriously believe what you're saying?"

They both nodded. "Especially since he's already threatened me once," Jason said.

"Threatened you? How?"

"It was right before he sent Tiffany away. Told me that if I continued to see his daughter against his wishes, he would, quote, punch my lights out, unquote."

Tiffany shuddered. "I don't know how he did it, but he found out that I'm staying at the Petrowskis now," she said. "So far, he's just called on the phone, but we're terrified he'll come looking for Jason."

I didn't want to discount their fears, but I thought they were overreacting and told them so as gently as I could.

"You don't understand, Kellie. Daddy has changed a lot from when you lived next door. We used to be so close, closer even than Mom and I. Then he just went nuts for no reason." She shuddered again. "I'm so scared of him now."

Jason patted her shoulder. "Don't worry, Tiff, my dad won't let him get anywhere near us."

"Do you know where your father is?" I asked Tiffany. I had some real doubts about his hiding-in-plain-sight story. Even if true, he couldn't last much longer. According to Kingston, the search for him had intensified significantly—the longer he was on the run, the more embarrassing it looked for the department.

She shook her head. "I don't even want to know where he is—unless it's jail. But you might ask that lady in Personnel at grandpa's firm. Everyone knows she's madly in love with Dad. She'd do anything for him, including hiding him from the police."

Our hot chocolate had cooled, along with the good mood we'd enjoyed during our sail. "Do you want a refill?" I asked. They declined and took their leave.

• • •

THE PHONE RANG.

"May I speak with Kellie Montgomery, please?" The man's wheezy voice was unfamiliar.

"This is Kellie."

"Good. I called Sound Sailing School first but all I got was an answering machine. So I thought I'd try you at home."

I'm going to throttle Tom Dolan, I thought. This wasn't the first time he'd given out my home telephone to a potential student. He seemed to think he was personally responsible for fixing my client base as well as our fleet. "I'm sorry, but you'll have to call back tomorrow at Sound Sailing if you want to register for lessons. My scheduling book is at the school."

"Uh, I'm not calling about sailing lessons. My name is Sammy Ortiz," he said. "I'm a deputy sheriff in New Mexico."

A deputy sheriff? In New Mexico? This did not sound good. I clutched the receiver tightly and waited for him to continue.

"Are you the mother of Cassie Montgomery?"

Oh, my God. I knew it was bad news. "Tell me, please. Has there been an accident? Are the girls all right?"

"Cassie and Deena are just fine," he said quickly. "I'm sorry if I worried you. I tend to forget that people often assume the worst when the police call."

I wasn't relieved. "Then why are you calling?"

He cleared his throat. "Well, I may be your daughter's uncle. She and her twin are claiming that my sister is her birth mother."

I couldn't think of anything to say.

"But the thing is," he said after getting no response, "Renée never had any children, let alone twin girls."

"Are you saying that Cassie and Deena made a mistake? That your sister isn't their birth mother?"

"Well, I'm not sure. Renée wasn't always . . . well, let's just say she wasn't always close to the family. There's a whole lot we don't know about her life after she left here. Anyway, the girls want me to arrange a meeting with her. So before I did that, I thought I'd call you."

"How can I help?"

"I hoped you could verify that your daughter and her twin are who they claim to be. As an officer of the law, I guess I'm a little suspicious. They seem like nice kids, but you never know. I'd hate to get mixed up in some kind of hoax or scam."

"You can rest easy, Sheriff. Cassie and Deena are indeed adopted and searching for their birth mother. I won't go into all the reasons why they feel such a search is necessary, but I will say that they are sincere and very motivated to discover their true heritage."

"Glad to hear that. And you're okay with their search?"

"I'm not thrilled that Cassie dropped out of college, but as far as reuniting with her family goes, yes, I am. I can't speak for Deena's mother."

"And I can't speak for the rest of the family, but I'll tell you this: If Renée does turn out to be their birth mother, the Tewas will welcome those two girls with open arms."

"The Tewas? I thought you said your name was Ortiz."

He chuckled. "It is. I was referring to my people. We're Indians. Tewa from the San Juan Pueblo."

After we disconnected, I sat with my hand on the receiver for a few minutes and wished I'd asked a few more questions. Cassie an Indian? With her coloring I'd always thought that she was probably Hispanic. I hadn't even considered the possibility of a Native American heritage. I was so stunned by the call that I didn't even think to ask him to give Cassie my love. Nor did I ask if he'd called Deena's mother. I would have to call her. But first I had another call to make. I consulted my directory and dialed.

"Hi, Diana. This is Kellie."

"Hey, there. What's up?" She sounded like my new best friend. I guess after spending an evening pouring wine and sharing secrets, she felt we'd bonded or something.

"I met Chip a.k.a. Bill Starkey today. Did you know that he owns Emerald City A & E?"

"Yes."

"Why didn't you mention that the other night?"

She hesitated a little too long. "Well, I don't know. It didn't seem all that important."

"And Martin?"

"What about him?"

"Bill said that it was Martin, not Paul, who beat him up in high school."

Long pause. "Really? Well . . . that might be true."

"Why do you think Paul took the rap for Martin? It doesn't make any sense."

"It does to me."

"How so?"

"Think about it. Paul probably did it for Amy. If Martin had gone to jail, he wouldn't have been able to take care of his wife and newborn. I told you Paul was loyal."

I wondered about her own loyalty. "I heard something else today that surprised me."

"What?"

"I talked to Terry Lindstrom at Shelton RE-PC. He told me that you paid him to retrieve data from Pierpont's disks before they were cleaned. Why would you do that?"

"Jeez, what is this? Twenty questions?"

"I'm just trying to help Paul, Diana."

"So am I!" she said huffily. After a pause she added, "Okay, I paid Lindstrom for the data. But I was just trying to recapture Colin Dawson's E-mail. He was making such a fuss about his wrongful termination, threatening to sue the company over it that I had to do something. I hadn't thought about his E-mail until after we'd already gotten our new computer system. I figured that if I had the data from his disks I could prove without a doubt that he'd been corresponding with Emerald City A & E."

"Bill Starkey denies that he's ever had any contact with Dawson or Terry Lindstrom. He said he knew nothing about any confidential data from Pierpont."

"Of course he'd deny it," Diana said. "He was a sneaky kid in high school, and nothing has changed. Now, if you don't mind, I've got to run." She didn't sound like my best friend anymore.

"Just one more question, Diana. Do you know where Paul is?"

"No! Absolutely not. Why on earth would you ask that?"

"Oh, no particular reason."

I hung up believing that there was a lot more to Diana's involvement in this mess than she'd disclosed. And I was right.

TWENTY-FOUR

"WHAT CAN YOU tell me about the Tewas?" I asked Kingston. This was the first time we'd been together since our sunset sail, and we were at the Topside satisfying our sweet tooth with a chocolate sundae. Not that we needed the caloric overload. We'd already stuffed ourselves with lasagna and garlic bread at the Spaghetti Factory. Dessert at the Topside was just an excuse to extend the evening.

By mutual agreement, we'd succeeded in avoiding any mention of the Crenshaw case—a real accomplishment on my part since I couldn't stop thinking about my conversation with Diana and the one I intended to have with Martin. We'd also skirted around anything that bordered on the state of our relationship. Although politics and religion weren't necessarily off limits, our conversation had been pretty much limited to critiquing a movie we'd both seen (thumbs up), the weather (thumbs down), and Seattle's potholes (definitely thumbs down).

Given these hot topics, it was probably inevitable that we wound up talking about family matters.

I'd already told Kingston about Cassie's trip to New Mexico and the phone call I'd received from Deputy Sheriff Ortiz. He seemed interested enough, but when I asked about the Tewas, he snorted abruptly, spraying coffee all over the front of his shirt.

"What'd I say?"

Grabbing a napkin, he dabbed at his coffee-splattered shirt. "White people," he said with a shake of his head.

"What about us?"

"You assume that just because someone is an Indian, he automatically knows all about every Indian nation."

He had a point, but I wasn't inclined to admit it. "Excuse me? Don't you claim to be French and English, too? Sounds a little white to me."

Kingston snorted again. "As Will Rogers once said, 'I have Indian blood in me and just enough white blood for you to question my honesty.' "

"Will Rogers was an Indian?"

"Cherokee."

"So, what are you trying to tell me? That I shouldn't believe you?"

"Hey," he said with palm upraised as if he were swearing in court. "You can believe me. I'm an officer of the law. And I know about the Tewas—just not personally."

"Well, what about generally?"

He scooped out the last dollop of ice cream from his dish and swallowed it. "Generally the Tewa people live in northern New Mexico on several separately recognized pueblos. There are also some Tewas in Arizona, living on the Hopi reservation."

"Sammy Ortiz said he was from the San Juan Pueblo."

Kingston smiled. "I went down to Santa Fe once to

pick up a prisoner. Didn't have much time for sightseeing, but I made a point of going to the San Juan Pueblo before attending to business."

"Why?"

"It was February. The Winter People were performing the Deer Dance." He noted my confused expression and explained, "The pueblo has a two-part social system, the Winter People and the Summer People. The Deer Dance is a ceremony the Winter People conduct to ensure prosperity for the coming year." He smiled again. "I helped them out by dropping by the Oke Owinge Arts and Crafts Co-operative. Spent a tidy little sum on pottery and baskets before I got out of there."

"Did you get a feel for what the Tewas are like as a people?"

Kingston frowned as he eyed me over his coffee mug. "You mean, does Cassie come from good stock?"

I felt my face flush. "I know she comes from good stock, Kingston," I said indignantly. It hurt that he assumed I would think otherwise. "I was asking about their everyday life. Cassie's uncle said he was a deputy sheriff. That's the extent of my knowledge."

After signaling for a refill on his coffee, he said, "You're going to have to ask Cassie about her particular family. Many people find work outside the pueblo and return only for ritual occasions and ceremonies. On the pueblo, the economic base is primarily agricultural, supplemented by raising livestock and the sale of handicrafts. 'Course, they have a casino, too." He smiled broadly and added, "Not that I had time to check it out, you understand."

"Not even for a little bingo?" I teased.

He laughed. "Especially not for bingo."

"What can you tell me about the living conditions?"

His smile faded, and he said, "Not good. Unless you

consider low incomes, poor health care, poor schooling, and unemployment good."

I was starting to feel depressed. "How do they get along with the whites?"

He waited for Janey to refill his coffee cup and then said, "Given their history, I suspect there's some resentment and anger. Bound to lead to a few clashes."

"I wonder how Cassie and Deena will fit in. Their uncle said the family would welcome them with open arms, but . . ."

Kingston shrugged. "Don't worry about it. If those girls really are Tewa, they'll be welcome."

I nodded, but I wasn't as confident as Kingston. Why had their mother kept her daughters' birth a secret from her family? Would she be upset that they'd revealed a part of her life that she obviously didn't want exposed? *Oh, Cassie, what have you gotten yourself into?*

We sat quietly, thinking our own thoughts, until I caught Kingston glancing at his watch again. It was the third time in the last half hour. "Bored?" I asked.

He grinned. "With you? Never!"

"So, what's up? You have a hot date later?"

"As a matter of fact . . ."

I raised an eyebrow and waited.

"I have an appointment with Diana Sunn-Burton."

"Let me guess. You think she knows more about the Crenshaw case than she's led you to believe."

His turn to raise an eyebrow. "I shouldn't ask this, but what's your take on the woman?"

"I think she's madly in love with Paul Crenshaw and has been ever since they were kids."

"My gut tells me she knows where he's been hiding."

I'd already told Kingston what Paul had said about living on the street, and he hadn't bought it. Nevertheless, the department was keeping close tabs on all the shelters and other hangouts that the homeless were known to frequent.

"Tiffany seems to think so, too," I said.

He swallowed the last of his coffee and prepared to leave. "Well, there's only one way to find out."

"Can I come with you?"

"You know the answer to that."

"Then could you ask her a few questions for me?"

He gave me a wary look. "What questions?"

I told him about Colin Dawson and Diana's visit to Terry Lindstrom. "She said she was just trying to prove that Dawson's firing was justified, but I think there was more to it than that. Ask her about those disks."

Deep frown. "Anything else?"

"Well, her sister was married to Martin Petrowski. I think you should press Diana for more information about him."

Deeper frown. "Why?"

"He lied about something really important."

His frown was a full-blown scowl now. "Care to fill me in?"

I related what I'd learned from Bill Starkey. "Paul's stint in juvie was because of Martin."

Still scowling, Kingston heaved a weary sigh. "You've been doing a lot more investigating than I thought."

"Enough to wonder about Martin Petrowski's motives."

"Damn it, woman!" he blurted. "How many times do I have to tell you? Keep your nose out of this case!"

"Okay, okay," I said, holding up my hands in surrender. "I get the message—loud and clear."

"Kellie, I mean it," he said sternly. "It's dangerous out there." As he stood to leave, he paused and looked at me without frown or scowl. Instead, his face registered such tenderness that it nearly took my breath away. He kissed me lightly on the cheek and said softly, "In case you've forgotten, Kellie, I love you. Very much."

After he left, I lingered over my tea and thought about what he'd said. I loved him, too. Maybe I couldn't say it yet, but he had to know it. If I really loved him, though, I'd butt out of this case like he wanted. Wouldn't I? I was still pondering that puzzle when Bert Foster stopped by my table.

"What's up, Kellie?" he asked. Before I could invite him to join me, he eased his bulk into the chair Kingston had vacated. Spotting our empty ice cream dishes, he declared himself starving. When the business of ordering his dinner was taken care of, I asked him whether it was true that Pierpont Engineering had lost the marina contract.

He nodded. "Blame it on old man Larstad. I can't remember when he's been in such a dither."

I flashed on the protest scene with Danielle Korb and her ever-present microphone. "Rose warned me this might happen. I just didn't realize that the contract would go to Pierpont's biggest competitor." I told him about my meeting with Bill Starkey.

"Bill Starkey owns Emerald City A & E?" he asked.

"You didn't know?"

He shook his head. "That explains a lot. Rose thought Starkey was just another rich yacht owner the Weasel was chumming around with. But I didn't think that was the case since Starkey didn't have a yacht registered with us. Rose said there was always another explanation—he could be a spy for that new Coho Marina."

"Sounds like she's getting a little paranoid. I don't want to add fuel to the fire, but tell Rose she should be prepared. Wilmington is going to take all the credit he can for this deal." A new thought occurred to me, and I said, "I guess the good news is that with Starkey taking over the contract, I'll be back in the charter business again."

Bert sighed and shook his head. "I guess you haven't watched the news on TV lately."

I'd been avoiding the news media ever since my photo appeared on page one of the *Seattle Times*. It was sort of like sticking my head in the sand, but it did wonders for my stress level. "What now?" I asked.

"Rose should be the one to tell you this, not me."

"Come on, Bert, what's up?"

"Well," he said slowly, "Danielle Korb has been on the tube every night this week with a report on the Crenshaw case."

"And?"

"Her reports haven't sat well with old man Larstad— especially since she is claiming that you've been interfering with the police investigation of Sharon Crenshaw's murder. Larstad told Rose that if what Korb says is true, you'd be out of the charter business *and* the sailing school."

"But," I protested, "surely Rose doesn't think Korb's allegations are true?"

He shrugged as Janey brought his dinner. "Rose said she doesn't know what to think." As he cut his steak, he added, "You have to admit you've been snooping around, asking a million questions. Besides me, you've talked to Charlie and just about everyone else here at the marina. Korb says you've been doing the same thing all over town."

I didn't bother denying it. "I've just been trying to help Paul."

Bert nodded. "I know that, Kellie. Your heart is in the right place, but maybe you should consider helping yourself."

"Meaning?"

"Meaning don't give old man Larstad a reason to order Rose to fire you."

When I didn't respond, he tackled another unpleasant issue—the activists protesting the marina's proposed expansion. "If they have their way, Starkey's new contract might be in jeopardy as well."

I usually enjoy Bert's company, but all the problems facing the marina—and me—were more than I could handle for one night. When his dessert arrived, I excused myself and headed for home. But I only got halfway down K Dock when I spotted a new problem. As I passed *Sweet Rewards,* one of the J22s in the sailing school fleet, I noticed that the prop looked bent. That was my first mistake. The second was leaning out over the water to take a closer look. The third was not realizing that someone was watching me. As soon as I leaned over, they made their move quickly, quietly—and violently.

It happened so fast that I had no time to scream when the fist slammed into my back. A gentle push would have accomplished the same result, but the force of the blow was calculated to cause as much damage as possible. And it worked. My forehead hit the prop with a hard thud as I tumbled into the cold water.

Although dazed, I knew I was in trouble. Blood gushed from my forehead when I bobbed to the surface and my limbs felt so heavy I could hardly move them. Resorting to a slow but desperate dog paddle, I managed to struggle back to the dock.

I'd almost gained enough purchase to pull myself out of the water when my attacker, a dark-clothed figure in cowboy boots, stomped on my shivering fingers. The pain was agonizing, and I screamed for all I was worth. The boot lifted, and for an instant I thought my screams had thwarted a further attack. Surely someone would come to investigate. But my assailant was determined to silence me—permanently.

Before I could move out of the way, the boots' owner kicked my bloody forehead, plunging me under the water again. I thrashed about in a wild attempt to get back to the surface, but my efforts were no match for the strong hands holding me in a watery death grip. I had no air left. My life didn't pass before my eyes, but I knew with every fiber of my being that I was about to die. Death by drowning.

No! I wouldn't give up. I couldn't give up. Summoning a last burst of strength, I fought against my attacker's hands.

I was still fighting, flailing my arms and kicking my feet, when I realized that I could breathe again. Gulping in the fresh air as fast as I could, I swung my fists at the two big hands trying to grab me. But it was futile. My body was shutting down, exhausted and beaten. I felt myself being dragged out of the water and onto the dock. Shivering uncontrollably, I wrapped myself into a tight ball and waited helplessly for my attacker to hit me again.

TWENTY-FIVE

"KELLIE! CAN YOU hear me?"

The voice was familiar, but I was afraid to look up.

"It's me, Charlie," the voice said. "You're going to be all right now."

Good old Charlie the Tuna. He had never sounded so good. It's always nice to have a live-aboard around when you need rescuing from a watery death. Within moments, he'd draped a blanket over my shoulders and handed me a towel to stem the blood still oozing from my forehead. Although Charlie repeatedly assured me that I was safe, I didn't believe him. Surviving a near-drowning was one thing. There was still a good chance that I'd freeze to death. Shivering uncontrollably, I was vaguely aware that a crowd had gathered on the dock. I could hear sirens wailing in the distance, but I was too busy trying to keep warm to care.

By the time the paramedics arrived, I just wanted to go home, but they didn't give me a choice in the mat-

ter. After taking my vitals and inspecting the gash and
bump on my forehead, they decided that a trip to the
emergency room at Harborview Medical Center was
just the ticket. The police eventually showed up, but
I'd already been loaded onto the Medic One van and
missed them.

My recollection of the events immediately following
my arrival at Harborview is a little fuzzy, but it's probably just as well. The emergency room was crowded, as
always, and, after a brief inspection by the triage nurse,
my medical condition was deemed a low priority. While
the staff attended to the sick, the maimed, and the dying,
I was wheeled into a tiny examining room to exchange
my wet clothes for a hospital gown. After a quick trip
via gurney to the X-ray lab, I was returned to the examining room to wait my turn for a physician. Unfortunately I wasn't allowed to wait alone. Besides the
police who'd followed me to the hospital, my relatives
descended en masse. I had Bert Foster to thank for that.
He'd called my sister Mary Kathleen who in turn had
burned up the telephone wires with the news of the incident. There's nothing like an attempted murder to
launch a spontaneous family reunion.

Although it was well-meaning, I didn't feel up to dealing with their solicitous comments, especially when they
were interspersed with "I told you so" remarks about my
lifestyle. Ever since I moved aboard my sailboat, they've
been predicting some disaster would strike. The fact that
this was the second time I'd wound up in a hospital
because of an incident at the marina was proof, in their
opinion, that their fears for my safety were justified.

I tried downplaying the seriousness of the whole episode, but my older sister, Donna, took it upon herself
to give me a piece of her mind. As far as I was concerned, she didn't have a lot of pieces to go around.

"You know, Kellie," she said, "you should just sell that awful old boat and move into a decent house on the Eastside. It's time you gave up that ridiculous job and started living like a civilized person."

At fifty-three, my sister was not only the oldest of my siblings, but also the best-looking. And thanks to all the nips and tucks, lipo, and collagen, she was likely to stay that way. She had the same reddish-blond hair, the same size six figure, and the same peaches-and-cream skin of her youth. Even her attitude hadn't changed over the years—it stunk when we were kids and it stunk now.

I mumbled an uncivilized retort that she chose to ignore.

Mary Kathleen, seeing my discomfort, came to my rescue. Sort of.

Donna has always been able to browbeat my siblings into submitting to her whims. The fact that she controls the purse strings on the settlement we received after our parents were killed has a lot to do with her power.

"Donna," Mary Kathleen said, "I don't think Kellie needs to think about moving right now."

My three brothers and their wives were silent on the matter, which Donna took as support for her position. "Of course she needs to think about it right now. She was almost killed tonight. I don't think Kellie should even go back home after she's released."

Donna would've kept on lecturing ad nauseam if the police hadn't arrived and ordered everybody out of the room. Given a choice, I'll take a visit from Seattle's finest over my sister's haughty posturing any day. "Thanks," I said to the uniformed officers after the family had left. "A whack on the head wasn't enough for my sister. She thought she still needed to knock some sense into me."

The officers laughed, which I took as a sign that we'd get along. They were courteous and sympathetic to my plight, which also helped. The one who did all the talking was a pretty brunette with hazel eyes and a soft yet confident voice. I didn't have much to tell her. No, I didn't get a good look at my attacker. No, I didn't know who would want to harm me. No, he or she didn't say anything. About the only information I was able to give them was a description of the boots that had stomped on my fingers—big with pointed toes and black leather. I could tell by their expressions that the interview had been a disappointment.

"Sorry," I said. "But I just can't think of anything helpful."

They smiled, thanked me for my cooperation, and left just as the emergency room physician—carrying my X rays—finally came to check on me. The good news was that my fingers weren't broken, I didn't have a concussion, and my skull wasn't fractured. "But that's quite a bump you've got on your head," she said. "Scalp injuries tend to bleed profusely, even little nicks."

I looked at the blood-soaked towel Charlie had given me. "Some nick."

She smiled condescendingly and then, shining a penlight into each of my eyes, asked me a series of questions. "Did you lose consciousness?"

"No."

"Are you nauseated?"

"No."

"Headache?"

"A little."

"Dizzy?"

"No."

After testing my reflexes by tapping on my wrists and knees, she announced that she didn't think a CT scan was warranted. "But you might have a slight concussion. If you get any of the symptoms I asked you about in the next couple of hours, you should call. Is there anyone who can keep an eye on you?"

Thinking of Donna and the rest of the gang, I chuckled, "Eyes are no problem!"

She patched me up with some kind of glue (it supposedly doesn't scar like stitches), taped on a bandage, and gave me some Tylenol for the pain. The entire treatment took no longer than ten minutes. "So many patients, so little time," she said as she hurried out the door.

Free to leave, I dressed in the dry clothes that Mary Kathleen had brought for me and wandered out to the main waiting area. I wasn't looking forward to another encounter with Donna et al. but I needed a ride home. The room where family and friends gathered to wait for word on the status of their loved ones was packed. Too many worried people squeezed into a confined space are bound to cause some commotion, but the room was unusually chaotic.

It occurred to me that there were an inordinate number of uniformed police officers in the crowd. At first I thought they'd come to the hospital to arrest someone, but it soon became apparent that they, like the rest of the people in the room, were waiting. As the officers milled about, talking to each other in low, serious voices, I noticed that Melody Connor was among the group. My surprise at seeing her suddenly turned to apprehension when I realized that she was talking to Sergeant Brian Saunders and another detective from Kingston's unit.

Donna called to me from across the room. I acknowledged her with a brief wave and mouthed "just a minute" as I headed toward where Melody and the other detectives were standing. When Melody saw me approaching, she broke away from the group to greet me. I've never been at the top of her hit parade, but she seemed uncharacteristically distracted. If she noted my bandaged forehead, she didn't comment. "What's up?" I asked.

Her beautiful face was ashen and her voice unsteady. "I was hoping you could tell me. Have you heard anything new about Allen's condition?"

"What are you talking about? What condition?"

My confused reaction was not lost on her. "You didn't know? I thought that's why you were here," she said. "Allen's been shot."

I felt as if she'd punched me in the gut. "No!" I cried. It wasn't possible. Not Kingston. "Where is he? I need to go to him," I gasped frantically.

"Calm down, Kellie," she said. "No one is allowed to see him yet." I started to protest, but she kept on talking. "The information we have is sketchy, but I'll fill you in if you don't go ballistic on me. Okay?"

I gave a brief nod and then listened in shocked silence as she told me that Paul Crenshaw was the suspected shooter. "He also shot a woman," Melody said.

Once again, I had trouble processing what she was saying. "When . . . where did all this happen?"

"At a town house in Bellevue. Allen went to see Diana Sunn-Burton for a follow-up interview and was ambushed by the suspect." She eyed me closely. "I understand you've been in contact with Crenshaw lately. If you know where the creep is, I suggest that you tell me right now," she added sternly.

I was still reeling from the news that Kingston was wounded. "I don't care about Paul Crenshaw! All I want to know is how Allen is doing."

She shrugged off the question and glanced at Sergeant Saunders. He was talking to two more detectives who had just arrived. The room was practically overflowing with police now. Their show of support was gratifying, but it made me frantic. What did they know that I didn't? "Please tell me about Allen," I begged Melody.

"He was taken to Overlake Hospital first, but they felt he could be treated better here. Allen's being prepped for surgery," she said grimly.

"Surgery? Oh, my God. It's real bad, isn't it?"

She didn't say anything for a moment. "Gut wounds are the worst."

I felt as if I were underwater again, desperately trying to breathe. My head throbbed, and my stomach churned, but I couldn't let myself fall apart. I took a deep breath and asked about Diana. "Is she alive?"

Melody nodded. "She's expected to survive. As soon as the doctor okays it, we're going to take her statement."

"They brought her here, too?" I asked.

"Under guard."

"Heavy guard," Brian Saunders said as he joined us. "I'm sorry about Allen, Kellie. But don't you worry, we're going to get the S.O.B. who shot him." The young, muscular sergeant was Kingston's former partner, and I'd gotten to know him fairly well. The two men hadn't always seen eye to eye, but they respected each other. Allen always said that Brian could be counted on in a crunch. *Well, Kingston,* I thought, *this certainly qualifies as crunch time.*

"I'm glad you're here, Brian," I said, fighting back tears.

He eyed my bandaged forehead. "Are you all right?"

"Just a scratch," I said.

One of the detectives who'd been talking to Saunders earlier approached him. "We've got to go now, Sarge."

I was confused. "You're leaving?"

"We want to donate blood for Allen," Brian explained. "But they told us we had to go to the Puget Sound Blood Center."

I knew they had a lab at this hospital, because my cousin was the head technician. "Why can't you do it here?" I asked.

"They're not set up for donations."

As soon as the group departed, Donna hustled across the room. With both hands on her hips, she glared at me like an angry schoolmarm. "Do you have any idea how long we've been waiting for you?" she asked.

"Don't start, Donna."

"Listen," she said. "I know we're just your family, but we deserve a little more consideration. We came here to help you. And how do you thank us? By putting us on hold while you chitchat with your friends."

I turned abruptly and walked away.

"Where do you think you're going?" she called.

MY COUSIN, HILLARY Young Thompson, had been Harborview's head lab technician for several years. At fifty-five, she was aging gracefully with a salt-of-the-earth goodness and wisdom that my sister sorely lacked. But she didn't beat around the bush when I asked about donating blood for Kingston.

"I don't care how badly you want to help your friend, Kellie. It's just not going to happen tonight." She softened the refusal with a sympathetic smile that reminded me of my mother. Disappointing as her words were, I knew she was right. While the blow to my head hadn't been life-threatening, it probably wouldn't be a good idea to donate blood right now. With my luck, they'd give *me* the transfusion.

When I told Mary Kathleen and the others about what

had happened to Kingston, they were genuinely concerned. They also understood my need to stay at the hospital. But Donna, as usual, wouldn't let me off that easily. She refused to leave when the others went home and instead followed me into the lab.

"Of course you can't donate blood," she said, rolling her eyes. "You've suffered an injury yourself tonight." She gestured toward the door and added, "Besides, half the police department is out there tonight. It's *their* duty to help their comrade, not yours."

On a good day, Donna doesn't get to me. Even on a bad day, I can usually ignore her. But this day was so far off the charts that all she had to do was look at me and I could feel myself losing it. Nevertheless, I'd managed to hold it together until she mentioned Kingston. "Stuff it, Donna," I said. "You don't know what you're talking about."

She reared back as if I'd hit her. "Well, for heaven's sake. I was just looking out for your best interests."

"Really? Then feel free to look elsewhere."

No one talks back to my sister and gets away with it. She pursed her collagen-filled lips together and gave me one of her "who do you think you are" stares while she thought of a put-down to top mine. Before she could get the words out, though, Hillary intervened.

"Donna, we know you want what's best for your sister," she said escorting her to the door. "But right now I need to talk to Kellie—alone."

"Thanks," I said to Hillary after Donna had huffed her way out of the room. "But you could've waited until I slugged her before you kicked her out."

Hillary laughed. "I did that once when we were kids. Believe me, it didn't shut her up."

I pictured Hillary pounding on Donna and smiled. "Did you really want to talk to me?" I asked.

"Yes," she said, putting an arm around my shoulders. "I wanted to tell you not to worry, Kellie. I know things don't look good for your friend, but Donna was right about one thing. Detective Kingston has plenty of blood donors."

"I realize that," I said. "It's just that I wanted to help him, too." I touched the bandage on my forehead and gave it one more try. "Maybe I should join the others over at the Blood Center. I wasn't really hurt all *that* bad."

She shook her head. "You still don't get it. When you donate blood nowadays it doesn't go directly to the intended recipient. The blood has to be tested first, and it takes at least four days for that process to be completed. So Detective Kingston won't be receiving the blood his friends give tonight."

"Then why donate?"

"It shows support for the injured party, but mainly our supplies need to be continually replenished. The officers' blood will replace what the detective is given here at the hospital tonight. Besides, even if the system was set up so that you could donate to him directly, you'd be refused, injury or no injury."

"Why?"

"You aren't the right blood type." She walked over to her desk and consulted some paperwork next to a computer terminal. "According to my records, Detective Kingston is type A. And you, if I remember correctly, are type B."

"It makes that much difference?"

"Yes. Your blood types are incompatible."

The wrong blood type. Suddenly something clicked that had been nagging at me for a while. "Do fathers and sons always share the same blood type?"

"No," she said. "Nor do mothers and sons. Same with daughters."

I thought a moment. "So . . . if a parent's and child's blood types were not compatible, they wouldn't be able to donate blood for each other?"

"That's right. Only those with type O negative can donate to anybody. It's called a universal donor. Type AB positive is a universal recipient."

"Any other reason why they might not be able to donate?"

"Well, there may be Rh factors and other hereditary considerations." She pointed to my forehead. "Or injuries and illnesses. My mother was too anemic to donate blood for me when I needed surgery a while back." She loaded some empty tubes into a tray as she talked. "Matter of fact," she said with a chuckle, "they wound up giving her a transfusion, too."

I glanced at her computer and asked, "How far back do your records go?"

"It depends on the physician involved, the disease or injury—a lot of things. Why?"

I made a "no big deal" gesture. "Just curious. What about blood type records for deceased persons? Would you have those records?"

"No, but I could probably get them from the Cross-Match Lab at the Blood Center. If the person donated or received blood in Seattle, they'd have a record."

She set the tray of tubes on the counter near the door and retrieved another tray to load. I stuck around a few more minutes and chatted with her while she worked. I had an idea rattling around in my head, but it wasn't until the phone rang that it all came together. "Kellie," she said after she hung up. "I have to run an errand for a few minutes."

"No problem," I said as she hurried out of the room.

As soon as she was gone, I lifted a white lab coat off a coat rack and slipped it on. Then, retrieving the tray of empty tubes from the counter, I left on an errand of my own.

TWENTY-SIX

SERGEANT BRIAN SAUNDERS hadn't lied. The guard outside Diana's hospital room was fortified with enough firepower and metal gadgetry to outfit a small army. Just the size of the guy's biceps straining the fabric of his uniform was enough to give me pause. But I was on a mission and couldn't let him see me sweat. I marched right up to the folding chair on which he'd perched his burly body and announced my intentions. "I need to draw some blood," I said, nodding to the tray of blood tubes I carried.

He straightened his already ramrod-straight shoulders and gave me the eagle eye. His gaze lingered on my bandaged forehead for so long that I mentally scrambled to think of some plausible explanation. But the only question he asked was, "Name?"

"Hillary Thompson. Same as on my badge." The official hospital ID badges had a photo attached, but Hillary's lab coat just had a small plastic nametag clipped to the chest pocket. I hoped it would suffice for my purposes.

The guard glanced briefly at my bogus nametag and then consulted some type of roster that was attached to a clipboard. He flipped through several pages until he found what he was looking for. "Hillary Thompson, Supervisory Lab Technician," he read aloud. "Okay," he said, standing. "You're cleared to enter."

I smiled as he opened the door for me. "Thanks, this won't take too long."

Once inside, I closed the door and breathed a sigh of relief. Posing as a job applicant was one thing. This was the first time I'd ever impersonated a specific person, and my heart was pounding like crazy. My unauthorized visit was probably a dumb idea, but it was a little late to back out now. Once again, I was winging it and hoping for the best.

Diana's private room was a no-frills affair with the standard hospital fixtures. The TV mounted on the wall in front of her bed flickered with some sitcom, but the sound had been muted. I doubted that Diana cared one way or the other since she appeared to be either asleep or unconscious. The bullet hadn't killed her, but you had to wonder if she'd survive the treatment. There were more tubes attached to her body than noodles at a pasta factory. I approached her bedside cautiously, but she stirred and opened her eyes.

"Diana? It's me, Kellie."

She turned her head slightly and moaned.

"Can you hear me, Diana?"

"Yes," she said in a soft, barely audible voice.

Since I didn't have a lot of time, I got right to the point of my visit. "The police say that Paul shot you and Detective Kingston. Is that right?"

She grimaced and then blurted, "No!"

"Who, then? Who was your attacker?" She didn't respond, so I posed another question. "Was Paul at your house tonight?"

"Yes."

It was such a struggle for her to talk that I was beginning to feel guilty about questioning her further. Although I was afraid that I might make her condition worse, I had to ask, "Where's Paul? Was he hurt, too?"

"He . . . not hurt . . . left before . . ."

"Diana, this is very important. Are you sure Paul didn't attack you?"

"Yes!" Her voice was surprisingly strong. "He's going to turn himself in . . . knows who framed him now . . . and . . ."

"Who was it? Who does he think framed him?"

Her eyes fluttered briefly and then closed. I listened to her breathe for a minute or two and then let myself out of the room. The guard was reading a newspaper, but he glanced up when I shut the door. "Get what you needed?" he asked.

"Yes, thank you," I said, smiling sweetly. If he noticed that the tubes I carried were still empty, he didn't comment.

While I still had the lab coat on, I found a nurses' station down the hall and picked up the phone and dialed the operator. "Cross-Match Lab, please."

I RETURNED HILLARY'S lab coat and the tube tray without detection and then headed back to the waiting room. I was thankful Donna was nowhere in sight. The crowd had thinned, but there were still a significant number of uniformed officers and detectives present. The mood was somber and quiet as they drank coffee from paper cups, read the newspaper, and talked to one another. I'd just settled into a vacant chair when Melody Connor entered the room and nodded to one of the detectives. He threw his newspaper aside, grabbed his overcoat, and followed her into the hallway. I jumped up and made it a threesome.

"Where's Brian?" I asked.

Melody has always been reluctant to divulge information, no matter how innocuous, to a civilian. That she didn't hesitate to answer told me a lot about how upset she was. "We got a tip on Paul's whereabouts," she said. "Sergeant Saunders is coordinating the search."

I swallowed, fighting back the urge to disclose what Diana had told me. "Is that where you're going? To help with the search?"

She glanced at the tall, dark-haired detective beside her. "No," she said, "we're going to question the Sunn-Burton woman. The doc says she's conscious now."

"What about Allen? Do you know anything more about his condition?"

"Just that he's still in surgery." She nodded to the waiting room. "You might as well find yourself a comfy spot in there. It'll probably be a long night."

I suddenly felt very tired. Trudging down the hall to the cafeteria, I bought a cup of hot tea and sat down to drink it at the first table I came to. My head throbbed, but the pain couldn't deaden the fear that had enveloped me ever since I'd heard about Kingston. For the first time in years, I found myself earnestly praying. Terrified that I was going to lose him, I pleaded with God to spare his life. *I love him, God. He can't die. He means everything to me. Everything.*

"Here you are! I've been looking all over the hospital for you!" Donna's piercing voice so startled me that I dropped my teacup. She jumped back from the table as the hot liquid dripped onto the floor. "Jesus, Mary, and Joseph," she exclaimed. "What's the matter with you, Kellie?"

I stared at her a moment, too stunned to respond. When I finally gathered my wits, I blurted, "What's the matter with me? Is that what you asked?"

She nodded as a flicker of uncertainty crossed her unlined face.

Worry does strange things to people. That's the only explanation I can give for what happened next. "I'll tell you what's the matter with me, Donna. You're *still* in my face."

"Well, I never!"

"Exactly. You never get it. So let me make it perfectly clear. Get the hell out of here!"

"Fine," she said. "You can just take a taxi home."

THREE HOURS LATER. Kingston was out of surgery, but I wasn't allowed to see him for another two hours. The nursing staff had orders to admit only relatives and the police into his room—and then only one person at a time. Melody Connor, of all people, intervened on my behalf. "Kellie's not a relative," she explained, "but she's the closest friend Detective Kingston has. Closer, in fact, than any relative." The head nurse waffled somewhat, but eventually approved my visit. The fact that Kingston has no relatives—close or otherwise—probably helped.

"Thanks, Melody," I said. "I owe you one."

"You owe me two," she said with a slight frown.

"Diana?"

She nodded. "But we won't talk about that little visit of yours right now."

I thanked her again, grateful (and surprised) that she'd

cut me some slack. I wondered if Diana had told her that Paul wasn't the shooter, but I didn't bother to ask. Kingston was my only priority now. Although trembling from fear, fatigue, and too much caffeine, I moved quickly to his bedside. They'd told me he wasn't conscious, but I wasn't prepared for how bad he looked. Like Diana, he was hooked to a zillion tubes and machines. His closed eyes were puffy, and his face so pale that if it weren't for the beeping heart monitor, I'd have questioned whether he was still alive. I wanted to take him in my arms and hold him, but I was so afraid that I couldn't even touch his hand. I felt the tears starting. . . .

"Kingston," I whispered. "I'm here for you." He didn't stir or moan or give any indication that he'd heard me. I leaned in closer to him, so close that my tears brushed his bruised face. "I . . . I want you to know something," I said softly. "I love you, Allen. I've loved you from the first moment I saw you." I pressed my lips lightly against his cheek. "And I'll always love you."

A few minutes later, the door opened, and the head nurse said, "You'll have to leave now. Your five minutes are up."

I pulled a tissue from my handbag and wiped my tears. "Be well, my love," I whispered. "Be well."

IT WAS ALMOST five o'clock in the morning when the taxi delivered me to the marina. I was so keyed up that I didn't think I'd be able to sleep, but as soon as I climbed into my bunk, I was dead to the world. I'd probably still be sleeping if the phone hadn't rung. My first thought was that someone was calling about Kingston. I bolted out of bed and grabbed the phone on the second ring. "How is he?" I asked.

"Huh?"

"Detective Kingston! What is his condition?"

"Kellie? Is that you?"

"Yes! Who is this?"

"Flora Hampton. I'm calling about Cassie and Deena."

Certain that they'd been hurt or worse, I cried, "No!"

Anyone other than a mother might have wondered about my sanity. But Flora knew intuitively what I was thinking. "Kellie, they're all right! The girls just called me. They're on their way home."

The relief was overwhelming. "Oh."

She started talking again, but I had trouble focusing on what she was trying to tell me. Sleep deprivation, coupled with worry and my own brush with death, had seriously warped my ability to concentrate. When Flora paused to take a breath, I asked, "What about their reunion?"

"You mean with their birth mother?"

Who else? "Yes, of course. How did it go?"

"Well, I'm not sure. The girls didn't say."

I felt myself growing irritable. "What *did* they say, exactly?"

"Just that they were coming home. They should arrive in Portland later today."

I asked a few more questions, but Flora couldn't add anything more to what she'd already told me. I hung up feeling frustrated and angry. Why hadn't Cassie called me? Was she still that upset with me? So upset that she couldn't pick up the telephone? She had to know that I'd be worried.

A cup of strong tea did nothing to calm my jangled nerves. I forced myself to accept the fact that there was nothing I could do about Cassie—at least right now. What I could do was get my act together. I had things to do, places to go, people to meet. First on my list was a phone call to the hospital. Kingston's condition was listed as guarded. "Has he regained consciousness?" I asked the duty nurse. The answer made my heart soar. "Tell him Kellie Montgomery is on her way over."

I showered, dressed, and applied a fresh bandage to my forehead in less than fifteen minutes. Breakfast was a bagel as I hurried to the car. The Weasel spotted me just as I reached the parking lot. "Kellie! Wait up!"

Ignoring him never seemed to work, but I gave it a valiant effort. He caught up with me at the Miata. "Hey! I need to talk to you," he said between gasps of breath.

"I'm in a hurry, Todd."

"This will only take a second." He glanced at my forehead. "Hear you had a little mishap last night."

"Something like that."

"Yeah, well," he said. Then, pointing to the Miata, "You going somewhere?"

"No, I just like to sit in my car. Of course, I'm going somewhere!"

He folded his bony arms across his chest. "You can't."

"Watch me," I said, opening the door.

"I guess your job means nothing to you."

I turned to look at him. I had no classes scheduled for today, and he knew it. "What are you talking about?"

"Your future here at the marina. From what I hear, it's on shaky ground," he said with a smirk.

Shaky ground? It was all I could do to keep from shaking *him*.

He mistook my stony stare for interest and continued. "Of course, you still have the opportunity to redeem yourself."

"And I'm sure you're dying to tell me how."

"Well, it's obvious that you've forgotten the anniversary celebration."

He had that right.

"It's today, Kellie. If you handle the dinghy races well and do whatever else I ask of you, I'll make sure my uncle hears about it." He winked and added, "Play it right, and I could save your little ass."

Climbing into the car, I said, "Don't bother, Todd. I can save my job *and* my ass without any help from you."

"Suit yourself. But the celebration starts at noon. Just make sure you're here—or there won't be any job to save."

TWENTY-SEVEN

KINGSTON WAS ASLEEP. His breathing was labored and raspy, as if he were sucking air through a ripped straw. I stuck around for as long as they'd let me, but he never did wake up. "It's the meds, honey," the nurse explained. "He'll be doing a lot of sleeping in the next few days." Whatever it takes for him to recover, I thought.

My next stop was Shelton RE-PC. I had a couple more questions to ask Terry Lindstrom, and I couldn't get there soon enough. As I drove across I–90 to the Eastside, I tried not to think about how messed up things were—I'd almost drowned, my job was on the line, my name was on the news every night, Cassie wasn't speaking to me, and Kingston was lying in a hospital bed. But I just couldn't stop my investigation now. If anything, the laundry list of troubles made me more determined than ever to solve the case. My hunch was that my attacker and Kingston's was the same person. I also believed that he or she had killed Jewell Jessup and Sharon Crenshaw. The big questions were who, and why. I felt that the puzzle pieces were all there. I just had to assemble them.

I didn't have an appointment with Terry Lindstrom this time around, but no one questioned me when I strode purposefully through the cavernous room to his makeshift office. He didn't seem surprised to see me. In fact, I got the impression that he almost expected me. He sat at his desk fiddling with some sort of camera attached to his computer terminal but stopped as soon as he saw me. "Hey," he said. "The marina lady, right?"

"We need to talk," I said bluntly.

"Let me take an educated guess," he said. "You have some more questions about my dealings with Pierpont Engineering."

"Why do you think that?"

"Ever since you were here, I've been doing nothing but fielding calls about Pierpont."

"Calls from whom?"

He ticked off the names on his fingers. "Diana Sunn-Burton, Maury Kranich, Colin Dawson, some dude named Martin, and even that Crenshaw guy. You know, the one they say murdered his wife and some other woman. Seems like everyone in town is suddenly interested in the computer recycling business."

"What kind of questions did they ask?"

"What makes you think they were all asking questions?"

I sat down on a folding chair. "I think you'd better explain."

"Look," he said irritably. "I don't have to explain nothing. But I will say this. You'd better watch your back. Some of those calls were threats." He refused to say anything more.

"Okay," I said. "At least tell me about the time Diana first contacted you. Do you know what was on the disks that she bought back from you?"

He shook his head. "Nope. I just transferred the data onto a backup disk and gave it to her. The original disks were cleaned and resold."

I thought a moment. "Did any of the people who called you later know what was on the disks?"

He smiled. "Well, some were only guessing. But Colin Dawson knows for sure."

"Because it was his data?"

"Maybe. But I'd say it was because I sold him the very same data I sold Diana."

COLIN DAWSON WASN'T on his favorite stool at Joe's Pub & Ale House. The bartender told me—after I'd slipped him a ten spot—that he hadn't been around for several days. "The word on the street is that Cryin' Colin isn't crying anymore," he said.

"What's that supposed to mean?"

He ran a thin, dark rag over the counter and smiled. "Whatever you take it to mean."

"What do *you* take it to mean?"

He eyed my handbag, and I put another bill on the counter. "That his ship has finally come in," he said.

His cryptic remarks weren't getting me anywhere except on a fast track to a flat wallet. I left the pub and headed for the apartment Dawson shared with his grandparents. The sun was out for a change, and Seattle's skies were as blue as the song, but somebody forgot to tell the Cambridge. Everything about the building was as dreary as the first time I'd visited. But there was one major difference: It was moving day. A nineteen-foot U-

Haul truck was parked in front of the building. I pulled in behind the truck and waited.

A few minutes later, Colin Dawson walked out the front door of the Cambridge wheeling a dolly stacked with several cardboard boxes. His white T-shirt was drenched with sweat, and he was breathing hard. When he got to the rear of the truck, he left the load on the dolly and leaned against the tailgate.

I climbed out of the Miata as he withdrew a rag from the back pocket of his jeans and wiped his forehead. "Moving's not much fun, is it?" I said.

He grinned. "Only when you're moving out of the Cambridge."

"I hear things are looking up for you now."

Dawson squinted into the sun at me and asked, "Do I know you?"

"We met at Joe's Pub."

"My drinking days are over."

"What about your days at Pierpont?"

He grinned broadly. "Well, it looks like I'm going back."

"What happened? The last time we talked, you were pretty down on the personnel director. Did she hire you again?"

"Ha!" He laughed. "She's on her way out."

"How so?"

"The bitch got me fired just to cover her own hide. I thought that was the case, but nobody would believe me. She spread a false story about me giving confidential information to Pierpont's main competitor. Turns out she was the one slipping confidential information."

"To Emerald City A & E?"

He shook his head and grabbed a box off the dolly. "Nope. She was giving it to her lover."

"What lover?"

Dawson grunted as he carried the box into the truck's interior. When he came back out he said, "Martin Petrowski, our construction supervisor."

"How do you know all this?" I asked.

"It was in the E-mail she sent to Petrowski."

"What E-mail?"

He grabbed another box and then set it down. "What's your interest in all this?" he asked.

"I'm a friend of Paul Crenshaw's."

"Then you're a friend of mine. That man is a saint. He said he's going to hire me back personally."

"Right now he's wanted by the police."

"Yeah, but not for long. He called and told me that he knows who was framing him for those murders."

"Who?"

"That he didn't say. But he knows that Diana paid Terry Lindstrom to retrieve the data off the hard disks. Data that supposedly proved that I'd sold out Pierpont. I guess she didn't figure that Lindstrom would duplicate the data and sell it to me, too. I told Crenshaw about her relationship with Martin. He said that explained everything."

It might have explained everything to Paul, but I still had a few pieces of the puzzle to fit together. If what I suspected was true, though, the remaining pieces would be a perfect fit.

IT WAS ELEVEN-THIRTY when I pulled up in front of Emma Donnelly's house. She was sitting in a rocker on the front porch, her eyes closed and her face turned toward the sun. I thought she was asleep, but she greeted me as soon as I'd climbed out of the car. " 'Tis a grand day to be alive, Kellie darlin'."

It tickled me that she still remembered my grandfather's favorite expression. "That's a fact," I said as I bounded onto the porch.

She smiled warmly. "Is this a social visit or are you up to no good—like that TV reporter's been saying?" She winked and added, "I hope it's the latter."

"Well," I said, "I don't know whether I'd put it like that, but I need a favor, Emma."

She sat forward in the rocker and looked me square in the face. "Oh, Kellie darlin', you've just made this sunny day even sunnier. What can I do for you?"

"Do you still have a key to the Crenshaws' house?" In the past, Emma had been the keeper of spare keys for all her neighbors.

"Sure do. As a matter of fact, I still have *your* old house key."

"I just need the Crenshaws' key."

Ignoring the yellow police tape still attached to the front door, I let myself inside. Despite the bright sunlight pouring in through the front window, the Crenshaws' home had a dark, creepy feel to it. A death house, I thought. Shivers ran up and down my spine as I glanced toward the kitchen. There was no way I could force myself to go back into that room. Fortunately I didn't have to. What I sought was still in the living room where I'd last seen it.

I sat down on the couch and flipped through the pages of Paul's high school yearbook until I found the photo I remembered. It wasn't a posed shot like those taken with teammates on the football field or a group of student body officers. This was a candid shot of Paul and Martin standing near a locker. Something about the photo had been bothering me ever since I saw it. I examined it more closely now.

Yes! The ring on Paul's finger was exactly the same ring that I'd found on the sailboat. The same ring that he'd said wasn't his. The same ring that didn't fit Martin's finger. I flipped through a few more pages, skimming the autographs and verses that his classmates had written. It didn't take long before I found what I suspected would be there. *"Yours til the sun no longer shines . . . S,"* the verse read.

I reached for the telephone and dialed. "May I speak to Detective Connor, please."

TWENTY-EIGHT

I KNEW I'D be late getting back to the marina but I had no idea that it would be a big deal. The celebration, that is. There was such a hullabaloo going on that no one—not even the Weasel—noticed when I arrived half an hour after the official starting time. The crowds were overwhelming, and the parking impossible. Danielle Korb and her TV crew were jostling the print reporters for exclusive coverage of the event. Not that celebrating Larstad Marina's fifteenth anniversary was so newsworthy. Controversy always makes the headlines, and the antimarina expansion group was doing their part. They'd seized on the day's activities as the perfect public forum for their cause.

What had seemed like a major rally the day I returned from the San Juan Islands was a genteel gathering compared to the raucous protest now in progress. If it hadn't been for a contingent of Seattle P.D. officers, the marina's security team would've been seriously outnum-

bered. As it was, the noise and confusion that the
protesters generated was equivalent to a small riot.

Once I'd pushed my way through the crowd of spec-
tators lining the parking lot and entered the main gate,
it occurred to me that I had vastly underestimated the
Weasel. He had turned a simple celebration that no one
else had wanted to spearhead into a three-ring circus
with himself as the ringmaster. A large stage complete
with banners, balloons, and flags had been erected in
front of the administration building. A high school band
performed a loud rendition of "Happy Birthday" while
the Weasel, the mayor, Bill Starkey, and several city
council representatives stood like candles on a raised
platform decorated as a birthday cake.

I spotted several familiar faces in the crowd that, for
the most part, was upbeat. The notable exceptions were
Bert Foster, Rose Randall, and a few live-aboards who
recognized the celebration for what it was—a blatant
example of Todd Wilmington's ego run amok. I
should've seen it coming. All his planning committee
meetings that I missed or slept through were but a pre-
lude for his day in the sun. His need for recognition was
so great that I almost felt sorry for him. Especially since
the primary person he wanted to impress—Old Man Larstad—didn't even seem to be present. And his so-called
girlfriend, Danielle Korb, was occupied covering the
protest outside the marina.

Someone thrust a program into my hand, and I
skimmed over the day's agenda. Since the dinghy races
were scheduled to begin immediately following the
ground-breaking ceremony led by Bill Starkey, I decided
that I had a perfect excuse for not sticking around any
longer. The wisdom of my decision was reinforced when
the Weasel stepped up to the microphone to deliver his
welcoming speech.

I noticed that I wasn't the only one who'd suddenly found something better to do with their time. But Wilmington held most of the gathering intact by promising that the drawing for a Jet Ski would follow his remarks. I spotted Jason and Tiffany among those who apparently found the possibility of owning such a watercraft compelling enough to suffer through whatever the Weasel had to say. "We can't miss this!" Tiffany chirped excitedly when I stopped to say hello.

"How about you, Kellie?" asked Jason. "You going to wait for the drawing?"

"Guess I'll have to pass," I said. "The dingy races are coming up soon."

I didn't say it, but from what I could tell, Wilmington's audience was mostly confined to the young and those who didn't know any better. Being neither, I made my escape.

The dinghies that I'd planned to use in the races were housed in an eighteen-by-twenty-foot structure at the far end of the marina. The fastest way to get there was via a shortcut through the parking lot next to the sailing school. The protesters and the associated razzamatazz were camped out at the other end of the lot, so I didn't anticipate any congestion problems. I was a little surprised, though, to see that the airporter, Shuttle Express, had pulled into the parking lot next to the school.

The marina wasn't a regularly scheduled stop for the van, but then, the goings-on today weren't exactly what anyone would call regular. My first thought was that the Weasel had arranged the airporter to transport some dignitaries to the festivities. Just what we needed today— more stuffed shirts who . . .

A shout caused me to stop my grumbling and take a second look. The two passengers who disembarked from the van were no dignitaries, but I held them both in high esteem. What I couldn't figure out was why they were here.

Cassie and Deena waved enthusiastically when they saw me. *"Mom!"*

I waved back and joined them as the van prepared to pull out of the lot. The sight of the two girls almost took my breath away. Cassie's long hair had been cut to match Deena's short style, and Deena's bleached bob had returned to its natural blue-black hue. They'd looked identical before the hairstyle change but now they were like mirror images of each other. When I found my voice, I said, "What are you two doing here? Flora was expecting you in Portland today."

"Change of plans," Cassie said. She tossed her backpack over her shoulder and looked at me warily. "Is it all right if we stay with you tonight?"

"I'd be delighted. Stay two nights, three nights, stay as long as you—"

Deena's laugh cut me off. "See, Cass," she said, "I knew Kellie wouldn't be mad."

"You thought I'd be mad at you?" I asked my daughter.

She shrugged. "We didn't exactly part on a high note."

"True," I admitted. "But I'm thrilled to have you girls here. I was hoping I'd get to hear all about your trip." I glanced at the departing van. "What happened to your car?"

Deena laughed again. "That bucket of bolts? It broke down right after we called my mom. We had to ditch it in New Mexico. Our new family pooled their resources to make sure we left town on the first available airplane—a direct flight to Seattle."

What was that supposed to mean? Their family didn't want them? My alarmed expression made both girls laugh. "Relax, Mom. They were wonderful to us," said Cassie. "You should've seen it. They had this big dinner for us, a feast actually, and everybody came. We have a zillion relatives down there. And we look exactly like them."

"And your mother?" I asked cautiously. "Do you like her, too?"

Cassie and Deena's expressions turned sad. "We didn't meet her," explained Deena. "Uncle Sammy thinks that it'll just be a matter of time, though. He is convinced that her reluctance to meet us is because she's ashamed."

"Ashamed?"

"That she didn't tell her family about our birth and adoption," Cassie said.

"But she *is* your mother, right?"

The girls nodded. "She told Uncle Sammy that she has our birth certificates," said Deena. "We're hoping that she'll send them to us, but . . . Anyway, we did see photographs of her."

Cassie added, "She's beautiful, Mom. Stunning."

"Of course she is," I said, smiling. "Just like both of you."

AS SOON AS the girls left to stow their gear and freshen up aboard *Second Wind*, I hurried off to get the dinghies ready. The building where they were housed had been specifically designed for storing the craft with easy access to the water. It was a covered bridgelike building that straddled a slip. One end had been left open for a water entry, while the other end was accessed through a standard door. The twelve dinghies were stored three-deep high on racks lining two sides of the structure. I'd left instructions for Tom Dolan to remove the dinghies

from the racks and step the masts. Stepping the masts is
sailor talk for erecting the tall pole that holds the sails
and rigging upright.

After all that had happened lately, I felt a little uneasy
about entering the dimly lit building by myself. The storage facility was located too far from the sights and
sounds of the rest of the marina for my comfort. Usually,
I don't mind working by myself, but this day I would've
preferred a little crowd cover. I also would've preferred
that Tom Dolan had done what I asked. He'd only removed and stepped the mast on three of the dinghies.

My unease quickly turned to irritation as I realized
just how much of a job I had ahead of me. On the other
hand, I welcomed the extra labor. There's nothing like
working up a little sweat to keep the mental demons at
bay. The worry that I'd been shouldering about Kingston
was beginning to take its toll. But if Melody Connor
acted on the phone message I'd left for her, there was a
good chance that part of the burden would soon be lifted.
The problem was Melody. Leaving a message for the
woman hasn't always been a winning proposition. As
best I could, I shook off thinking about her and set to
work.

I'd only gotten one of the dinghies ready when I
thought I heard a noise. I stopped and listened, but it
was just a duck flapping its wings. He'd swum to the
end of the water inside the structure and decided to fly
out. I watched him take off just as a dark figure stepped
inside the building.

TWENTY-NINE

"WHO'S THERE?" I shouted with more courage than I felt. My tough-girl act was just that—an act. Fear had wrapped itself around my vocal chords so tightly that my shout wasn't much more than a squeak.

"It's me, Kellie. Paul Crenshaw."

Still wary, I was ready to run if need be. As the man moved toward me, I saw that it was, in fact, Paul, wearing the same outfit that he'd worn when we went sailing, including the gray beard and wig. "What are you doing here?" I asked.

"I'm on my way downtown," he said. "I'm turning myself in."

"Good. You should've done that a long time ago."

His rounded shoulders drooped, and he hung his head. "I know . . . It's just that I had to prove . . . Well, it's over now. I'm sorry about the detective and Diana. How are they doing?"

"Diana will recover. I'm not so sure about Allen."

"I'm so sorry. It's all my fault."

"You should've told me up front what was going on, Paul. It would've saved us both a lot of grief."

"You're right. Maybe Tiffany wouldn't hate me so much, either."

"She's got to be told right away."

Paul looked at me, his eyes weary and defeated. "How did you figure it out?"

"The ring. At least, that's the first indication I had that something wasn't right. You denied owning it, but you were wearing it in a photo in your high school yearbook. It didn't register the first time I saw it, but I think that's what Sharon found the day she was murdered. The inscription on the ring was the same verse written in your yearbook."

"Amy gave it to me when she found out that she was pregnant. After she died, I never wore it again. But I always had it with me. I kept it in my briefcase, wrapped in a small lace handkerchief that belonged to her. I don't know how I lost it on board the boat."

"Diana told me that you loved her sister. The name threw me off until I remembered that she said you called Amy your little sunshine. The "S" in the yearbook stood for sunshine."

A sad, wistful smile formed at the corner of his mouth. "Little Amy Sunshine. It was a play on her last name, Sunn-Burton." He was quiet a moment and then asked, "How did you know that her baby was mine?"

"Sharon's father said that you'd donated blood when Jason had his emergency appendectomy. I didn't think too much about it until I was at the hospital. I grew suspicious when I was told that my blood type was incompatible with Allen's. On a hunch, I phoned the Cross-Match Lab at the Blood Center. Luckily they believed that I was a lab technician at Harborview and gave me the information I sought. Their records confirmed that Martin couldn't have been Jason's father. His blood type is O positive. Jason's is A negative. Amy's was B."

"And mine is A negative, same as Jason's."

"Right. So, there was no way a child with type A negative blood could've been the offspring of Martin and Amy. That's why you've been so adamant about keeping Jason and Tiffany apart. He's her half-brother."

He heaved a weary sigh. "I couldn't bring myself to tell Tiffany that—or Sharon, either. Amy and I didn't plan on falling in love," he said, shaking his head. "She was my best friend's girl. But it just happened. Tiffany thinks I don't know anything about young love. I know that you can love so deeply it wounds the soul. I would've married Amy in a heartbeat if she'd agreed."

"Why didn't you tell Martin?"

"We didn't want to hurt him. Amy insisted that we keep our romance a secret until after the baby was born. But her parents were staunch Catholics. When they learned of her pregnancy, they insisted that Martin and Amy get married right away."

"But you still didn't say anything?"

"Believe me, I wanted to. I wanted to shout it to the whole world: I loved Amy. I was the father of her baby. And I would marry her. But Amy was too afraid of hurting Martin, who was deliriously happy and . . ."

A noise behind us caused Paul and me to turn around at the same time. Neither of us had heard him enter the building. His boots were surprisingly quiet on the concrete dock. "Go on with your little story, Paul. Tell her how deliriously happy I was to lose my wife—and my son."

Martin pointed a gun at Paul, who seemed more sad than stunned or frightened. I, on the other hand, was furious. Once again, Melody Connor had not come through. I'd identified Martin Petrowski as the killer in the message that I'd left for her. She either didn't get my message or, more likely, didn't think an amateur detective was a credible source.

"Go on, tell her," repeated Martin, but he didn't wait for Paul to pick up the story. Turning to me, he said, "Did he tell you how much I looked up to him?" Then to Paul, "My God, you were my hero back then."

Paul hung his head as if ashamed.

Martin snorted disgustedly and directed his comments to me. "He saved me from going to juvie by taking the rap for the beating I gave Chip. For years I thought he was my best friend." A vicious, evil sneer accented his words. "Some friend!"

He pressed in closer to Paul, who stood motionless. "I know now that you were just guilt-ridden. The way you stood by me, the job you gave me, the interest in Jason's welfare—all the actions of a man with a guilty conscience." He glared at Paul, his voice growing louder and meaner. "You stole everything from me!"

"When did you find out that you weren't Jason's father?" I asked, hoping to diffuse his building rage.

Momentarily distracted by my question, he turned his glare on me. "When he had his appendectomy. I'd always had a little suspicion in the back of my mind about Paul and Amy, but I'd refused to believe it. I did a little digging into the medical records that day and discovered that I'd been right all along. I couldn't have been Jason's father. Not with my blood type. But what do you know? Paul's blood type was a perfect match."

"What made you suspect Paul? Couldn't the father have been one of your other high school chums?"

His face reddened as he shook his head. "Never! It was Paul, all right. He had everything that should've been mine—the college education, the rich wife, the beautiful daughter, *and* my son." He paused for a moment to catch his breath and then, as if energized by his internal rage, he continued to rant and curse at Paul for his deceit. "You stole my whole life from me!"

"But you stole them back," I said.

He laughed bitterly. "It was so friggin' easy. All I did was fake a romance with Diana, and she got me everything I needed to open up new credit accounts in his name. She thought she was retrieving E-mail love letters I'd sent her, but I needed Paul's financial records off those disks. Lucky for me he kept his personal records on the company's system. I already knew how to forge his signature."

"Why buy the yacht? Why kill an innocent woman?"

"Ah, that was payback. Amy was innocent until Paul got hold of her. Spilled his seed and took her life. Jewell wasn't exactly an innocent, but what can I say? Our relationship was delicious while it lasted—even though she believed I really was Paul Crenshaw."

"So you strangled her aboard the yacht you purchased using Paul's name and ID?"

"The yacht was just a little whimsy on my part. Did you catch the name I gave it? His name for Amy— *Sunshine*."

"And Paul's fingerprints? How did you manage that?"

"Simple," he said with a self-satisfied smile. I just swiped a champagne bottle from their liquor cabinet when they weren't home. Paul's fingerprints were all over it."

Paul looked up. "You bastard," he hissed. "You killed Sharon, too."

I thought for a moment that Martin would shoot Paul on the spot. His face contorted into a vile smirk. "Had to, my friend. She'd discovered that goddamn verse in the yearbook matched the inscription on the ring Kellie found. When she called me to ask about Amy, I realized that it was just a matter of time before she figured out that I was behind all her dear hubby's troubles. She might have been scared of her own shadow, but she wasn't stupid."

"That why you came after me, too?" I asked.

He nodded. "You kept snooping around, asking questions, making yourself a real pest. Same with that idiot cop."

"And Diana? Why'd you shoot her?"

"You have yourself to thank for that. All your questions had her wondering about what my real motives were." He stared at Paul with a hatred that was almost tangible. "And now it's time to bring down the final curtain."

Paul seemed resigned to his fate, but my heart beat wildly as I frantically searched for a way out of this madness.

Martin ordered the two of us to stand side by side. Noting my expression, he said, "Don't worry. I'll make this quick. Too bad I got here too late to save you. But I'll be a hero anyway. They might even give me a reward. After all, I brought down a serial killer."

Martin aimed the gun at Paul first, his finger poised on the trigger. "Say goodbye, old pal."

THIRTY

PAUL STIFFENED SLIGHTLY and stared straight ahead, the condemned prisoner stoically awaiting his fate.

Too terrified to watch his cold-blooded execution, I closed my eyes. My mind flashed on that infamous photo of the Vietnamese prisoner as he was executed in the street. I cringed inside, knowing now exactly how he must have felt right before he died. I held my breath, helplessly waiting for the explosion that would end Paul's life. For a fleeting moment, I wondered if I'd even hear the second shot. But instead of gunfire, I heard someone call my name. "Kellie! You in there?"

Desperate to believe that help had somehow arrived, I opened my eyes. But it was not a rescue team that came barreling through the door. Jason and Tiffany rushed into the building like two eager puppies. "We came to help you get . . ."

Jason's unfinished sentence hung in the air as he suddenly realized something was amiss. It took a moment for the scene to register. Even then it was clear that neither he nor Tiffany could comprehend what they saw.

"Dad, what's going on?" Jason asked, staring wide-eyed at the gun.

However resigned Paul had been to accepting his own fate, he was obviously not prepared to let anything happen to his children. Fearing for their safety, he yelled, "Get out of here! *Now!*"

I echoed Paul's panicked yell. "Run!"

Martin, too, seemed anxious for them to leave. "You heard them, kids. Hit the road!"

But Jason and Tiffany just stood in the doorway, frozen by their confusion.

Beside me, Paul trembled. *"Run!"* he yelled again.

Martin must have thought the situation was quickly getting out of hand, because he suddenly waved the kids inside. "Shut the door, *son*," he said coldly. "We're just settling some old unfinished business."

"Don't do this, Martin," Paul blurted. "Let the kids and Kellie go."

"Sorry, old chum. This is even better. I'll really be a hero now." He ordered the kids to move away from the door and stand next to Paul and me. We were lined up facing Martin like ducks in a shooting gallery: Jason, Tiffany, Paul, and me.

Tiffany glanced at Paul's wig and beard. "Daddy, is that you?"

"Oh, that's your dad, all right," Martin said. "And Jason's, too."

"What are you talking about?" Jason asked, looking from Martin to Paul.

"Just what I said. Paul is your father."

Tiffany's face blanched. "I don't believe you!"

"Tell her, Kellie," Martin ordered.

She stared at me, waiting for the denial that I could not give. "It's true," I said.

"But that means . . ."

Martin laughed, a sickening guffaw that turned into a leering smirk. "Gotcha! Now you know why your little romance was a no-no."

Tiffany and Jason exchanged horrified looks.

"Too bad you didn't know sooner, huh? Might've saved your lives."

Tiffany looked at Paul again and began to cry. "I . . . I don't understand. I thought you killed Mom."

"Stop the blubbering," Martin said. "He killed Jason's mother. My wife. So I killed his. It's what we old folks call tit for tat."

Jason's eyes bored into Martin's. Ignited by anger and fear, he yelled, "No, it's called murder!" and lunged at his so-called father.

Paul instantly leaped between Jason and Martin to push his son out of harm's way.

The struggle that ensued was violent but over quickly as the gun went off. The explosion was so loud that it seemed almost as if the building had been rocked by dynamite. My instinct was to run, and that's what I yelled at Tiffany and Jason. But Paul's body, lying face-down in a pool of blood on the concrete deck, was like a magnet. They couldn't take their eyes off him. My God, I thought, Paul's really dead.

Sweating and breathing hard, Martin waved the gun at us. "Now it's your turn," he said.

Once again, Jason courageously intervened. Stepping in front of Tiffany and me, he asked Martin, "Why are you doing this?" The shock and hurt in his voice was heartrending, but Martin wasn't moved. Fighting back tears, Jason continued. "He was your best friend. He loved you."

"Ha! If you call that love, you're just as fucked up as Paul." Martin had totally unraveled now, a man possessed with unfathomable rage. "He deserved to die! He took the one precious thing I had in my life and killed it. But that wasn't good enough. He had to poison my love for you, too. And now you'll have to pay the price."

Jason stammered, "What are you saying? Don't you love me?"

"Let me tell you the facts of life, kid. I owe you that much."

While Martin related his cruel and twisted version of Paul and Amy's story, I grabbed Tiffany's hand and squeezed it. She looked at me, and I nodded toward the rack of dinghies near where we stood. If Jason could keep Martin talking a little while longer, I thought we might have a chance. I just wasn't sure if Tiffany understood what I had in mind. When I squeezed her hand again, though, she squeezed back.

Confident now that she'd follow my lead, I silently mouthed, "One, two, three," and we darted behind the wooden dinghy rack. With one strong push, the rack toppled forward.

Jason, who'd kept Tiffany in his peripheral sight, caught on to what we were doing and jumped out of the way in time. But Martin had been too engrossed in destroying his son's life to notice us. The rack hit him square on the back and plunged him headfirst into the water along with a couple of the dinghies.

He popped up like a cork, sputtering and shouting, "Help me! I can't swim!"

Jason grabbed the gun that had skittered across the deck when Martin took his nosedive. "Why should we, *Dad?*" he asked sarcastically.

Martin spit out water as his arms flailed uselessly in

the air. "Please!" When that plea didn't work, he cursed us.

In the end, he saved himself by latching onto the hull of one of the overturned dinghies. Clinging to it like a turtle that had just found his shell, he continued to curse and yell at us. We ignored him and tended to Paul, who was still breathing—barely.

"Jason," I said, "Go get some help! There're plenty of cops on that picket line outside the marina. Tell them we need an ambulance. And see if they can get hold of Detective Connor."

Martin was still yelling when Melody Connor and company arrived. Jason reported that she'd been in the crowd looking for me. She immediately took command of the situation and directed a couple of the uniforms to fish Martin Petrowski out of the water.

Meanwhile, the paramedics attended to Paul. Despite what looked like massive blood loss, they reassured an anxious Tiffany and Jason that his wound did not appear to be life-threatening. The youngsters received permission to accompany their father to Harborview in the Medic One van. I told them that I'd see them there later.

When Martin had been handcuffed and led from the building, I allowed myself a relieved sigh. Grinning at Melody, I said, "I guess you got my message after all."

"Nah," she said, returning my grin. "I just showed up here on my own. You know, to check out the marina's anniversary celebration."

"Oh, really?" I said, playing along with her. "And how was it?"

"Not bad until that Wilmington fellow grabbed the microphone. As soon as he started droning on and on about himself, I figured I had two choices: shoot the guy or come save you."

"Maybe you should've shot him first and then saved me."

"Do you think he's still talking?"

"Probably."

"Let's go."

IT TOOK THREE long months before life returned to some semblance of normality. Thanks to Danielle Korb, my name was a steady item on the nightly news for the first month after Martin Petrowski's arrest. The print media had a field day as well. Some local crime writer expressed interest in writing a book about the case. At one point there were even rumors that a Hollywood major motion picture deal was in the works. That might still happen, but probably not before the TV movie of the week was broadcast.

I guess all the media attention was inevitable. The public seemed fascinated by every detail of the Crenshaw case, especially the revelations about Tiffany and Jason's relationship. Paul and Amy's love affair provided a second star-crossed lovers element to the tale that proved irresistible. But then, as is often the case, another scandal erupted, and the public lost interest. The TV news reports eventually died out, and the only articles in the newspaper were buried on the back pages.

"How does it feel to be out of the limelight?" asked a grinning Rose Randall as she handed me a beer.

We were at Herman Pierpont's retirement party—a backyard barbecue at his Lake Washington view home that, despite cloudy skies, had attracted a fair-sized crowd of well-wishers, both personal and professional. Although he was still coming to terms with his daughter's death, Herman was determined that his impending departure from the workday world would be as upbeat and festive as possible. A good old country boy at heart, he'd hired a party planner (a recent transplant from Montana) to give his posh lakeside estate a Western hoe-down look. One of the best bands in the area serenaded us while waiters dressed in cowboy attire served up the chow.

"Great," I said, returning Rose's grin. "Almost as good as being snubbed by the Weasel."

"He still not speaking to you?"

My grin got a little wider. "Not since his big anniversary celebration fizzled. He holds me personally responsible for the shooting. Unlike some of us, he liked being the center of attention."

Rose nodded. "I think he's also pissed at what all the publicity did for you."

She meant my job. As unwelcome as the media attention had been, it was good for business. My sailing classes have never been in more demand, and old man Larstad even gave me the green light for resumption of my charter business. "Yeah," I said, sipping the cold beer, "but it's Danielle Korb that he's really pissed about. Her interest in him fizzled right along with the anniversary celebration."

Rose laughed. "Oh, well."

"What's so funny?" asked Bert as he joined us. Deftly juggling two paper plates piled with ribs and chicken smothered in barbecue sauce, he handed one to Rose and then perched himself on a nearby bale of hay with the other. He didn't wait for an answer before digging in. "This is great stuff," he said, smacking his lips between bites.

Rose rolled her eyes at me and mouthed "that's my man" and then gave his shoulder a squeeze. "Hey there, big guy. Did you leave anything for the rest of the party?"

He looked up at her with a dazed expression as sauce dripped from his chin. "Huh?"

Rose and I laughed. Bert shrugged as if to say, "Women!" and kept on eating.

"Hey," Rose said, suddenly distracted. "Isn't that Diana Sunn-Burton over there by the bandstand? I thought she was headed for jail when she recovered from her injuries."

I followed Rose's gaze. Diana, dressed in a white cowgirl hat and boots, had definitely recovered— enough, at least, to dance the Texas two-step. "Her attorneys worked out some kind of plea bargain. So, despite her role in Martin's credit-card fraud, she's a free woman."

Rose watched her dance a moment. "But why was she invited to the party? I'd have thought Herman would've fired her. She was playing awfully fast and loose with the company records."

"He would have, but Paul intervened on her behalf. He said she had suffered enough and deserved another chance."

"So Paul is back at work, too?"

"Yep. And so is Colin Dawson."

"I wonder how Dawson feels about working with Diana again?"

"I don't know, but Paul also hired Maury Kranich to oversee the installation of an advanced security system for their computers. That should allay any fears anyone might have about history repeating itself."

"What's the word on Martin these days?"

"It's a sure bet he's not eating as good as we are," Allen Kingston said. He carried two plates piled almost as high with goodies as Bert's had been. He handed a plate to me and added, "But he probably doesn't have much of an appetite anyway. Petrowski was denied bail on the murder charges, and the prosecutor is going for the death penalty when his case comes to trial."

Kingston gestured to Bert. "Hey there, partner, how about making room for some company? This broken-down old Injun is starvin'." Bert scooted over, and Kingston eased himself onto the hay bale.

Noticing the way he'd winced when he sat down, Rose asked, "How're you feeling, really?"

Kingston shrugged. "I've felt better," he said candidly. Then, with a grin, "But you can't keep a good man down . . . With a guy like me it just takes a little longer."

Although he'd never come right out and admit it, Allen was still in a lot of pain. He had a second date with the surgeon's knife a month ago that his physicians assured him would be the last. After some serious reflection, he decided to take the disability retirement that the police department offered him.

Bert stopped eating long enough to ask, "What're your plans once you're back in shape again?"

Kingston glanced at me and then, shrugging again, said, "Future's a little uncertain at the moment." The truth was, Kingston was at sort of a crossroads. As soon as the word got out about his retirement, he'd received several tempting offers from some big-name investigative services in town. He'd told me just last night that he hadn't made up his mind yet what he was going to do. Said it depended on getting a few things settled first. What those things entailed was anybody's guess, but I had a feeling it concerned me somehow.

We'd finished eating the last of our barbecue ribs when Paul Crenshaw approached our group. After a few pleasantries, he asked, "Would it be all right if I took Kellie away from all of you for a few minutes?"

Kingston shot me a playful look. "Just as long as she comes back with a couple more beers."

Paul and I headed toward the refreshment tables. As we walked, he said, "I never got a chance to thank you properly for all that you did for my family."

"That's nice of you, Paul, but I really didn't do anything."

"Nonsense. Tiffany told me how you disabled Martin at the dinghy shed."

"She helped, too. And Jason. Not to mention the police."

"But it was you who figured everything out. Detective Connor told me your phone message is what brought her to the marina in the first place."

"Okay, I accept your thanks." Slowing my pace a bit, I asked, "How're you doing, Paul?"

"I'm okay."

Yeah, right. I stopped and faced him. "Just okay?"

"Work is good therapy." He gestured to his father-in-law who—forbidden cigar at the corner of his mouth—stood talking to his secretary, Beatrice. "With Herman bowing out, I've got my hands full. Which is exactly the way I like it."

He didn't look as pleased as he tried to make it sound. "But?"

"But . . . Well, let's just say that I've got a lot of regret and guilt to work through. I keep feeling that if I'd just handled things differently, Sharon would still be alive."

"You talking to anyone about this? A professional, I mean."

"At a hundred an hour. Tiffany and Jason are also seeing a shrink. In fact, they're doing real well. A lot better than I'd expected."

"I understand Tiffany went back to school in San Francisco."

He nodded. "We thought it best for the time being. Jason is living with me in a condo downtown. As soon as he finishes his senior year he's going to U Dub. He says he wants to be a family therapist and some day sail around the world on his own boat."

"I hope he does," I said, smiling. "Jason's a great kid, Paul."

Paul returned my smile. "Yeah, he is."

We resumed walking in silence for a moment. Then he asked, "How about you, Kellie? How're you doing?"

"Great. My job looks secure for the time being."

"What about the marina's expansion project?"

"We're still getting some flak from a few die-hard protestors, but interest in their cause died about the same time the EPA said the proposed expansion met all their guidelines. Then, too, old man Larstad's attorneys won a restraining order that significantly limited the picketers' access to the marina."

"Bill Starkey will do a good job for Larstad's."

"So far that seems to be the case. He's right on schedule for the completion date." I didn't mention it to Paul, but the general agreement is that the improvements to Larstad's Marina will give the new upstart, Coho Marina, a serious run for the yachting dollars. Talk is that the owners of Coho are so worried that they've approached Larstad about a buyout.

We found ourselves at the refreshment table. I grabbed a couple of beers from a cooler. "This is a great party, Paul."

"Yeah." He sighed. "Sharon would've loved it." He turned away slightly and coughed. His heart was breaking, but when he turned to face me again, he was smiling bravely. "I see Cassie's here today," he said, gesturing toward the dance floor. "She's quite the dancer."

"Can you believe she learned line dancing in college? A Phys. Ed. class!"

Cassie and I'd had some rough bumps to get over, but I was encouraged that she'd stuck around after Deena left to "work things out" with me before going back to college. The loss of her scholarship that I'd been so worried about never happened. In fact, she received some additional monies from her school's social sciences department for a research project she proposed on adoption searches and reunions.

"Tiffany told me that Cassie found her birth mother."

"Well, not exactly. She and her twin found their birth family. But they still haven't met their mother."

"I guess it'll just take time," he said. "At least, that's what everyone tells me. Time is the great healer."

"You're right, Paul. You're absolutely right."

CHRISTMAS FOUND US in the New Mexico sunshine. Cassie and Deena's official welcome to the San Juan Pueblo was scheduled to coincide with a celebration known as the Pine Torch Procession, and Flora Hampton and I had been welcomed along with the girls. Although Flora Hampton was still coming to terms with her adopted daughter's heritage, she and I were pleased to witness firsthand the warm reception the girls received from their newly acquired extended family.

Allen Kingston had volunteered to accompany us on the trip, and we found his presence both comforting and helpful as the unofficial intermediary between the girls' Tewa and adoptive families. His presence was especially beneficial when it came time for Cassie and Deena to receive their new Indian names. The secret and sacred ceremony was limited to Indian peoples only, which Flora had a hard time accepting. But Kingston reassured her that it was nothing to be concerned about. To allay her fears, he went with the girls as our representative.

When they returned to the hotel where we were staying in Santa Fe, Kingston had a protective arm about each girl. "Ladies," he said, addressing Flora and me, "I have the great privilege of introducing your Tewa daughters, Summer Star and Yellow Flower."

Later, when we were alone, I thanked him for all that he'd done for us. "You probably don't remember this, Allen. But when you were in the hospital, I told you that I loved you."

He grinned and waited.

I gazed into his dark eyes. "I just wanted to tell you that I meant it then and I mean it now. I love you, Allen Kingston. I love you!"

"You know," he said, taking me in his arms, "I've waited a long time to hear those words. They have a nice ring to them."

Our kiss was tender and sweet, but no more so than what followed. Later, still holding me in his arms, he said, "I like the girls' new names. But I sort of like the sound of Kellie Kingston better. What do you think?"

ABOUT THE AUTHOR

VALERIE WILCOX WAS born and raised in the Pacific Northwest. She currently lives in the Seattle area. A graduate of the University of Oregon, Wilcox was a teacher and management training consultant for over twenty-five years.

Much like her Montgomery protagonist, Wilcox is a lifelong boating enthusiast. She and her husband David were living aboard their sailboat when she began the sailing mystery series.

As the mother of three adopted daughters, Wilcox drew upon personal experience to help her character, Kellie, deal with her adopted daughter's search for her birth mother. During the course of writing her first novel, *Sins of Silence,* Wilcox teamed with her own daughters to locate their birth mothers.

Sins of Deception is her third novel, following *Sins of Silence* and *Sins of Betrayal.*

Valerie Wilcox welcomes reader feedback and may be contacted via e-mail (vjwilcox@nwlink.com) or in care of Berkley Prime Crime. Readers are also encouraged to visit her web site (www.nwlink.com/-vjwilcox).

EARLENE FOWLER

introduces Benni Harper, curator of San Celina's folk
art museum and amateur sleuth

❏ FOOL'S PUZZLE   0-425-14545-X/$6.50

Ex-cowgirl Benni Harper moved to San Celina, California, to
begin a new career as curator of the town's folk art museum. But
when one of the museum's first quilt exhibit artists is found dead,
Benni must piece together a pattern of family secrets and small-
town lies to catch the killer.

❏ IRISH CHAIN   0-425-15137-9/$6.50

When Brady O'Hara and his former girlfriend are murdered at the
San Celina Senior Citizen's Prom, Benni believes it's more than
mere jealousy–and she risks everything to unveil the conspiracy
O'Hara had been hiding for fifty years.

❏ KANSAS TROUBLES   0-425-15696-6/$5.99

After their wedding, Benni and Gabe visit his hometown near
Wichita. There Benni meets Tyler Brown: aspiring country singer,
gifted quilter, and former Amish wife. But when Tyler is murdered
and the case comes between Gabe and her, Benni learns that her
marriage is much like the Kansas weather: bound to be stormy.

❏ GOOSE IN THE POND   0-425-16239-7/$6.50
❏ DOVE IN THE WINDOW   0-425-16894-8/$6.50

28 ~~14~~ DAYS

MYSTERY
Wilcox, Valerie.
Sins of deception